THE WHISTLER'S OMEN

A gripping mystery about a very strange murder

IAIN HENN

Published by The Book Folks

London, 2023

ISBN 978-1-80462-114-1

www.thebookfolks.com

THE WHISTLER'S OMEN is the second standalone book in a series by Iain Henn about a special FBI unit set up to investigate seemingly unsolvable mysteries. Look out for the first, THE PIPER'S CHILDREN, and the third, THE STORM KILLINGS!

Details about Iain's other novels, the mystery DEAD SET ON MURDER and the romantic thriller THE GREATEST BETRAYAL, can be found at the back of this book.

"When you hear his whistling coming close,
El Silbón is far away.
But when his whistle is far off… he is close…
and death is near…"

Venezuelan legend

Prologue

The past

Every night the boy wondered what it would be like if he was still with his mother and father, living like a normal family in a normal house. Memories of that other life flashed through his mind at lightning speed. He often tried to slow the rush of those images so that he could experience them all over again, but they slipped through his mental grasp, whisked away through a shifting, churning kaleidoscope.

He learned to take deep breaths to calm his heart rate.

Memories of the events that led him here were vague, the images tinged with dark edges. He didn't like this place. He didn't like these people and he had no friends.

He remembered being angry and confused, he remembered raised voices, and he recalled being in the back of a large black sedan.

He often felt lonely and fearful.

The only thing he looked forward to were the visits from the tall, friendly man. The visitor seemed strong, and his wide, warm smile was the only smile that ever seemed real to the young boy.

The man told him jokes and spoke to him about his own parents and how he, too, had once been alone. He asked about the boy's well-being.

"I miss my *mamá* and *papá*," the boy once blurted out.

"You have to be strong," the man said, "and your memories of them can give you that strength."

The boy nodded, although he didn't feel that way and he wasn't sure he understood.

"What do you miss doing?" the smiling man asked.

The boy told him.

"One day soon you'll be free to do whatever you want."

The man then told the boy the one thing he really wanted to hear, the most important thing in the world to him. "I have something to tell you, a secret for only you and me to share." The visitor leaned in, whispering. "One day soon I'll be coming to take you away from here."

PART ONE

Chapter One

The wharf alongside the marina was a popular place, often busy with walkers, runners, and cyclists. The fisherman and two of his friends were chatting, casting their lines into the sunlit waters of Puget Sound. Nearby, a small group of homeless men and women, who had shelters a block away, ambled about catching the sun and on occasion sharing easy banter with passers-by.

The fisherman's attention was constantly drawn to a boy – who looked to be about twelve years old – sitting quietly on the edge of the wharf. The boy's eyes flicked up and down the walkway, watching, as though waiting for someone. The fisherman, an Afghan vet, had seen haunted expressions like the boy's during his time in the war-torn country. He knew that even on a day like this, in a free country, with the sun sparkling across the water, darkness was always near – a constant undercurrent, never far away.

Though the scene was lively, he imagined that for the child the time dragged. Perhaps to help pass the hours, the boy sometimes pulled a mouth organ from his pocket and played. Each time he played, a few people would gather, clapping along to the livelier of the tunes, and some of them dropped coins onto the ground in front of him but the boy ignored them.

By late afternoon as the groups began drifting off, the fisherman, his concern for this child rising, approached him.

"Hi there, buddy. You doin' alright?"

The boy eyed him suspiciously. "I'm okay," he replied in a lightly accented voice.

"We enjoyed your music," the fisherman said.

The boy shrugged but said nothing.

"You got a home to go to, buddy?"

"A place is always found."

The fisherman, a large man, seemed puzzled by this but shrugged and asked, "What's your name?"

The boy didn't answer, and his eyes narrowed further in suspicion.

The fisherman smiled broadly as though unbothered by the lack of response. "So, who always finds a place for you to stay?"

"El Silbón." The boy's voice lifted as he said the name.

"El Silbón, eh? And what kind of name is that?"

The boy considered this for a moment. "It's not a name."

"No? Okay, you've piqued my curiosity." The fisherman laughed in a jokey fashion. "What *is* El Silbón?"

"It's what he is." Even as he replied, the boy's eyes darted to a point behind the fisherman, and all of a sudden, he jumped up and dashed past the man. Running.

"Hey, where are you—"

Ignoring the fisherman's startled reaction, the raggedy boy rushed up to a middle-aged man dressed in smart, casual dress jeans and a polo shirt. The man was walking along the wharf, heading for the private, gated entry to the marina where the boats and yachts were moored.

The boy took something from his pocket and thrust it into the right hand of the unsuspecting man.

The fisherman heard the boy say, "A message," and then saw him run off, across the street, to a corner further up a hill. A figure in a long coat and a wide-brimmed straw hat was waiting there.

The fisherman called out to the well-dressed man, "Do you know that boy?"

"Never seen him before," the other man called back.

Concerned for the boy's welfare, the fisherman strode quickly after him.

He saw the boy and the tall, shabbily dressed man turn into an alley between two older-style, multi-level brick buildings. When the fisherman reached the alley, he stared into a long, wide space with a brick wall at the far end, and no doorways and no street-level windows along the walls. His brow furrowed in confusion. This didn't make sense.

The man and the boy had vanished into thin air.

Chapter Two

Day one

Migrating eagles ride the thermal air currents at speeds of up to thirty miles an hour and can travel over two hundred miles in a single day. True freedom, I thought, my eyes turned skyward. The kind of exhilaration I craved more often than was good for me.

I watched as the eagle glided high above, a rare sight over the city of Seattle. Rare sights, however, weren't so uncommon when you watched the skies as much as I did.

I had always prided myself on my ability to tune in to the true nature of people. An intuition I believed was the result of the ordeal I'd endured as a teenager. A trauma that led to constant dreams of the soaring freedom that those eagles enjoyed. It had stood me in good stead as an FBI agent, picking up on the subtle signs that people exhibited, I was alert to danger, primed to recognize and follow the smallest of clues.

I looked out at the city skyline; 5 a.m. Soon the first rays of dawn light would touch the glass and steel of the skyscrapers. This was the quietest of moments before the sky lightened, before the moon and the stars faded from view, before the sounds of a bustling city began.

I had to shake off this unsettling shadow of self-doubt.

I've come too far to be dragged back down. Time to get back on the horse.

Another case.

My need to get back to work at the Unsolvable Crimes Unit also put Will McCord squarely in my thoughts. We'd been a couple, working together as agents until two years ago when he'd taken a promotion and moved to DC. We'd thought we could handle a long-distance relationship, that it would be a piece of cake – *yeah, right* – but neither of us had had any idea what was involved – how could we? – and we'd split soon after.

Will had returned to Seattle as a Supervisory Special Agent, spearheading the newly formed UCU and enlisting me along the way.

I snapped out of my reverie as I stepped into the shower, letting the hot spray ease the tension in my shoulders, and then toweled myself dry and pulled on my work outfit – a light crimson blouse, dark jacket, and suit pants.

I'd mostly recovered from the bruises and cuts I'd suffered on the first UCU case and my physique was as honed and as fit as it had been in my Quantico training days.

I brushed my shoulder-length chestnut hair into place, applied just a trace of eyeliner and lipstick, drank some strong coffee and had a slice of toast – I never ate a big breakfast – and then my phone pinged with an incoming text.

It was Clara Benson, my BFF from my Washington DC teenage years. With me and Clara, it was as though no time had ever passed.

Yep.

I texted back.

Go show 'em what you're made of, girl.

Bright and bubbly Clara always made me smile. I was about to respond when the phone rang.

Will McCord. It was almost as though he'd tuned in to the conversation.

At the closure of the first UCU case, the DC directors persuaded me to stay with the new unit as second-in-charge. They also insisted that I first take leave for some R&R and attend peer support sessions with the Bureau's internal Critical Incident Stress Management service. I told them I didn't need it but they responded with their usual deaf ears and insistence in these matters. I'd managed to cut those sessions short by returning temporarily to my previous unit in the CCRSB – Criminal, Cyber, Response, and Services Branch – assisting with the wrap-up of an old case. In retrospect, those last six weeks had given me the right amount of space and distance to shake off the events surrounding the Piper case, before fully embracing my new role. I'd just texted Will the night before telling him to expect me back in the UCU office.

"I got your message. How have you been?" he asked gently.

"I'm ready to get back to work. I'm keen to know if Themis has anything on its radar."

"It does," he responded, *it* referring to the artificial intelligence program that Zoe Marshall, agent and tech guru, had created for the FBI and named Themis. "A murder victim, yesterday, in Seattle."

"I thought you were calling awfully early just to ask how I was," I said drily. "And why does Themis predict this particular murder is potentially unsolvable?"

"Because this man shouldn't have been a murder victim yesterday," Will said. "He died twenty years ago."

Chapter Three

I walked into the front lobby of the Seattle Field Office at the same time as Marcia Kendall, the middle-aged translator and analyst who'd worked with us on our first case. Marcia, with her sensible spectacles, ash-blond bob, and warm, motherly smile was always a welcome sight.

"Great news you're still on board but I heard you cut your peer support sessions short," she chided.

"The stress management was stressing me out."

Marcia laughed. "Anyway, I was thrilled the ADs convinced you to stay with us," she said as we reached the elevators.

"I didn't need as much persuading as they might've thought. But don't tell them that."

Initially, I'd resisted the idea of working alongside Will again. For both our sakes.

Marcia pressed her right forefinger to the side of her nose, grinning. "Need to know."

The Unsolvable Crimes Unit had its own specially constructed workplace on the second floor of the building. A suite of offices that intersected at varying angles to the main command center, housing the computer system around which the UCU had been formed.

Zoe Marshall was already at the broad console in the command area. She gave a wave to Marcia and me as we stepped from the elevator and headed into Will's office.

"I still think that young woman – or should I say 'girl' – is too young to have created something like Themis," Marcia said as an aside.

"Agreed." I flashed a knowing smile and then spread my hands. "And yet Themis wasn't even her first or second act." We both knew that the street-smart, young African American had grown up in Harlem, mucking around in her teenage years with local gangs while attending college. On the side, she'd created games software. She'd then gone on to be the Young Entrepreneur of The Year and the founder of the *Virtour* online travel site which made her, as Marcia joked, "a rich young thing."

"Not the usual FBI recruit," Marcia said.

Will, engrossed in the report on his monitor, looked up as we entered his office. "As you've already no doubt discovered," he said to me, "in addition to her translating assignments, Marcia has agreed to take on a part-time role with us. Assisting with research and admin and working closely with Zoe in programming Themis."

I nodded my approval, smiling at Marcia, and then diverted my attention back to Will. "Themis has red-flagged a case? A murder victim you said died years ago?"

Zoe Marshall's artificial intelligence system analyzed the details of every newly reported crime across the US and cross-referenced them against the data held on cold cases. Themis then predicted which of the new cases was most likely to remain unsolved. When I called it, "A digital Nostradamus on steroids," Zoe had quipped, "Oh, she's a hell of a lot more than that."

"A murder yesterday at the Seascape Marina," Will said, dragging me back to the present. "For starters, this is a highly unusual MO. The victim, Ken Rossi, was chained to a sack full of heavy stones and pushed through a broken railing into the ocean. His girlfriend was on his yacht. She called 911 and then ran over and dived in but she couldn't release the chain and couldn't lift Rossi from the seafloor."

"Who attacked him?" Marcia asked.

"Description is of a tall man in a worn-looking long coat and straw hat."

"And Themis honed in on this because…?"

Will rose from his chair. "Zoe can fill us in further."

Marcia and I followed him out to the open-plan operations room. Zoe Marshall, dressed in a short, patterned tunic dress over skinny blue jeans, stood surrounded by a wide, horseshoe-shaped bank of computers. A series of widescreen LCD monitors filled the wall beyond that.

"What have we got so far, Zoe?" Will asked.

"A man who shouldn't have become a crime statistic yesterday," she responded, "because he was one of the one hundred and fifty passengers on board Ven Air Flight 387."

"Flight 387–"

"The very same," Zoe cut across me, and then with an impish smile, continued. "Why don't we let Themis remind us of all the details." Her hands flew across her keyboard with a rapid series of commands.

Zoe had named her AI software after the Greek Goddess of Justice and had programmed the system's voice-activated responses to sound like a Greek-accented professional woman. "Hello, Zoe," the machine said.

I grinned to myself at the uncannily natural-sounding voice. I wasn't certain I'd ever get used to it.

"Ven Air Flight 387 was an international passenger flight that departed Caracas Airport, Venezuela for Miami, Florida on 17 May…"

I was well aware of the flight even though it was twenty years since it had vanished. It was one of the most famous and mysterious plane disappearances in the history of aviation.

News footage from the time appeared on the screen as Themis continued. "The captain last communicated with air traffic control approximately thirty minutes after takeoff, and a short while after that the signal was lost from ATC radar screens. Military radar tracked the aircraft for another twenty minutes before it too lost the signal. The plane had deviated from its course and is believed to have crashed into the North Atlantic in the region known as the Bermuda Triangle."

I arched my eyebrows at this, exchanging a glance with Marcia.

"Despite an exhaustive search carried out for over a year by military and rescue operations from several countries, no bodies or wreckage have ever been found and there remains no known cause for the disaster."

"Thank you, Themis," Zoe said.

"You're welcome, Zoe," the AI responded.

I shared a brief, bemused stare with Will.

Zoe faced us. She enjoyed the reactions we showed to her cyber creation, but her grin quickly morphed into a far more serious expression as she elaborated on its findings. "Themis has established that Ken Rossi, the man who was drowned late yesterday at the Seascape Marina, was one of the passengers on board that plane."

"How did Themis come to that conclusion?" Marcia asked.

"When a newly reported crime feeds into our system," Zoe explained, "Themis, as you're aware, cross-references the crime with a wide range of data from multiple sources. Just one of those sources is the database of deceased persons' social security numbers."

"Isn't the same process being followed by local police?" asked Marcia.

"Not traditionally," Will said, "although it's being done more and more with the automated systems now in place. But government agencies do not necessarily check a person's ID against the deceased SSN database."

"So, Themis ran that check," I stated, "and matched these two Ken Rossis as being one and the same."

"Yes." Zoe's eyes wandered to her computer screen and back. "Themis then accessed the coroner's photos of the deceased man. She compared them to the National Transportation Safety Board's photo of the man on the plane. When Themis recognized in that photo a younger version of the murder victim, her schematics propelled her to scan for other instances of the same thing." Zoe glanced in turn at each of us, her eyes intense. "She selected an initial parameter of the past twelve months and ran the SS numbers of all murder and accident victims against the SS numbers of the people on that plane."

"And found other instances," I guessed.

"One other. A parachuting fatality, just a week ago. A man who was also on that same flight."

"Can't possibly be…" Marcia's voice trailed off.

"No, it can't," I agreed.

Will's gaze was centered on me. "Are we on the same page?"

I nodded. "We need to take this case."

Chapter Four

It was a twenty-minute drive along 15th Avenue West to the Seascape Marina. As Will pulled his blue Ford sedan into the parking area, I surveyed the cruisers, unmarked police vehicles, medical examiner's and news vans at the crime site.

Police tape cordoned off the spot where Rossi had been pushed off the wharf.

Before we'd headed out, Will had phoned the police officers on the scene and ascertained that Rossi's girlfriend, stricken with grief, was at times reverting to her native Italian language.

"I can help with that," Marcia had said and so she'd joined us on the drive over.

The officer stationed at the marina security gate let us through and Will, Marcia and I approached the yacht. There were two other Seattle Police officers on the wharf. The officer in charge – a fit, middle-aged man, his dark hair flecked with grey at the temples – turned as we walked up.

"I was told just minutes ago we'd be answering to a special FBI unit on this," Senior Detective Paul Radner said, "although I didn't know it would be the team that solved the Piper case. Good to see you again." He shook hands with Will, who said, "This isn't one of those jockeying for jurisdiction things, Detective, it's part of our remit to take on certain cases."

"No worries there," Radner said with a shrug, "though this doesn't seem anything like your previous investigation."

"Believe me it has its oddities," I said with a smile.

I introduced Marcia to Radner and his offsider and then we boarded the yacht.

"What have we got here so far, Detective?" I asked.

"Rossi's girlfriend, Luisa Moretti, is understandably distraught. She was sedated last night, and she's not been easy to interview this morning. She's Italian American, spent a lot of time growing up in Rome, her parents alternated between the two countries, and she was living in a largely Italian neighborhood here in Seattle, doing a lot of modeling work, when she met Rossi at a party."

We boarded the craft starboard side and Detective Radner led us aft to the spacious teak deck. "What we've learned from her is that Ken Rossi was an independently wealthy early retiree, and she's lived with him on this yacht for the past eighteen months. Rossi spent most of his time sailing the coast from one marina to another, spending anything from a few days to a couple of weeks at each port."

"How the other half lives," Will quipped.

"But not how they die," Radner said. "The emergency services got here in record time, but Rossi had drowned."

"I can't imagine what she's going through," Marcia said. "Trying in vain to lift her boyfriend from the seafloor and having to continually surface for air."

"And just within reach of the wharf," I noted. "She must've screamed for help. Any other witnesses?"

"She thinks, but she's not sure, that there could've been a small group of homeless men on the other side of the street," Radner told them.

"Homeless people?" I said, surprised.

"There's a tiny community with makeshift shelters and old RVs, in a derelict parking lot a few streets back."

"If there were a few of them nearby, clearly no one came to help," said Marcia.

"Might not be able to swim," the detective suggested. "And if they were already heading off, they might not have seen or heard anything."

"Could Luisa shed any light on Rossi's family or friends, or for that matter, enemies?" Will asked.

Radner lowered his voice, taking a step closer to us. "Frankly, Agent McCord, she doesn't seem to know very much at all about her rich, older lover."

"You think she could've been involved with the killer?" I asked him.

"Early days on that." Radner cocked his head toward the sliding glass doors that ran alongside the cabin facing the deck. "The lady is in there, in the main living area, with one of our policewomen. Oh, and a news reporter. Luisa refused to let the newspeople on the boat, but she recognized this reporter, and the reporter talked her into allowing her to come on board."

"Recognized her?" I said. "Who's the reporter?"

"The young woman who was reporting your Piper case. Apparently, she's just joined one of the metro papers here."

"Brooke Goodman?"

"Yeah, that's her."

* * *

Red-eyed and with her raven hair in disarray, Luisa Moretti sat at the table in the spacious cabin that served as the main living area. She was dressed in a loose-fitting white dress and sandals, and she sobbed as the policewoman spoke quietly in an attempt to soothe her. Brooke Goodman was sitting further away, uncharacteristically tight-lipped, taking notes, her face partly obscured by her long, dark hair.

Biding her time, treading carefully, I thought. I knew that Brooke was not just an ambitious, idealistic journalist but also a highly intelligent and emotionally aware young woman. Brooke had suffered grief of her own and, like me, her way of dealing with it was to keep busy, immersing herself in her work. Given the ordeal shared on the recent UCU case, I would always have a special bond with the young reporter.

Brooke showed her surprise as we entered. "Ilona?"

"Hi, Brooke, you remember Agent McCord?"

"Of course."

"How have you been?" I asked.

"Coping." There was a distance in her tone.

I nodded my understanding.

Will took a step toward the table where Luisa Moretti was seated. He introduced us all. "Miss Moretti, would you be up to answering a few questions?"

The woman tossed her hair back and dabbed her eyes with a tissue. She sucked in a deep breath. "*Sì, certo.* Anything… anything I can do to help."

Will shot a glance at Brooke. "You're going to have to step outside for a few minutes, Miss Goodman."

"Of course."

Will pulled up another chair. "Miss Moretti–"

"*Per favore*, call me Luisa."

Will gave a gentle nod. "Luisa, in your statement to the police last night, you said that Mr. Rossi arrived back from an afternoon out with friends, but then headed out again almost immediately. You said it was something to do with a boy that he'd seen outside the marina on the public wharf?"

"*Sì.*"

"Why did he need to go back out to see this boy?"

"I never saw this boy," Luisa said, "but there was a message and it… it didn't make sense."

"What message was that, Luisa?" I asked, standing behind Will, and flanked by Marcia.

"It was the USB." Becoming alarmed again, she reverted to Italian, the words spilling out in a torrent. "*Era spaventoso, confuso.*"

"She said it was scary, confusing," Marcia translated.

The woman was falling in and out of the two languages. "The message…" Her voice was breathy, and then it rose to a shriek. "*Il tuo tempo è arrivato.*"

"…your time has come," Marcia whispered.

"Who said this to Mr. Rossi?" Will asked.

"L'uomo sull'USB."

"She's saying it was on the USB," said Marcia.

"Nothing was said in the statement last night about a USB," Radner pointed out.

The policewoman placed her hand on Luisa's shoulder. "It's alright, deep breaths, take your time."

I stepped forward, kneeling beside the stricken woman. "Did the boy give Mr. Rossi the USB stick?"

"*Sì.* The boy."

"You didn't mention the USB in your statement," I said.

The woman shrugged and stared blankly as though not understanding the comment. I suspected that the distraught, grieving woman had overlooked some of the details when speaking to the local cops the night before. Not uncommon.

"You and Mr. Rossi listened to a recording on the USB?" I pressed her for the details.

"*Sí.*"

"Do you know the names of the friends Mr. Rossi spent yesterday afternoon with?"

"No, I don't," she replied. "I never met any of his friends."

"Did Mr. Rossi do anything else before he went looking for the boy?"

There was a pause as she considered this. "He made one of his phone calls on the deck."

"What do you mean 'one of his phone calls'?" Will asked.

"He sometimes made private calls, in his office or on the deck, never long. He never told me what they were about."

I glanced at Will and Marcia. "The phone was on Rossi when he went into the water, but we can get a list of numbers he called from his phone provider."

"I'll get it underway," Marcia said, stepping away to make the call.

"Luisa," I said, with my eyes flitting briefly to the policewoman with an expression that said, *good work, you're keeping her calm, keep it up.* "Did Mr. Rossi ever speak to you about being on a flight from Venezuela to Miami?"

"No." The woman was confused by this question, glancing at the policewoman and then back to me. "Why do you ask? What has that got to do—"

"Luisa, did he ever say anything about visiting Venezuela, or has he ever spoken about being in any accidents?"

The confusion etched itself even deeper into the woman's features. "No."

She doesn't know anything about this Ken Rossi having been on a missing flight, I realized. "And where is the USB now?"

Luisa looked toward the cabin that housed Rossi's office.

* * *

I stayed with Luisa, as did the policewoman, while the others headed to Rossi's office. With fewer people surrounding her, I hoped she might relax a little more. I asked her to take me through the events of the previous afternoon once more.

Luisa closed her eyes, her heart beating rapidly. I could see that the questioning had thrust her mind back into the horror of her boyfriend's death. Luisa recounted how she'd been lounging, bikini-clad, on the deck of the seventy-foot craft when Rossi had returned.

Rossi had told her about the boy and the USB stick. Luisa had followed him into the cabin he used as an office, and he'd played the audio track that was on the USB. A whistle had come through the speakers. It had been short and simple and yet, repeated several times, there had been something strangely unsettling about it.

And then Luisa and Rossi heard the voice of the boy saying something, followed by the seven notes of the whistle.

"What happened then?" I asked.

"He went to find the boy, but he was long gone. A few minutes later I saw Ken walking back."

Luisa continued. It was twilight, she was startled when she saw a tall man in a hat step out from behind a pylon on the marina. She could just barely hear the man's whistle in the distance, the same short, eerie notes. She told me that she saw a large sack propped against the pylon and a gaping hole in the wharf's wooden railing. Before the approaching Rossi could react, the whistling man had grabbed hold of his arm. He viciously wrapped a chain around it and snapped shut the padlock.

Luisa had screamed out as the long-coated man slammed into her lover and thrust him through the hole in the railing, the large, heavy sack attached to the chain being pulled in as well. Luisa leaped from the yacht and sprinted desperately along the wharf to where Rossi had gone into the water. She hadn't seen where the straw-hatted man had gone.

Leaving the policewoman with Luisa, I joined the others in Rossi's office. A brief search of the cabin hadn't turned up anything unusual. The USB was still inserted into the PC just as Rossi had left it the night before.

Marcia reached across to the keyboard and navigated to the USB drive. "An audio track." She clicked Play.

A short, eerie whistle, just seven notes, starting low and rising with an urgency to a piercing, unsettling pitch, then quickly fading. It was followed by the boy's voice, reciting three short lines.

> *The years have passed*
> *Your time has come*
> *Listen for the whistling of El Silbón.*

And then came the whistle again, this time the voice morphing on the last note into a snake-like hiss. An otherworldly sound that sent a sudden, sharp chill shooting from my spine to the nape of my neck.

Radner looked at the intense expression on my face, and the faces of Marcia and Will. "What the hell is this?" he said.

Chapter Five

Detective Radner's phone rang, and he glanced at the display as he answered. "It's my officer on the wharf." He spoke briefly to the voice on the other end of the line, then ended the call and turned to us. "A fisherman's arrived who says he spoke to the boy yesterday."

The policewoman remained with Luisa, and Brooke stepped back in from the deck. The others and I made our way to the public access area of the wharf. The three fishermen were setting up their gear and the larger of the three was talking with the officer on site. Radner identified himself and then asked the fisherman about the boy.

The man told him what he'd seen the previous afternoon.

"He'd never been here before?" Radner asked.

"No. Never seen him."

"And you spoke with this boy?" I prompted.

"I wanted to make certain the kid had somewhere to go. He said El-something-or-other always finds a place."

I exchanged glances with the others.

"El Silbón?" asked Will.

"Yeah. That's it." The fisherman's eyes lit up with recognition. "El Silbón. And then the kid ran over to some fellow who was headed to the marina. Thrust something at him." His gaze wandered to the crime scene tape a few feet along. "The news reports about the murder here... Was it that guy?"

"Yes," said Will, "so anything you can tell us about that boy, anything at all, could be vital to our investigation."

The fisherman shrugged. "He said the strangest thing when I asked him about that name. He said El Silbón is *what* he is." The man then turned toward the street and pointed to the intersecting road that ran up the hill. "A man in a wide-brimmed hat appeared on the corner and the boy went with him. I followed, just to make sure the kid was alright, but they turned into an alley and when I reached it there was no sign of them anywhere. I didn't think any more of it until I saw that news report this morning."

I nodded, realizing that the hatted stranger must have returned to the scene soon after, and hacked a hole in the railing, most likely with a small ax that was probably on the sea floor now.

"Those homeless folk" – the fisherman looked to the far end of the street – "they might be able to tell you more."

I thanked him for his help and as we headed to the cars, Radner turned to me. "What was all that, back on the yacht with Miss Moretti, about flights to Venezuela and accidents?"

I flashed a glance at Will, and he nodded. "This is something we're keeping under wraps for now, so it goes no further, not even to any of your officers working the case this morning."

"Understood," Radner said.

"You know of Ven Air Flight 387?"

Radner took a moment to run the name through his memory. "Ah, the plane that went missing between Caracas and Miami quite a few years back."

"Twenty years," I specified. "Social security number tells us this Ken Rossi was a passenger on that plane."

Radner stared at me. "What?"

"And from the photos of the corpse we see a strong resemblance between the victim and a younger Rossi," Will elaborated. "That's the reason our team is taking on this investigation."

* * *

There was limited parking in the area immediately adjacent to the wharf. A few streets further back, away from the main thoroughfares, stood the neglected parking lot that in recent years had been taken over by the homeless community with their old-style RVs, tents, and makeshift cardboard and canvas shelters.

As Will's car, followed by Radner's, pulled into the parking lot, I observed a couple of the homeless men seated outside their tents. They scrutinized the cars, stood up and shuffled back inside. I saw a face appear at the window of one of the old RVs and then promptly disappear.

Alighting from the car, Will called over to Radner. "If you and Ilona start from the southern end, Marcia and I will start from the north. It won't take long to cover all the shelters here."

Radner signaled, "Got it."

"I don't think we'll be getting any joy here," Radner said as we approached the first RV. "These people keep to themselves and then some."

"Let's see if you can charm them into cooperating."

"Not my strong suit," he deadpanned.

The clear sky of just minutes before became shadowed by dark clouds and there was a smattering of drizzle. It brought a fresh tang to the parking lot air that was otherwise dry and dusty. I glanced skyward and could tell that it would soon pass. I suspected it was going to be one of those four-seasons-in-a-day kinds of morning.

The first man to open his RV door was reed-thin and raspy-voiced, aged around mid-fifties, I guessed.

"Never saw no man in a hat," he said sharply, "and that boy, don't know who he was, never seen 'im before. Can't help." He closed the door abruptly.

None of the others we approached had been on the wharf, and they'd neither seen nor heard anything out of the ordinary.

"Tough crowd," Radner said drily as we met up with Will and Marcia back at the vehicles.

We returned to the marina. The Seattle Police CSI team and a diver had initially checked the wharf and the seafloor the night before and returned this morning. They'd been joined in the last half hour by a couple of Bureau forensics men, searching for anything that could shed further light on the crime. The ax had been found but that was unlikely to provide any clues. The coroner would provide us with fingerprints and DNA samples from Rossi's corpse, but we were going to need something from before the time of the plane's disappearance to match those against. I knew that would involve a visit to Rossi's family.

The CSI and forensics officers were packing up now, preparing to leave. The sky had cleared and a brisk wind had sprung up, coming in across the water. I breathed in the sea air and my eyes wandered over the cityscape in the distance, the high-rises brightening under the return of the sun, light glinting in the windows of the buildings. I felt the craving to indulge in the one thing that brought me a surge of exhilaration like nothing else. I thought I'd suppressed it and that being back on the job would divert me from it. And yet here it was, as unrelenting as always. *Later.* I shrugged it off.

"Let's have a final word with Luisa Moretti," Will said. "I want to make sure she knows she can get in touch with us at any time if she remembers anything else."

Brooke was on the deck and approached us as we boarded the yacht. "You'll want to have a listen to this." She handed over a piece of paper with a web address scribbled on it.

My eyes took in the address. "A podcast?"

"This guy's been attracting a following for several months," the reporter explained. "He's based in Seattle and this morning his podcast is trending all over the web. He takes calls from the public and he's had calls about this crime."

"What kind of calls?" Will asked.

"I haven't listened to it yet," Brooke said. "I just had a call from a colleague back in the office to tell me to check it out."

I looked again at the name of the podcast. *One Voice.*

As Will and I headed back to his car, he slipped his phone from his pocket.

"Who are you calling?" I asked.

"Not calling, googling. El Silbón."

I walked around to the driver's side. "Why don't we go one better than Google?" Eyebrows raised cheekily, I shot Will a knowing grin. "Let me drive."

He knew that look and responded with a frown. "Silverstein."

Chapter Six

Standing in the wings of one of the University of Seattle's lecture halls, Will and I watched as Professor Zach Silverstein wandered the wide dais as though he was in an illusory study, surrounded by imagined books, shelves, maps, and wall charts, constantly centering his movements back at the lectern. There was nothing illusory however about the elevated widescreen behind him and the audio-visual presentation that accompanied his words.

A professor in history as well as criminology and forensic science, Zach was also a self-styled expert on a range of diverse subjects including myths and legends. I had called him in to consult with our team on the Pied Piper case.

A student had once referred to his lectures as a verbal roller coaster, at one point building in a measured pace as though rising a steep slope and then racing headlong into overdrive and excitement before slowing down. Pausing. Then repeating. I smiled inwardly at the memory of that description.

"Just as we now use psychological profiling and forensic techniques to solve crimes," the professor was saying, "so I believe we can use current and ultimately yet-to-be-developed sciences to explain strange phenomena throughout the world. And in the process, we will make discoveries about nature and the universe that we never thought possible."

He half-turned and excitedly extended his right arm toward the screen. "Mankind has only known about DNA since the middle of the twentieth century. Now we've mapped the entire human genome and new light is constantly being shed on old crimes. For example, in the last twenty-five years, in the US alone, more than four hundred people in prison, some on death row, have been released because DNA advancements have shown them to be innocent."

A slideshow of images on the screen detailed the history of DNA with pictures of its pioneers, Watson and Crick, in their lab, images of the DNA helix, and press reports of early cases where the new science was applied back in the 1980s.

"And psychological profiling" – Zach was on a roll – "saw the advent of the FBI's Behavioral Science Unit, as it was previously known, it's now the Behavioral Analysis Unit, making it possible to determine the characteristics of various serial killers and leading to their arrests. Anything remotely like that was considered impossible a century ago." On the screen, images of the capture of Ted Bundy appeared, changing then to pictures of various creatures in the wild. "Another example" – Zach was speedily changing the impetus of his lecture – "is that each year the scientific community discovers new species of insects and animals that we didn't know existed or that seem to be newly evolved."

I couldn't help but raise my eyebrows at the familiar form of the professor, tall and lanky with his mop of longish, springy black curls, dressed simply but strikingly in a black polo skivvy and a long, slimline coat that could almost be mistaken for a cape.

"What's with this wearing of a long coat while lecturing?" Will mused.

"Dramatic effect," I suggested with a laugh.

Will grimaced. "He's not a rock star."

"He is to many of these students," I said.

One of the students stood, hand in the air, and Zach nodded, waving in the student's direction, encouraging her question. "And so you predict that every aspect of the unknown, Big Foot, ghosts, UFOs, *everything* will eventually be found to be scientifically plausible, part of the natural world?"

"Absolutely."

"I suppose," said the student, a twinkle in her eye, "you're going to remind us that we only use a small percentage of our brains and if we open up the rest it will expose us to extraordinary possibilities and insights."

Just like that young woman, I couldn't help but admire the professor's exuberance. I could see the effect it had on all of his students.

"Yes." Zach snapped his fingers in excitement, as though he'd just made a major scientific breakthrough.

His assistant strode across the hall and onto the dais, leaning in to tell him that the FBI was on the premises, waiting to speak with him.

He quickly wrapped up the lecture with a reference to the following week's subject and then followed his assistant to the side annex where Will and I waited.

* * *

"Hello, Zach."

"Hi, Ilona." He nodded in Will's direction. "Hi, Will. I'm told there's something urgent—"

"Do the words El Silbón mean anything to you?" I asked.

There was a momentary pause and I grinned as that long, rubbery face with the John Lennon glasses squinted while its owner dug deep into his memory.

"El Silbón," he said, his voice betraying growing excitement at the question, "is the ghostly, murderous whistling man of South American legend, most specifically from Venezuela but also Colombia. And you don't ask questions like that out of the blue unless you have a very, very good reason."

I was familiar, by now, with Zach's unusual trait of speaking faster and faster as he became more and more passionate about the subject.

"We need very specific details about this legend, Professor," Will said. "Can you meet us at the field office in an hour?"

"I can be there in half," Zach said.

* * *

Zach was waiting in the UCU command room with Zoe when Will, Marcia, and I entered.

"What have you got for us, Zach?" I asked.

He was seated at the console, with Zoe standing alongside. "Zoe tells me this is about the murder at the Seascape Marina yesterday."

"Yes." I quickly filled him in on the USB message.

"There are various versions of the El Silbón myth," Zach said, "but I'll keep it brief–"

"That would be a first," Will cut in, suppressing a grin, his irritation pushing up from just beneath the surface. He'd previously conceded that the professor's expertise in both folklore and criminology had been useful. However, I knew that he wasn't totally on board with calling in Silverstein regularly.

Zach laughed and shot back a bemused stare but didn't miss a beat. "El Silbón, which means 'The Whistler' in Spanish, is both a Venezuelan and Colombian legend – a lost soul, an omen of death, a tall, thin ghostly man in a long, dusty coat that carries a sack of bones over his shoulder. He preys on drunks, the homeless, and the corrupt."

"A sack of bones?" Marcia queried, surprised.

"Yes," said Zach. "Relevant?"

"We haven't released the details of the murder to the media," Will told him, "but the victim, an American Venezuelan, had a sack of not bones but stones chained to him, to weigh him down, before he was pushed into the water."

"Okay…" Zach ran his fingers through his shock of hair and fiddled with the glasses on the bridge of his nose as he took in the gruesome detail. "The legend has it that if you hear El Silbón's whistle up close you are safe, but if you hear it far away then he is close and your time has come."

"Well, that part doesn't fit," Will said. "The whistle was on the USB and Rossi listened to it not long before the attack."

"But it was a recording," Zach pointed out, gesturing animatedly, "so the original whistling as it was being recorded was actually far away."

"Interesting point," I said.

"The legend first came to light around the middle of the nineteenth century," Zach informed us. "The story goes that the El Silbón spirit was that of a boy whose father murdered his mother for being a whore. The father himself was a drunk and a womanizer. The boy retaliated by murdering and disemboweling his father; yeah, I know, it's a pretty horrific legend, but it doesn't end there. The boy's grandfather was furious with the boy for what he had done. He tied the boy to a post, whipped him until his back was in shreds, and then sent him away, cursing him to carry the bones of his father in a sack for the rest of time."

"Just a nice little bedtime story, then," Zoe quipped, leaning back against her console, arms crossed.

I noticed that Marcia's face had drained white.

"What kind of folk tale is that?" The older woman shook her head in disbelief.

"The question is, what does it tell us about this killer?" said Will. "It seems he identifies with the legend. He's targeted an American Venezuelan. But his victim can't possibly be the person his SS number indicates – unless he wasn't actually on that flight."

"Ven Air 387," Zach said. "Zoe was filling me in…"

"We've got Rossi's DNA," I said, "but what we need now is something to match it with, from the Rossi of twenty years ago."

"A search is underway for dental records, or items that could have traces of his DNA from before his disappearance," Marcia said.

Zach stood up and stretched his long limbs. "If this guy Rossi was on that plane twenty years ago, then what was going on in the years since then?"

"What Themis has established," Zoe weighed in, "is that a paper trail on Rossi doesn't appear until five years after the plane vanished. From that point on, for the past fifteen years, he's been living off bank investments, but he's been largely off-the-grid. No tax returns, loans, property purchases, credit cards, no social media, not even a cell phone account. It seems he was using a prepaid, and his internet access was in the name of a private commercial entity simply named after his yacht, *Sun Chaser*."

"But surely," said Zach, the wrinkle forming across his forehead showing his disbelief, "a connection would have been made that this guy from the plane was still out there?"

"There's no reason for anyone to think that a Ken Rossi sailing the coast would be the same Ken Rossi who died in that plane crash twenty years ago," I said.

"There are hundreds of men named Ken Rossi in this country alone. But even so…" Zoe turned to her keyboard, quickly tapping out instructions. The monitor above the console began displaying a slideshow of images. "I've called up news articles on the disaster from the time. Take a look."

Zoe waited while we scanned the articles on the screen. "What's missing?" she asked presently.

There was silence as we glanced again at the articles.

Will was impatient and, as always, straight to the point. "Enough of the cloak and dagger, Zoe. What are you getting at?"

"Reading through those news items," Zoe explained, her words measured, "you will see the names of the airline captain and his co-pilot. You'll come across the names of a few of the victims from interviews with their loved ones."

I looked at her, realization dawning. "But there's no listing of all of the passengers and crew."

"Not in the general media, no." Zoe was standing behind her chair now, hands gripping its backrest, rocking it gently. "The general public knows of the tragedy but doesn't know the individual names of the passengers. And, Zach" – she eyed the professor – "Rossi is not the only example. Themis uncovered another recently deceased man with the same SS number and the same appearance as someone on that plane."

"Two men from that flight going about their lives, unencumbered and unknown." Zach bit down on his bottom lip, fascinated by the anomaly.

"So it seems," Zoe said.

Marcia expelled a breath. "Beggars belief. How could a man on a plane that plunged into the North Atlantic over three thousand miles away, come to be a murder victim in Seattle, two decades later?"

Chapter Seven

I drew the piece of paper with the web address from my pocket. "Brooke Goodman is now working for the *Seattle Chronicle*," I told Zach and Zoe, "and she was at the crime site this morning, talking with Luisa Moretti." I held up the paper. "She gave me this web address for a podcast called *One Voice*. Anyone know it?"

"Some of my students have mentioned it," Zach said.

"Isn't he the guy who calls on the public to come forward with any info they have on corruption and conspiracies, that sort of thing?" Zoe asked him.

Zach grinned. "That sort of thing."

"I like him already."

"Let's give it a listen," I said.

Zoe nodded, leaning into the console, pressing keys.

The screen came to life with the silhouette of a man's face, in shadow, behind the outline of a newspaper's front page. On that page was a moving, swirling montage of images from famous crime headlines, the kaleidoscope of shapes and colors forming the words of the podcast's title as a theme played. The title and the images then faded to reveal the podcaster in his studio.

The host was constantly leaning forward to his mic and then lounging back, gesturing with both hands, and then repeating the process with his face running the full gamut of expressions. I had the impression of a chameleon that was laid-back and chatty one moment, hyper and intense the next.

"I'm Aiden Sharpe and welcome to my podcast. Except that it isn't just *my* podcast. It's yours as well. I encourage you to phone in or post comments or email me because we are a community, and this is our safe forum. *Our* podcast."

I noted that he looked to be in his early thirties, with close-cropped hair, receding hairline, glasses, and facial fuzz that was more designer stubble than beard.

"I know there are many people out there who are hesitant to come forward if they have information," Sharpe continued, "and it's no surprise why. Every time a police officer or a politician is exposed as being corrupt it damages the law enforcement brand. It creates fear and mistrust in the wider community. It empowers a belief that it's not safe to approach authorities with whatever knowledge or information you might have."

"He has a point," Zach said.

My eyes widened and I admonished him with a schoolteacher's stare. "*Listen.*" I ignored the sheepish grin he exchanged with Zoe.

The podcaster's video was enhanced by a slideshow of images that ran in the background, constantly changing to suit his narrative, and a series of front-page newspaper headlines depicting corporate world scandals slid by.

"Whistleblowers are a prime example of this. People who put their safety and privacy on the line to expose the corrupt or the immoral, only to find themselves ridiculed or accused of crimes and be driven to despair. Understandable, people. I get it. And *that* is why I'm here, on this podcast, offering anyone out there, anonymously or otherwise, the chance to come forward with what you know about any crime, large or small, epic or petty, and I will listen. I. Will. Listen."

I was aware that everyone in the room was riveted to the screen. Aiden Sharpe was unarguably a charismatic presence.

"Everything on this podcast is sent through, whether they like it or not, to various levels of our law enforcement and our so-called political leaders, and my promise to you is that I'll follow up and I'll keep following up."

Sharpe's fingers poked at the air, driving home his point.

"I'm annoying like that. I'm everywhere, whistleblowing for all of us, campaigning for justice."

There was the briefest of pauses, and then the infectious voice of the podcast host resumed.

"Even if you remain anonymous, the people, the government, and the police *need* your information, need your eyewitness accounts, and this podcast provides you with a line of communication. This podcast represents all the voices in the wilderness, the innocent and not-so-innocent bystanders. United here as one. I'm Aiden Sharpe and this is *One Voice*."

Sharpe's voice took on a darker tone as the theme music played quietly.

"Just yesterday, a man was purposely drowned in a Seattle marina by an unknown assailant. I've had a call this morning from someone who witnessed that crime, someone who, for whatever reason, will not speak directly with police. This caller told me that the strange-looking assailant whistled before and after this senseless killing. Just seven notes, rising and then descending, and then repeated. And the assailant was accompanied by a mouth-organ-playing young boy. If anyone else out there knows anything about this pointless crime and this unusual duo, then know this: you can speak to *One Voice*. I can and I will help."

"I suspect one of the homeless people knows about this podcast and made that call," Will observed.

"Which means this podcast vigilante could prove a problem," Marcia said, "if his callers reveal more about the killing than what we want the public to know at this stage."

Will agreed. "We'll pay Sharpe a visit and ask him to keep certain details under wraps."

"Actually," I said, "we might be able to use him to do something more than that."

Chapter Eight

As Will and I headed down to the parking station, Will said, "And by the way, it probably goes without saying, but it means a lot to me that you decided to stay with the unit."

"The assistant director can be more than a little persuasive. Gave me a promotion and the freedom to have a say in the cases we take on." I shot him a glance, raising my eyebrow. "Your suggestion, I expect?"

"He wanted you on the team, and when you declined he asked for my input." We reached Will's car but before he unlocked the door he stopped and faced me. "I was so gung-ho about launching this unit and wanting you on it, that I didn't consider any awkwardness between us. It's just that I thought we had… or could get past all that."

"We have."

He gestured with his right hand. "Here's the thing. You're the right agent to make the UCU work during this trial period. But if you think you and I are going to be a problem, there are other projects I can move to–"

"Will, it's all fine," I said. "Really. After everything that happened on the Pied Piper case, I was so… My emotions, my perceptions, everything was so jumbled up."

He offered a conciliatory smile. "Understandable."

"But if we're going to be a team, working closely together every day–"

"Then we need to keep it strictly professional," he cut in.

I could see in his eyes that he'd anticipated where my head was at. This reminded me of the Will McCord I'd fallen for over two years ago. There were moments when I thought he knew me better than I knew myself until, and this saddened me, the day came when we both realized that the emotional intimacy between us had faded. At that time, living and working in another State, Will had become close with another woman, another agent. We'd officially split and he'd started spending serious time with her. That other relationship hadn't lasted and in the meantime, I had moved on, and yet…

"Yeah…" I said.

He pressed the remote, unlocking the car, and minutes later we were traveling south along the I-5 to the home address of Aiden Sharpe in Kent.

* * *

Aiden Sharpe's home was a modest bungalow with an extended garage in which he'd built his podcast studio.

Most people confronted with federal agents on their doorstep would exhibit concern, but Sharpe was beaming.

"I started the podcast six months ago and I've built a subscriber base of over a hundred thousand, a vast majority of those in just the past six weeks." He led us through the side door of the garage and into the studio. "I've made countless approaches to police divisions, bureaucrats, and politicians, but this is the first time I've had a callback." He sat down behind his studio desk and indicated for us to pull up chairs.

We remained standing.

"This isn't a callback," Will said.

Sharpe's infectious mood didn't dampen. "Maybe not, but you're here so I've made an impression, I've got your attention. This is the *first* of many firsts." He gave a slight tilt of his head, impressed by his own comment. "Now *that* line is going to make it into the next podcast." He spread his hands in a welcoming fashion. "You're here about this morning's show? The Seascape Marina murder?"

"Yes," said Will. "Do you know who made the call?"

"It was anonymous so no, no idea."

"Did you know there was a community of homeless people in the area, just a few streets away?" I asked.

"I didn't," he said, "but it would make sense if it was one of them. People living on the streets or in shanty townships are the least likely to trust the authorities with any information they have. But these are decent citizens, they want to help, and that is one of the reasons for my pod–"

"Did the caller give any specific details that you didn't broadcast?" Will interrupted, impatient with the man's bluster.

"I can play the callback to you," Sharpe said, his demeanor becoming serious. It seemed Will's dry, no-nonsense response had deflated him like a pin in a balloon. It struck me that beneath the showman-like bravado, Sharpe was a sensitive soul.

"The caller didn't say a lot, but clearly thought it was weird that the killer was whistling. I intend to play the full phone call on my next installment. Naturally, I have to create interest by building suspense, but…The caller mentioned that the whistling man chained his victim to a sack before pushing him into the water. And there was a boy who had approached the victim earlier, who seems to have been accompanying the killer."

"When is your next podcast?" I asked.

"It varies. Normally two or three times a week but right now, due to this, I'll be going out mornings and afternoons each day for a few days at least."

"We need you to keep the details of that call under wraps," Will said.

"What?" Sharpe leaned toward them, becoming more animated again. "I can't be expected—"

"It's vital to our investigation that we don't reveal all the details to the public," I said. "The less the killer thinks we know about how he planned and implemented the attack, the better chance we have of catching someone out who knows more than they should."

"And there's someone like that you plan to interview?"

"We can't divulge any details," I said. "As a crusader for justice you would appreciate that."

"Are you giving me a legally binding order?" Sharpe challenged.

"We're asking for your cooperation," I said, "but beyond that, we can apply for a court-issued public information blackout."

"But that would take time," Sharpe noted.

I sensed Will bristling alongside me.

"Your cooperation could help save lives," Will said with a hard stare, taking a step forward, "and we can offer to let you know in advance of anything else once it's safe to release details."

Sharpe didn't answer. He was mulling this over, but it was clear to me that the man wasn't convinced.

"There is, however, in addition to keeping the specifics of the attack quiet, something else you could do to assist us," I said, "something that could add a whole other dimension to your podcast."

Now I had Sharpe's attention. He stared back at me, intrigued. "What exactly do you have in mind?"

Chapter Nine

Back in the blue Ford, I grinned at Will's exasperated expression. "Look on the bright side," I said, "at least Sharpe doesn't know the victim was also on a flight that vanished decades ago. Nor that he wasn't the only one."

"Small mercies, then." Will turned the steering wheel, pulling out onto the road. "Either way, good work back there, persuading Sharpe to run with this idea of yours."

"Let's just hope it gives us the result we want."

My phone rang and I picked it up. It was Marcia.

"We've traced the number Rossi called yesterday," she said.

"Do we know whom it belongs to?"

"I called the number but no," said Marcia. "The receiver hung up when I spoke and now the number's been disconnected. As it was a prepaid SIM, we can't trace it."

"What about other numbers Rossi has called?"

"There aren't any from the past few months, so we're accessing the records further back."

"Thanks for the update," I said, "we're on our way back."

Half an hour later, Will and I reconvened with the others in the command center.

Will was restless. He was leaning against the side of the console, arms folded. "So, we still haven't been able to find anything on Rossi from the first five years after the plane went missing?"

"No," said Zoe. "His driver's license was reactivated fifteen years ago. His old one was presented along with an explanation that he'd been out of the country for five years. It's a common story and the license was issued without the social security number being detected as deceased. Since then, as we've already ascertained, there have only been very basic transactions that we can trace. He purchased the yacht. He opened a bank account with a series of sizeable cash deposits, although none of the monies came from his previous accounts. There's been no activity from him with any old accounts, or with any colleagues or friends from his old life. As for family, he was an only child, he wasn't married, and his parents have since died."

"Have we been able to trace any of the old dental or medical records?"

Marcia responded to this. "No joy there either."

"And yet the killer knew who he was and where to find him," I pointed out.

"So where on earth was he for those first five years?" Marcia said. "And how could he have been on that plane?"

"We need a consult on that," Will said, "and I've arranged an appointment for this afternoon with an aviation accident investigator. He's the same guy who looked into the parachuting accident victim."

"Any more details, Zoe, on the parachute victim?" I asked.

"Roger Islington. The other recent fatality who was also on Flight 387. And the major point here, that's just come to light, is that there's a connection between the two men." Zoe swirled toward the keyboard, hands skittering over the keys. "They were both partners in the same firm. A.V. Investments. Not so unusual that business partners are traveling together, but the fact they've both turned up now, murdered–"

"But Islington's death was a parachuting accident," Marcia corrected.

"Unless it wasn't."

The photos Zoe brought up on the screen were of Islington, a driver's license mugshot from twenty years before, and the coroner's shots of the corpse from a week ago.

"Once again an older version of the same man," Zoe commented. "No yachts or playboy lifestyle for Islington, though. He lived here in Washington State, in Madrona Beach, and he's been married for the past ten years. Once again, appears to have been living off investments."

Will glanced at his watch. Heading south out of Seattle, it was an hour and thirty minutes to Madrona Beach, near Olympia. "We'll talk with Islington's wife first thing in the morning. Right now, we've got a meeting at the National Transportation Safety Board."

"You're going to be talking to the NTSB guy about Flight 387?" Zach said.

"Yes."

"Let me tag along on this one. I've got a few questions of my own for him."

Will returned his stare. "Not about the location–"

Zach didn't let him finish. "With something this unusual and inexplicable" – he snapped his fingers, his eyes intense – "you're not going to be able to ignore the fact that these men were on a plane that went missing over the Bermuda Triangle. So yes, I want to pin down the aviation guy on some details about that."

"It's not a question of ignoring facts—"

"What's more, we need to face the fact that this killer appeared and disappeared like a will-o'-the-wisp, just like the legendary El Silbón."

"*Zach*" – Will suppressed his agitation – "we know you believe there's more to these legends than we understand, but surely even you couldn't be suggesting this killer has something to do with the Triangle? Or that he's a ghost from nineteenth-century South America?"

Zach shrugged, raising his hands. "For once I might have agreed but I've been researching the legend further since you called on me and this isn't the first time people have reported seeing El Silbón."

All eyes were on the professor, and I had never seen him look as serious as he did right at that moment.

"There have been dozens of random eyewitness sightings going all the way back to the nineteenth century."

I tried to hide a grin and failed. I certainly didn't buy into Zach Silverstein's outlandish beliefs and conspiracy theories. He had his idiosyncrasies, and he could get ridiculously excitable. At the same time, his knowledge, not just of myths and legends but also of historical and scientific facts and figures, combined with his unique take on all of those made him both a valuable collaborator and an ideal devil's advocate. Will was still on the fence about that, but I believed Zach's insights helped us narrow the field on which leads were worth investigating and identify what paths should not be followed.

"You're saying people have reported seeing the El Silbón of legend?" Zoe prompted.

"Over the years, many of the inhabitants of Los Llanos, that's the grassland region in Venezuela, claim to have seen a shadowy figure sitting in the trees, whistling." Zach barely took a breath, his voice rising excitedly as his speech sped up. "When they approached, the figure vanished.

Some of these sightings have been when murders, still unsolved, have occurred. These reports have never been taken seriously, after all, they're coming from a low socio-economic region, so the stories get buried, lost in the incredible mountain of police paperwork in a country that has one of the highest homicide rates in the world. Something like twenty thousand murders a year, although the government there stopped releasing violent crime data several years ago."

Zoe straightened, uncrossing her arms and frowning incredulously. "And you think there's a connection between this Whistler and the mysteries surrounding the Bermuda Triangle?"

"Not necessarily but we have a murder victim, possibly two; a whistling killer who identifies himself as a ghostly Venezuelan figure; and the impossible fact that both of the victims vanished over a place that's infamous for disappearances. *And* on a flight that came from Venezuela." Zach directed his next comment to me. "Ilona, when you asked about El Silbón, I didn't see this as a case that would prove any of my suspicions about the supernatural. But when it turned out the murder victim was on that plane, and that he wasn't the only one, and I did some research, I started to think... *two* suspiciously supernatural elements linking a killer and his victim... *something unnatural is going on here.*"

The professor was simply voicing what had already been on my mind. How could any of this be explained? As an agent, my colleagues and I were pragmatic, no-nonsense realists. We had to be. We were trained to think that way and it came naturally to me, as I knew it did to Will. That was why I wanted a consultant like Zach, who was the complete opposite. I raised my right eyebrow in acknowledgment that there were more strands to this case than initially anticipated.

Zach lifted his right forefinger, pointing to his own eyebrow to illustrate a point. "I see you're still doing that eyebrow thing," he said to me.

"What eyebrow thing?"

Zach grinned. "One of your quirks, when you're deep in thought or making a point—"

I cut him short. "Focus, Professor."

He shrugged, showing his amusement.

"Let's go see what an aviation expert can tell us about Flight 387," I said.

Chapter Ten

Federal Way, a coastal city within the greater Seattle metro area, was home to one of the NTSB's four regional offices. An independent federal agency, it investigated aviation, rail, marine, and other transport accidents in the US. It also participated with other countries in joint investigations into international incidents.

Will, Zach, Zoe, and I were ushered by the front desk clerk through an open-plan area to a corner alcove. Here, we were introduced to the head of the accident investigators. In his open-necked white shirt and suede jacket, and with his short, ruffled blond hair and piercing blue eyes, the late-thirtyish Ben Wheeler exhibited the persona of an everyman. I sensed he would be as at home out in the field as he was here, seated at a long bench littered with neatly ordered stacks of paper, a row of computer monitors, and a bookshelf topped with handbooks lining the adjoining wall.

He shook hands with each of us. "I'm Ben," he said, flashing a smile that hinted he took his work seriously but himself not so much. "Agent McCord, you said on the phone you wanted to consult with me about aviation accidents, with particular reference to Ven Air Flight 387?"

"That's right."

"Please, guys, pull up some chairs." Wheeler swept his arm toward the seats beside the bookshelf. "And I take it that the Ven Air flight is the reason you came to *this* office and asked for me?"

Will tilted his head, showing his confusion. "No. Our team is based in Seattle, so your office here was ideal for us to pick an investigator's brains. And I know you're busy, so I appreciate you sparing the time."

"Busy doesn't describe it," Wheeler declared. "We investigate over one thousand aircraft crashes, most of them small private crafts, and more than five hundred other transport accidents every year. Never stops. When you said you guys were a specialist team, I didn't realize you weren't from DC, and… I can see, as well, that you didn't know…"

"Know what?" Will asked.

Wheeler grinned. "My father was an NTSB investigator. He was based at headquarters in DC, and he was on the original US investigation team for the 387. I was a teenager at the time, and I saw my dad up to his armpits on that investigation. It had all of us completely perplexed of course. I guess it's one of the reasons, maybe *the* reason" – he shrugged – "that I followed him into this crazy-ass business."

"Is your dad still with the NTSB?" I asked.

Wheeler shook his head. "Hell, no, he retired ten years ago and lives down San Francisco; got a place by the water, always tells me he's got a hell of a lot of fishing to catch up on. But he still talks about *that* investigation."

Will leaned in, lowering his voice. "Ben, what I'm about to divulge I have to ask you to keep in the strictest confidence."

"Of course."

"We're investigating a couple of recent deaths where the victims have been identified as passengers on that flight."

Wheeler's response was immediate. "Impossible," he said abruptly, without blinking.

"Is there anything you can tell us about the investigation's findings that hasn't been widely reported, or that the NTSB has kept under wraps?"

"No official secrets, if that's what you're asking," he said. "Nothing that isn't in the reports."

"There were no passengers booked on the flight who weren't on board?"

I could see in Ben Wheeler's eyes that his curiosity was piqued. "No."

"Can you take us through the basics of the investigation?"

Wheeler pursed his lips and shrugged. "Well, let's see, you know the broader details." He spread his hands. "When a commercial airliner crashes, it leaves a massive trail of debris, not to mention the huge loss of life. Regardless of whether this happens on land or at sea, it's highly unusual for no wreckage, no bodies, no signs whatsoever to be found. And, as we all know, that's precisely what happened here."

"Which gives rise to plenty of conspiracy theories," Zach interjected.

Wheeler nodded, glancing at Zach. "Goes with the territory, I guess. And believe me, we've seen more than our fair share of those here." He took a deep breath. "As far as theories go, conspiratorial and otherwise; we'll come back to that. But right now, let's go through to what I call our all-purpose-conference-situation-whatever room."

He led us through to a narrow, windowless room with a long table, more PCs, and large wall-mounted screens. We pulled up chairs as Ben Wheeler leaned toward one of the computers, activating the screen. A map of the North Atlantic appeared.

"This is what we *do* know," he said. "The final radar contact was at 04.34 and the final automatic radar connection with the satellite, what we call a partial handshake, was a couple of hours later. The data shows that the flight had drifted from its course. From that moment the plane vanished. Another hour after that the Miami Area Control Center contacted Caracas to query the whereabouts of the flight as they'd not been able to establish radio or radar contact. The search-and-rescue effort was launched and focused on the area indicated. It was one of the longest search missions in aviation history, initially with ten vessels and over two hundred sorties by military aircraft, spanning just over a half-million square miles. And it included a sonar search of the seafloor."

"With no clues whatsoever to what happened," Zach stated.

"Nothing," Wheeler confirmed. "Ultimately, research from the International Transport Safety Authority put forward various suggestions. One of these is that the search was misdirected, that the joint agencies prioritized the wrong area."

"How would that come about?" I asked.

"The last position pinpointed by radar showed the plane off course. No storm activity to explain why the pilot made that change and no communication to advise a reason for it. The speculation is that there was some kind of event – maybe an engine failure or a collision with a bird flock – impacting communications and causing the pilot to maneuver off course. The autopilot's then been engaged but a further system failure, likely oxygen starvation, has rendered the crew and passengers unconscious. In that scenario, the aircraft would have effectively become a 'ghost plane,' flying for hours on autopilot."

"And at some point it crashes into the ocean…" Zach said, his voice trailing away, his eyes searching Wheeler's.

"It simply vanishes from the radar, confusing investigators as to how far the plane might have traveled while in 'ghost' mode."

I pressed for more information. "What were the Authority's other suggestions on why the search might have been in the wrong area?"

"Another possibility is that there'd been a radio and radar malfunction, and although unable to communicate with air traffic controllers, the crew was fine and the captain had decided his best bet was to turn back. And at some point, heading now in a different direction to what investigators anticipated, the plane had crashed into the ocean."

"Surely, though," I countered, "this would have been considered before that report, and the search parameters expanded?"

"Yes, down the line that did happen to some extent, although not to the degree many would have liked. And due to the passage of time, there was even less chance of locating any wreckage," Wheeler said.

"But they're not the only theories?" Zach urged.

Wheeler grinned. "I can see you've done your research, prof. There are certainly several other possibilities. Subsequent details came to light about the co-pilot. Inferences that he had financial problems, that his marriage was in trouble, that he'd been fighting depression, that he had a drug problem, and that he was suicidal."

"In which case this could've been deliberate?" Zoe said, alarmed. "He sabotaged the flight somehow?"

"There's no actual evidence to support that theory." Wheeler was quick to point out. "There's also no evidence, physical or otherwise, to support another theory that the co-pilot was influenced by Venezuelan insurgents, and that he sabotaged the flight as an act of terrorism."

"But any of those theories could plausibly explain the disappearance," I said.

"Yes."

"There are also other theories that the Authority doesn't like to be drawn on, that relate specifically to the region," Zach said.

"I was wondering when you were going to bring that up, professor." Wheeler tilted his head in Zach's direction and extended his arm toward the map. "The Bermuda Triangle, or as the sensationalists like to call it, the Devil's Triangle."

"But are they sensationalist? The Triangle's had this reputation ever since a military training aircraft disappeared over the Atlantic in 1945," Zach said.

Wheeler smiled, acknowledging the point.

"One of the search-and-rescue aircraft, a PBM Mariner with thirteen crew members, also vanished. And that's merely the tip of the iceberg." Zach rose from his chair, stepping forward and then back, counting off figures on his fingers, eyes widening, voice rising. "There have been over five hundred sea vessels and seventy-five planes reported missing, without a trace, without explanation — some of the vanished ships going back five hundred years. And Ven Air 387, one of aviation's greatest mysteries, is *just one* of these unexplained Bermuda Triangle incidents."

"Not all of those incidents are verifiable," Wheeler said, "but regardless, there's also been research confirming that there were just as many sea and air disappearances in other regions over the years."

"What concerns me," said Zach, "is that governments have agendas in denying or dumbing down both facts and speculation. They want to draw attention away from anything they can't explain."

"Point taken, Zach," Will said, clearly wanting to move the dialogue along. "There's a bigger picture concerning the region, but let's concentrate on Ven Air 387."

Zach rolled his eyes but didn't respond.

I looked at Ben Wheeler and gestured to the photos. "Ben, these are pictures of the murder victim from last night and the parachute victim from last week." My fingers traced the two photos and then moved to the two prints I'd placed alongside. "And these are archive photos of the two Ven Air 387 passengers with the same name and social security numbers."

Ben Wheeler scanned the photos. He raised his eyebrows and scratched his chin with his right forefinger, deep in thought. "They certainly look similar."

"Despite the fact they were booked on that flight, is there any possibility, however slight, that they didn't board the plane?"

"All seats and passengers were accounted for, and I've seen the interview transcripts with the families and friends left behind," he said. "In each and every case the people who boarded that plane were gone. Never seen again."

"Does the NTSB have cam footage of the plane being boarded?" Will asked.

"Yes. Every piece of physical evidence relating to the flight was archived and all the investigation agencies have access." He tapped a series of keyboard commands and clicked through icons, bringing forth the airport footage from twenty years before.

We watched as the flight was called and the one hundred and fifty passengers began to file past the boarding gate.

Catching sight of what looked like the younger Ken Rossi, I said, "There!"

Wheeler paused the video and enlarged on the man at the gate.

"One of the others in the frame," Zoe said, "is Roger Islington."

He glanced at her. "The parachute fatality?"

"Yeah," Zoe said. "The accident you investigated last week. Can you sweep the picture to the right?" Zoe moved forward, motioning to another three men and a woman. "There's a group of them traveling together, partners in the same company."

"Okay, so putting weird Bermuda Triangle theories aside" – Zach gesticulated and spoke faster and faster – "could those two men, or any passenger for that matter, have survived when the plane went into the ocean? It's not as though there haven't been crash survivors before."

Wheeler shook his head. "We're talking about a projected three hundred miles per hour impact which would break the aircraft apart, with shattered bodies and portions of the craft being tossed about. It wouldn't take long for the entire wreck to submerge. Most, if not all of the bodies would be in the sinking craft, in their seats, killed on impact, or already dead from oxygen deprivation…" He gazed intently at each member of the team. "In the unlikely event that someone survived, then they are a speck in an ocean that's anywhere from five to ten thousand feet deep and many miles from any land or passing ships. Anticipated survival in those conditions is no more than three days max but more likely just a few hours. So, in a nutshell, could they survive the crash? It's possible, yes, but only for a short time, and with massive internal injuries."

"Back in the 1970s," Zach said, "a teenage German girl, Juliane Koepcke, was the sole survivor of a passenger plane that was hit by lightning and crashed in the Amazon rainforest. More than ninety other passengers, including the girl's mother, died."

Wheeler reacted to the professor's exuberance with an exasperated grin. "Yes, here at the NTSB we know of the crash–"

"Still strapped in her seat," Zach continued, "she was flung out of the plane, and dropped over a mile through the forest canopy and the padding on the seat shielding her from the full force of the impact."

"What happened to her?" Zoe asked.

"She was injured, but as her parents were scientists in the region and she'd spent some time with them in the jungle, she had survival skills that other people would not have had. She managed to walk for days, at which point she was found, miraculously, by a team of fishermen."

"Incredible," said Zoe.

"And incredibly rare," Wheeler pointed out. "The Koepcke case involved an extraordinary set of circumstances, such as the jungle canopy and the fact she was still securely in a seat that was thrown clear before the plane plummeted. Those factors don't apply here."

I smiled inwardly as the professor continued to stress the possibility of something else, something unnatural.

"No," Zach said, "but other factors could apply. No one could have predicted the German girl's survival and likewise, we can't envisage unforeseen elements that might have come into play here."

"As an investigator, I understand that nothing can ever be ruled out" – Wheeler lifted his arms – "but at the same time, you need to consider that there was a twelve-month, multimillion-dollar search operation conducted jointly by half a dozen countries with experts from all over the globe. No stone was left unturned, Zach." His gaze widened to take in the rest of the group. "None of that helps you, though, determine who your murder victim was."

"We'll need to see the transcripts of the family interviews," Will told the aviation man.

"Of course," Wheeler said. "I'll organize copies for you. And what's more, Agent McCord, as this investigation of yours relates both to Flight 387 and the recent parachute death, the NTSB would, of course, be available to lend its expertise and work alongside you. I'm more than happy to help in any way I can. And there is something else you need to know."

"What's that?" asked Will.

"The parachute fatality last week. Our investigation is still underway, but I can advise that we're not ruling it as an accident, as first thought."

"Why?" I asked.

"The cord was twisted, which prevented the chute from opening. But on further examination, we now believe the extent of the cord's malfunction had to have been the result of tampering. We have interviewed the owner and all of the staff out there and, at this stage, there is nothing to suggest any of them were involved."

"We're going to need to talk to them," I said.

"The owner, Brendan Davis, is one of those Gen Z entrepreneurs. Bought the business a few years ago when it was just a skydive operation, expanded it to include helicopter rides, and then franchised it across several states. I'll give you a direct line for him."

"As well as reading those plane transcripts and speaking with Davis and his people," I continued, "we'll be conducting interviews with surviving relatives of the other passengers who were traveling with Ken Rossi."

"Happy to go along with you for those and, in fact, maybe go one better." Wheeler smiled broadly.

"How's that?"

"Since his retirement, my father has resisted any offers to consult to the NTSB. But as one of the original Flight 387 investigators, I bet my bottom dollar he'd jump at the chance to be involved with this."

Will nodded. "We'd appreciate his insights."

"Our next stop, this afternoon, will be to talk with the skydive people," I said. "And first thing tomorrow, we'll be calling on Roger Islington's widow."

"I spoke with her last week, after her husband's death. Would it help if my father and I were to accompany you to that as well?" Wheeler offered.

"Can't hurt," Will said.

"Surely, these murder victims must be…" Wheeler paused, and I could see he didn't want to pre-empt any aspect of the FBI investigation.

"Impostors?" I said.

He shrugged. "Possible…?"

"Or the men who originally boarded that plane were not who *they* purported to be," Zoe suggested.

Zach weighed in, embodying every inch of my devil's advocate. "*Or,*" he emphasized, "those men on that plane are also the men who've just been murdered, and something else happened to them in the years in between, something way beyond our understanding…"

Chapter Eleven

The sign at the perimeter of the property said 'SkyLife – Heli-Rides and Skydives', and there was a sprawling brick and aluminum structure at the end of the entry road. A light eight-seater aircraft stood on one side of the building, with a helicopter and its launch pad on the opposite side.

Brendan Davis strode out of the front of the building and held up his right arm in a semi-wave. There was a broad welcoming smile on his face and just a trace of designer stubble. I imagined it had been grown and styled to fit with his smart, sporty, casual shirt, jeans, and boots. His longish dark hair was swept back off his forehead, framing strong, angular features.

"I got Ben Wheeler's call to say you guys were coming over," he said, shaking hands with me and Will. "My team and I are devastated by what happened to Roger, so I really appreciate you working with the NTSB to look into this."

"Thanks for making yourself available to see us," I said.

Scattered shafts of sunlight filtered through the breaks in the heavy cloud as Davis led us into the building and through to his office. He gestured for us to pull up chairs. "That won't be necessary," Will said. "We have just a few questions for you, and then we'd like to speak with the other staff members and to be shown over your facility here."

"Of course."

"We understand your team members have all been with you for quite a while."

"Yes. Couldn't wish for more experienced and committed staff."

"Your staff prepare and check the chutes?" I asked.

"Absolutely," Davis said. "And in the case of our regular, more experienced clients, the customers will prep and store their own chutes but my staff will double-check those each time they're lodged."

"And that was the case with Roger Islington's?"

"Yes."

"Where do you store the chutes?" Will asked.

"Our storage area, down the end of the corridor at the back of the building."

"Let's take a look."

Davis took us to a large room where shelves were packed with parachutes.

I peered into one of them. "Your regular clients' chutes are labeled with their names," I observed.

"That's right."

"So if someone came in looking to tamper with Roger Islington's chute, finding the correct one wouldn't pose a problem." It was more a statement than a question.

Davis shrugged, his strained expression showing for the first time the shadow that the incident had cast over his operation. "I guess not."

"We'll be sending over forensics to dust for fingerprints," Will advised.

"Please do," he said. "And Agent McCord, can I ask why the Feds, and not the local police, are investigating this with the NTSB?"

"It's part of a wider investigation," said Will.

"Someone sneaking or breaking in would need to know where our parachute storage area was," Davis commented, "and they'd have to be aware Roger was a regular customer, that he had his chute prepped in advance of a dive, and that we have them labeled."

"But you haven't had any after-hours break-ins?" I said.

"No."

"What contractors do you use?" I asked him.

"My staff and I do all the internal cleaning," Davis replied. "I use contractors for the groundskeeping, and occasionally for a special event, I'll bring in caterers. And, of course, tradesmen for maintenance and repairs."

"Recent catering events?"

"None."

"Tradesmen?"

"An electrician, a couple of weeks back. We had some wiring repair work done."

"When was Roger Islington's previous jump?" I asked.

"A couple of weeks ago."

"The NTSB is following up with the contractors," Will said. "What about security?"

"My staff and I keep an eye on things."

"CCTV?"

"No," Davis said.

"You might want to consider investing in that," Will responded, his eyebrow raised.

I could guess what he was thinking: *Cowboy operation.* "I understand that your business has franchises across the country?"

"That's right."

"So you wouldn't often be on the site here yourself?"

"No, I move around the various sites keeping a close eye on our operations. But I have extremely competent franchise owners in each location."

"Let's get your local manager and then your staff in, one by one, so we can ask them a few questions."

"Sure," the skydive man said. "You know the NTSB guys already questioned them?"

"Yes," I replied, "but believe me, Mr. Davis, you'd be surprised how many times an eyewitness inadvertently remembers something crucial on the second or even third time they are interviewed."

He shrugged. "I can imagine, and please, Agent Farris, it's Brendan."

The twinkle in his eye was that of a natural charmer and I returned the smile, briefly, but said nothing further.

Later, as we left, Davis was solemn again as he walked out the front with us. "I have to put out a positive vibe for the sake of the staff," he said, "but, like them, I'm gutted that one of our customers died because our operation here was compromised. I just can't fathom who, or why, someone would have done this."

"We'll keep you informed of our progress," I said.

His eyes on me, he said, "I appreciate it, Agent Farris."

We drove back to the office, and Will said, half-jokingly, "He's much too young for you, Ilona."

I made a face at him. "He looks to be around the same age range, maybe a couple or so years younger than me."

"As I said, he's *way* too young for you."

My eyebrow rose suggestively. "And he's very successful," I teased. There was a brief pause in our conversation and I sighed. "Davis and his team are putting on a brave front but they're genuinely shattered."

"Which leads us," Will said, "to his contractors, and his other customers. Let's see what the NTSB investigation, and our fingerprinting, show up."

* * *

Will arrived at his apartment as the twilight faded. Despite the bizarre nature of this case, his thoughts drifted and the image which kept stealing its way back into his mind was that of Ilona. He felt charged not just by the dynamic of working alongside her but also by the buzz from their renewed camaraderie. He'd missed her being around these past six weeks.

He'd known that, after the completion of the unit's first case, it was important for Ilona to take some time off to heal from the trauma of facing off against the Piper. She needed to reinvigorate and return refreshed. He'd wanted to see her, but he knew it was essential that she had mental distance from him and the UCU, especially with part of that time spent helping out at her old unit.

If she wants to contact me or any of the others, then it's best she does it in her own time.

Or so he'd kept telling himself. He had to force himself not to pick up his phone and call her. Allow time to run its course.

Long before he returned to Seattle to head up the newly formed Unsolvable Crimes Unit, Will had regretted his split from Ilona. He'd let it be known, during their previous case, that he was interested in revisiting their relationship. Starting afresh. At the same time, he fully understood her resistance to going back over old ground, opening up to the chance of being hurt once more. And he shared her view that they needed to concentrate on making a success of this new unit without personal feelings getting in the way.

If he and Ilona were going to get close again, then it was something that would hopefully re-evolve naturally, over time, first as colleagues and then… and then only *if* Ilona would be open to it.

He knew she still harbored feelings for him, he sensed that there was still that spark there – even if it was being kept safely beneath the surface – but he also knew that Ilona had a fierce stubborn streak. She was determined to leave the past behind, to move on. In stark contrast, he'd felt his heart beating more rapidly when they'd met up after almost two years apart, and a swell of hope when she'd agreed to be part of this new team.

Or am I thinking and acting like a lovestruck teenager?

He grimaced at the thought and even as he did, his phone buzzed, signaling an incoming text. He glanced at the sender's name on the screen.

Ilona.

* * *

I'd kicked off my shoes as I entered my apartment. Mine was a living space that was comfortable and uncluttered, the neutral tone of the walls complementing the simple, wooden furniture of earthy hues and cozy-colored fabrics. The home of a young woman who didn't spend an excess of time there – not because I was out partying, there was no suggestion of that in this décor, but because I was mostly out pursuing my career with a single-minded focus. I peeled away the layers of my clothing and shook my shoulders to ease the tension when my phone rang.

"You need to listen to the podcast," Brooke Goodman told me.

"There's another posting?"

"Yes."

I rang off and googled *One Voice* on my laptop. The website materialized and I clicked Play.

The voice phoning the podcast was that of a young male. "I listened to your report on the wharf murder and the boy playing mouth organ."

"And do you know anything about that?" Aiden Sharpe, primed at his console on the screen, asked.

"I heard exactly that," the caller said, "a mouth organ. It was from a distance but I saw a boy playing one, and he was sitting with a lanky, straw-hatted man."

As I watched, I sent a text to Will. 'You need to listen to the new *One Voice* podcast. Now.'

"Are you one of the people from the shelter near that marina?" the podcaster prompted.

"No," said the caller.

"Okay, so when and where did you see this man and boy?"

"It was that same night," the caller elaborated, his voice tentative. I sensed he was nervous about making the call. "They were on a rooftop."

"A rooftop?" Sharpe responded. "And how were you able to see them there? From an apartment window?"

"There are no apartments there."

"So, no apartments. How did you see and hear this man and–?"

The caller hung up and I winced. *Damn.* Had Aiden Sharpe pushed too far too fast? Then again, without this podcast, information such as this would never see the light of day.

I wondered why this witness had called *One Voice* instead of the police. What did the caller have to hide? Why had he hung up so abruptly?

And almost as quickly as I asked myself that question, I knew the answer.

* * *

I parked a few streets away from where the homeless community occupied the parking station. It was a quiet, light-industrial area. It was late in the evening and the neon lights cast an eerie glow on the deserted, hilly, and winding street. In my jacket and jeans, peaked cap pulled low, and a duffel bag slung over my shoulder, I wasn't out of place here and could have passed for one of the disadvantaged locals. I was on the same street that the man and the boy had walked up when they'd left the wharf the day before, but approaching from the other end, beyond the rise of the hill. I reached the alley into which the fisherman had told me the man and the boy had vanished.

A narrow corner, old brick walls on either side, no windows or doors, and nothing visible anyway. The fisherman had been stunned. The man and the boy hadn't been that far ahead of him and yet when he turned into the alley there was no sign of them. I glanced at the uneven walls, at the piping, and at the tiny windowsills much higher up.

The fisherman wouldn't have craned his neck and cast his gaze way up toward the top of the buildings.

I slipped off the jacket, stuffed it into the bag, and rammed the bag into a dark recess in the far corner.

I walked back to the center of the alley, took a running leap at the wall, and gripped the slim pipe. Using my legs and feet against the wall like a springboard, I reached higher, partly pulling myself up, partly thrusting my body upward with my toes.

I reached the first of the narrow ledges, enough to take my whole foot and propel me even higher, even faster.

The caller had seen the boy and the man on a rooftop.

I realized that the caller hadn't wanted to reveal that he was an urban climber, or a parkour runner, roaming the steep rises and ledges and roofs of the city's wharf area at night, probably with friends. That was how he'd seen the man and the boy. And that was how the whistling murderer and his young companion had vanished so quickly from the ground in that confined space.

They'd been up above, scaling those walls. Rooftopping. In recent years, urban climbing and parkour had become popular with thrill-seeking youths around the world but I knew it mostly played out under the radar of police forces. Parkour was jumping, leaping, climbing, vaulting, and flipping, using the surrounding landscape of walls, roofs, balconies, tunnels, and the myriad network of pipes. It was a dangerous game, an extreme sport, especially in a rainy city like this one, and a world that I knew well. But none of this meant the ragged man and the boy were urban climbers. They may have simply been using the upper levels as a place to hide, and for moving about unseen.

I reached the top and pulled myself up over the rim of the building, feeling the heady sense of euphoria that came in a rush with the thrill of the climb. I bit down on my lip, cursing myself for even attempting this. What was I thinking? I could have come here during the day, entered the building, and ascended to the roof via stairs.

I'd resisted my craving this past week, reminding myself I needed to beat this reckless addiction.

I was on a sloped iron roof, with wood and metal casing and joints from much more recent renovation work. I wasn't expecting to find the man who called himself El Silbón, the Whistler, here. The man and the boy would be long gone, but I was looking for signs that they'd been here, to confirm my suspicion.

I moved cautiously across the roof. I found a screwed-up, grease-stained paper bag, something that had contained takeout food. Had it been cast aside and forgotten when they'd moved on? Even up here, away from the scrutiny of the public or the police, I suspected that this killer wouldn't have knowingly left behind any telltale signs. There was a partly covered alcove, ideal for shelter in the event of rain. Did they sleep here, perhaps in sleeping bags or did they have a tiny makeshift tent? Who the hell were they? Roaming the rooftops, safe from the prying eyes of the world below, seeking out hidden places, constantly moving on.

I glanced at the building across the narrow space. Was that the spot from which an urban climber had sighted the straw-hatted man and boy, from a distance, hearing the strains of the music the boy played?

I couldn't reveal to Will that I'd climbed up here to confirm my suspicion that the man and the boy had used the rooftops for their escape. I'd simply given in to my overwhelming desire to climb. Will knew, of course, of how I'd partly climbed out of a deep shaft where I'd been imprisoned as a kidnapped teenager. What neither Will nor anyone else knew, was that ever since that time, urban climbing had filled me with a heady sense of exhilaration. It was as though I was reaching out for my freedom, again and again. It was my escape, my release valve, and my most closely guarded secret. It was also a criminal offense, considered as trespassing and reckless endangerment. An arrest would call into question my suitability to continue as an agent, earn me a suspension, and likely dismissal, ruin my credibility and my career.

However, the anonymous call to *One Voice*, stating that the boy and the man had been seen on a rooftop, gave me a genuine reason to voice my suspicion to the rest of the team.

I took a moment for myself, sitting cross-legged in the alcove, gazing at the night sky and the smattering of stars. As I did, I couldn't help but think of the mysteries the sky held. And of one mystery in particular. What had happened all those years ago to Flight 387 and its passengers?

Chapter Twelve

Day two

Ben Wheeler had arranged to meet me and Will outside the house of Roger Islington's widow. Will and I discussed the previous evening's *One Voice* podcast while he drove. As Will parked the car outside the Islington home, I saw Ben Wheeler was already there. He was standing beside his white Volkswagen with a mature man who was craggy-faced with graying hair, partially bald.

The day was clear, the morning sun strong, and wafts of clouds were like sky trails sprinkled across the blue. Will stood back, answering a call on his phone, as I strode forward. Ben Wheeler introduced me to the other man.

"My father, Robert," he said, "flew up from 'Frisco on a red-eye."

The older Wheeler extended his hand. "Pleased to meet you, young lady. And thanks for allowing me to come along and observe."

"I've heard it's not that easy to drag you out of retirement."

He shot me a mischievous grin. "You dangled one hell of a carrot."

"I gather Ben has filled you in on the unusual aspects of this."

"Absolutely."

Even in his retirement, I could see that this man had an innate curiosity for anything related to his field.

"What Ben told me doesn't make much sense, but as you know I was on the original Flight 387 investigation. I'll stay in the background, but I'll certainly let you know if anything strikes an unusual note with me."

"Sometimes it's the smallest detail—"

"Oh, I know, I know." Robert Wheeler raised his right arm, gently waving his finger in my direction. "I know you're the agent who was interviewed on television about that Pied Piper case," he said, "but I've seen you somewhere else... *before* that..." He studied my face, searching his memory.

I smiled. "Maybe I've just got one of *those* faces."

"No, it's..." Recognition dawned in his eyes. "You're the agent who talked down that rooftop suicide jumper."

Ben Wheeler also registered his recognition. "Of course."

I grimaced. "My fifteen minutes won't seem to go away."

"You would've met Detective Paul Radner that night?" Ben Wheeler asked.

I nodded. "I've known Detective Radner for a while."

"I feel for the guy," he said. "Losing his daughter that way."

"Yes," I said.

"What happened to the detective's daughter?" Robert Wheeler asked.

"Her name was Sarah," I replied. "She became involved with a group of urban climbers. She fell to her death two years ago."

In my previous Bureau role, I'd assisted Radner and the Seattle Police Department in their crackdown on small groups of urban climbers who presented a danger to themselves and others. I was acutely aware that Radner had a powerful personal motive for the crackdown.

"Dear God," he said.

"And how do you know Detective Radner?" I asked.

"He attended a few of the accident scenes that the NTSB's been called to. Including Roger Islington's accident."

"Is the detective up to speed with your findings?" I asked.

"He is. And we'll be holding a follow-up briefing with the SPD later this morning." Changing the subject, he asked, "How did your visit to Brendan Davis at SkyLife go?"

"Nothing further to report on top of what you already know. We have a forensics team checking over the facility this morning, but other than that, the focus is on the contractors, tradespeople, and their customer base."

Will joined us and after introductions, he pulled me aside. "That was Zoe. She's programmed Themis to search the social security numbers for the other passengers who were business partners with Rossi and Islington."

"Anything current?"

"All four of the other partners – Morley, Garcia, Miguel, and Ramsay – have had some very minor activity on their SS number in recent years, but once again not for five years after the plane's disappearance," Will revealed.

"So there's more of these Flight 387 passengers out there."

"Let's see what we can learn from Islington's widow." Will led the way to the front door, Ben and Robert Wheeler following.

Once inside, the aviation men stood back, observing as Will. I sat with Beverley Islington.

She was aged in her early forties, tall and thin with long brown hair, her lipstick and eyeliner heavier than they needed to be. She seemed disinterested in our visit. "I told the local police everything I could last week," she said quietly.

"We'll try to take up as little of your time as possible," Will said.

"According to your statement, you last saw your husband, briefly, the night before his death," I said.

"That's right." A cast of sorrow fell across the woman's eyes. She was looking at me blankly as though not seeing me.

"Did your husband say anything to you, Mrs. Islington, about a young boy of around twelve years old that he might have encountered?"

The widow's eyes widened in surprise. "Yes. He said he'd been walking to his car in the city when the strangest thing happened. A boy came up to him with some sort of message."

"Did your husband say what the message was?" I asked.

Beverley Islington shook her head. "No. He seemed to think it was a mistake, that the boy was talking to the wrong person."

"Did he say whether there was a tall man anywhere in the area, maybe whistling?"

"Yes, he did." Now the woman's face showed alarm. "He heard an odd whistling sound, and it was coming from a tall, straw-hatted man, watching from up the street. I could tell Roger was spooked by the whole thing. The strange boy then ran off, to where the man was, and Roger was… mystified. What is this all about?"

"Did your husband say whether the boy gave him a USB stick?" I pressed on, injecting as sympathetic a tone as I could into my voice.

"No." The woman paused, searching her mind again, and then exhaled. "I barely saw him that evening. He was changing clothes, going straight out to another business meeting, a dinner. He came back from that later after I'd gone to bed, and he left early the next morning, to go…" Her voice trailed off.

"Would you mind," I said softly, "if my colleague and I took a look over your husband's possessions?"

"You're looking for a USB?"

"Yes."

There were tears in the woman's eyes and her voice rose. "But my husband died in a parachuting accident," she protested, her breath coming in heavy gasps now. "What has any of this got to do with the accident?" Her eyes widened. "You think it *wasn't* an accident?"

"If the USB we're looking for is here," I said, "then it would be a great help to us in a wider investigation." I stopped myself from revealing any more at this early stage. "We're also looking into an anomaly in your husband's background, Mrs. Islington."

The woman sighed. "What kind of anomaly?"

Will shifted in his seat. "How long have you and your husband been together?"

"Ten years."

"Would you know if Roger, before you knew him, ever took a flight to Caracas?"

"He never mentioned anything like that," the woman said. "Why do you ask?"

"If you could bear with us," I said, "we don't have anything more definitive at this stage—"

"But it would help your inquiries to search for a USB?"

I gave a gentle smile. "Yes, it would."

* * *

Robert Wheeler remained downstairs, speaking with the widow, while Will, Ben, and I entered Islington's study upstairs. Slowly and methodically, we looked through his drawers, his shelves, and his desk. Mrs. Islington hadn't touched anything since his death and it took only a few minutes to find the USB laying alongside the PC on Roger Islington's desk.

A password was scribbled on a strip of paper, taped to the side of the PC. Will fired up the computer and we listened to the audio file on the USB.

A whistle, followed by the low, calm voice of the boy.

> *The years have passed*
> *Your time has come*
> *Listen for the whistling of El Silbón.*

And then the man's whistle again, once again descending into the demonic hiss that sounded anything but human.

Chapter Thirteen

Our next stop would be to see the woman who had been Roger Islington's live-in girlfriend at the time of his disappearance two decades before. At the time, Islington and his partner had lived in Florida. The girlfriend, Jill Carson, had later married and in recent years had moved to Washington.

The Wheelers followed Will's blue Ford as we headed back through Seattle to the northern suburbs.

The night before, I had contacted Will, alerting him to *One Voice*'s newly posted installment. We'd discussed it briefly on the drive to Madrona Beach, but I had held back putting forth my suspicion. Biding my time. I didn't want to appear too quick to jump on the urban climbing subject.

Now, as Will drove us north, I said, "I've been giving more thought to the podcast caller's claim that he saw the Whistler and the boy on a rooftop."

"I'm listening," he said.

"It would explain how they vanished in that narrow alley."

He glanced at me as he drove. "You think they climbed to the roof of one of those buildings?"

"Makes sense," I said. "The police put out a description but have had no calls from anyone who's seen them. Local area CCTV didn't show them anywhere in the vicinity that night."

"But if they were on the roof–"

"They may not be urban climbers as such, Will, but it explains how they've moved around without being spotted" – I pointed a finger skyward – "and if they're camping up there…"

"You think the caller to the podcast was another climber, and that's how he came to see them?"

"Yes. And if we could get a drone up there, overnight, to scan the city's roofs…"

Will grinned. "Your detective friend Radner would love that. A drone might spot other climbers, the danger-lovers he wants to clamp down on. That'd give him the opportunity without it coming out of the SPD's budget." He frowned, unsure. "But regardless, it's a hell of a stretch."

"For God's sake, Will, everything about this case is a hell of a stretch."

"Fair point. But that's a lot of roofs and they could be anywhere by now."

"I know, but it's just for one night, in case they're still in Seattle."

"You think they'll be moving on?"

"This Whistler's killed Rossi and most likely Islington as well. There were four other business partners on that flight whose SS numbers have since been used, in three other states. What if this killer is tracking down every one of them?"

"I've been thinking the same," Will said. "Zoe's collecting current addresses and Marcia's finding out everything she can about them."

"*If* that's the case, then Rossi and Islington may be just the first two murders," I stated. "It means that the killer knew Islington lived here, knew he went parachuting and knew that Rossi would be sailing in and spending a few nights. Two birds with one stone in Seattle, so to speak."

"And no reason now not to move on."

"Yes. And if they are sleeping out on roofs, then why, when they could have been staying in motels? Money? And if that's a problem, how will they be traveling across the states?"

Will pulled the car over to the side of the road. He looked across to the modest bungalow with a small front yard. "Let's see if the lady who lived with Islington before he vanished can tell us anything new."

* * *

"My goodness," the woman declared on sighting Robert Wheeler. "You're the gentleman I spoke to twenty years ago…"

Wheeler Snr smiled broadly and shook her hand gently. "Retired now, and lending a hand to these fine young federal agents, and" – he gestured to Ben – "my son, Ben, also now with the NTSB."

Jill Carson, fair-skinned and red-haired, introduced herself as she ushered us through the front door and into her living room. "You have to understand that I haven't thought about Roger for a while now. With a husband, two littlies, a part-time job…" She shrugged, raising her arms. "It can get a little crazy at times."

"Our records show that Roger was born here in the US but spent quite a bit of time in Caracas," Will said.

"Oh yes, that damn job." She sighed with frustration. "Roger was a real up-and-comer at the bank where he worked. He dealt with international investments and had a lot of dealings with the Venezuelans. A group of them, some from Venezuela, some not, formed their own independent investment firm for South American clients."

"So he spent a bit of time going back and forth as part of that firm?" I asked.

"Not really," Jill Carson said. "Every few months maybe, but sometimes the partners met here in the US, and sometimes over there."

"And the flight they were all on together?" I queried.

The woman shrugged. "Some sort of campaign. As a team, they met with groups of investors in Caracas, and then traveled to the US to do the same at an event in Florida." There was a faraway look in her eyes, the painful memory dredging itself up. "Which, of course, never happened." As though to divert herself from that, she returned her gaze to Robert Wheeler. "You were the accident investigator who spoke to a whole group of the relatives. Oh, we were so angry, weren't we?"

"You had every right to be," he said.

"There'd been such a lack of information from the authorities," Jill Carson said. "We wanted answers and we weren't getting any. There was a meeting at the airport. Furious people, waving their fists, shouting at the investigation team. You calmed them down."

"Dad was always the charmer," Ben Wheeler interjected with a smile.

"He certainly was that day," the woman said.

"I remember that day quite clearly," Robert Wheeler said. "So many grieving people, so many faces in the crowd. I don't recall the names or the faces of the individuals of course–"

"Of course not."

"But I remember *yours*," he said. "We spoke."

"Yes," she responded. "You spent some time with a few of us individually."

Robert Wheeler frowned. "You seem more familiar than I would expect." And then recognition dawned, and he snapped his fingers. "You were the lady on crutches."

"Yes."

"That's why I remember your face. You'd been in a car accident just a few weeks after the flight disappeared."

"A minor accident," she elaborated, "but I'd broken my foot. I was so angry, I thought I must've been cursed. First, my boyfriend is on that damn plane, my older sister had a cancer scare, I'm in a car smash and then I had a break-in at my home, all in the month after the disappearance. Such a strange, awful time."

"Mrs. Carson," I said, "the FBI is investigating a case and Roger's name and the name of one of Roger's business partners came up." I waved toward the Wheelers. "That's why we've consulted with the NTSB. That's why we're talking to the families of each of the other business partners."

A puzzled expression crossed the woman's face. "What's this about?"

"We're simply asking if there was anything unusual you might have noticed in the time after the flight's disappearance, anything that might have been connected to Roger or any of his colleagues?"

"No," she said, "nothing at all."

Robert Wheeler spoke up, drawing on his connection with the woman. "Perhaps if you could cast your mind back to that period, Mrs. Carson, as hard as I know that must be. And especially after all this time."

She smiled gently at him, then closed her eyes, willing the past to replay. Presently, she said, "The firm was wound down, but I'd never had anything to do with any of that." She fiddled with a strand of her hair. "I had a phone call, and this must have been a few months later; someone with an accent, asking for Roger. I told them he'd died in the plane crash…" Her voice trailed away.

"What kind of accent?" I asked.

"South American. I figured it was something to do with the firm, someone who hadn't been in touch with them for a while, who didn't realize…"

"And how did they respond?" I urged.

"The caller said he didn't believe me and then he hung up." She was lost in the memory, her eyes glazing. "I remember it upset me… but I soon forgot all about it, and of course, it was all so long ago now. I married ten years later, had children, and we moved here to Seattle just a few years ago due to my husband's work."

"I'm sorry to have you drag out those unpleasant memories," I said.

"I just can't imagine what this investigation could have to do with Roger's firm."

"We're investigating the deaths of two men who have the same social security numbers and appearances as Roger and Ken Rossi," Will advised her.

Jill Carson shot him a confused look.

I held up a photo. "This is the Roger Islington who lived in Seattle and who died last week."

The woman stared at the photo. "He lived *here*, in Seattle?"

"Madrona Beach actually," I said.

"That face reminds me of Roger's father at the time," she said. "I never kept in touch with Roger's parents; I know they died a few years back" – she gestured toward the photo – "but that *can't* be Roger…"

"Do you still have any photos of Roger from when the two of you were together?" I asked.

She nodded. "Yes. In an old photo album."

Jill Carson led us through to a spare room that was packed tight with odds and ends and retrieved an album from a cupboard in the corner. She flicked through the album and handed the open book to me. "We weren't much into photos back then and I suppose, when I think about it, we'd only been together for less than a year. Looks like there's just this one that someone snapped at a party."

My gaze moved from the recent photo of Roger Islington to the snapshot from twenty years ago. And back again. The general cast of features was the same with relatively normal signs of aging.

I focused on the eyes, the most telling feature of any person at any age, but with just one recent license photo, and the eyes averted slightly in the older picture, it was hard to be sure.

"As with Rossi," Will stated, "we're looking at what passes for an older version of the same man."

Once again, we thanked Jill Carson for her help, and then the four of us headed outside to the cars.

Ben Wheeler's words seemed to have embedded themselves in my mind. He'd assured us it would be a miracle if anyone survived the crash of a commercial airliner plummeting into the North Atlantic. And even in the unlikely possibility that did happen, they could not survive more than a few hours in the vastness of that ocean.

How could this same man have been living in Seattle for the past fifteen years? If he wasn't Roger Islington, who was he? And if it was him, how could he have survived and where had he been for the first five years after the crash?

Chapter Fourteen

As I walked back into the UCU with Will, Zoe Marshall was pacing like a panther, ready to pounce.

"One of the other SS numbers currently in use belongs to Don Morley," she said as we entered, "and he lives in

Portland with his husband, Clarence Rawson. I figured you'd want to go see him, so I placed a call to Morley to confirm the address was current and that he'd be there."

"And?" I pressed, sensing more.

"The husband answered. He said Morley had gone out for his morning run and hadn't returned. He said it was out of character, that he tried to phone Morley but wasn't getting an answer."

"He was worried?"

"Yes. He wanted to report his husband missing and I said the police would consider it was too soon for that, and asked if there was anywhere, he might've gone–"

"There's something else?" I asked.

"Yes, he said he thought something odd was going on. Morley had been acting a little strange since the afternoon before. He said Morley ran twice a day, and the previous afternoon a strange boy had approached him with a message."

"Did he say there was a USB?"

"Rawson said he was going to call the police regardless and he hung up before I could get more information."

Will whirled toward Marcia. "Contact Portland Police, have them put out a BOLO on Morley," he instructed. "It's a three-hour drive down there. Marcia, see how quickly we can get a G-550 in the air."

"You think this Whistler has gone after Morley now?" Zach asked.

"If we're right," Will said, "then this oddball must've had a plan all along to go after each of these six passengers."

Zach raised his hands, frowning. "How does he even know about them?"

A flashing red light and an alarm erupted from the landline phone on Zoe's console. She flashed a look at me as she turned, reaching for the phone. "The signal you set up with the podcaster."

"What's that about?" Zach wondered.

"I suggested to Aiden Sharpe that he could create ongoing suspense for his podcasts if he put out a message to the Whistler, saying he knows he's out there, calling him a coward, and suggesting he phone the podcast to speak up for himself," I said.

"We didn't want Sharpe revealing details on air that the other anonymous caller had given him," Will elaborated. "This was Ilona's idea on something for him to run with until we gave him the clear on revealing more."

"But we've also rigged Sharpe's phone so that he could alert us if that happened" – my eyebrow raised in anticipation – "and Zoe's patched herself in to run a trace on the call."

Zoe tapped her keyboard and flicked a switch on the phone. The podcast came alive on the screen as she donned a headset.

"It's not the Whistler phoning in," she revealed.

"Who is it?" I asked.

"It's the boy."

I watched as Aiden Sharpe straightened in his chair, taking the call. I could see that he was surprised, excited, and fascinated all at once.

"You asked for the whistling man to phone you."

It was the voice of a young boy, his tone clear and confident.

"Yes," Sharpe said quickly. "You have something you can tell us, young man?"

"I have a message from El Silbón, the Whistler."

"Are you the boy who was at the marina in Seattle?" Sharpe asked, rapidly taking control of the conversation.

"Yes."

"And what is the message?"

"You should not speak about El Silbón, the Whistler. You do not understand."

I knew there were tens of thousands of viewers watching as Sharpe tilted back in his chair. "What don't I understand?" the podcaster fired back.

"Do not speak about El Silbón," the young voice repeated.

I knew that the best way to get answers was to engage the young caller in conversation and subtly steer him in the direction wanted, and Sharpe did just that. "Can I ask you your name, young man?"

"I've had lots of names."

The *One Voice* podcaster made a face which, I expected, was for dramatic effect. "Okay, but what is your name now, the name you go by? Can you tell me that?"

"No."

Sharpe tried a different tack. Will and I had told him to keep the caller on the line for as long as possible. Digital technology meant that landline or cell phone calls could be traced immediately but we expected that any call from the Whistler or the boy would be from a prepaid burner. Sharpe had been told it would take longer to triangulate such a phone's position off cell phone towers.

"Let me ask the question all of my listeners would want to ask you." The podcaster's voice swelled with warmth and friendliness despite the subject matter. "Can you tell me why the man at the marina was warned he was going to die?"

"It's so that he would know."

"Yes, I get that," Sharpe said, "but why did he have to die?"

"It was meant to be."

"Okay, but" – Sharpe spoke rapidly – "what can you tell me about the man who sent you to deliver the message? Do you know why he had to kill Mr. Rossi?"

Now you've given the victim a name, I was thinking, now you've made it personal. I hoped this would lead to the boy opening up more.

"It's so that they will know," the boy repeated, only this time he said *they,* and Sharpe's eyes widened at the use of the plural. "I give them the message so that they know The Whistler has come for them." And then the line went dead.

"Did we get it?" Will asked.

Zoe swung around on her chair. "Got it. The kid was calling from Portland."

Chapter Fifteen

It was less than an hour's flight in the G-550 jet from Tacoma Airport to Portland International.

Don Morley's luxurious, top-floor, four-bedroom apartment had views of the Tom McCall Waterfront Park and the Willamette River.

Photos of Morley from the archives had shown an African American man in his thirties, which meant that he would be in his fifties now, as was his husband, Clarence Rawson. On the flight across, I had been on my phone, scrolling through the details that Zoe had researched. Same-sex marriage had been recognized in Oregon since 2014 and Morley and Rawson had wed not long after. They'd been living together for several years before that. Morley, like the other five passengers who'd been his colleagues, had appeared fifteen years ago as a self-funded retiree, living off investments. His main interest was sports, and he'd taken part in a few local, amateur-level marathons.

Once again, there was absolutely nothing that would draw attention to his quiet lifestyle or for anyone to connect him with the Don Morley of two decades before. Even the official marriage document hadn't raised any suspicions.

"I phoned the Portland Police," Clarence Rawson told me and Will when we appeared on his doorstep. He was dark-skinned and portly, his hair flecked with gray. He opened his door wider, waving us in. "They said it was too early to list him as a missing person. I feel like I'm being paranoid. Am I? Am I being paranoid?" The man had the shakes and he sat down on his sofa, mopping his brow with a handkerchief.

"When did Don go out for his morning run?" I asked.

"He's an early riser: 7 a.m."

"And how long does he usually run for?"

"A couple of hours."

"Where exactly?" Will asked.

"The Esplanade, the Green Loop." Rawson shrugged. "All over. And sometimes he grabs a coffee with a few of the locals along the waterfront." He stared at them as though a long, sullen look might provide answers. "He would never be gone for half a day without letting me know what's going on."

"We've organized for local police to be on the lookout for him," Will said.

A questioning expression crossed Rawson's face. "You said you were federal agents?"

"That's right," I said.

"And you wanted to ask me about Don?" Alarm spread across his already distraught features. "Why would Feds be asking about Don? Why have you alerted the police when the local PDD already told me he couldn't be listed—"

"Mr. Rawson," I interjected, "we're here on another matter. We want to ask Don about the boy who approached him yesterday. And we need to ask him if, years ago, he had any connection with Venezuela."

"Venezuela?" Rawson shook his head. "He's never spoken about the past. Said it was painful for him to think about it, that his family was troublesome when he was a kid, that he... The only thing he ever mentioned, really, was that he was from the southern states."

I locked eyes with Will and our visual exchange said it all. We didn't believe a word of what Morley had told his husband. A cover. So that his real background wouldn't be suspected. Or was the cover for another reason entirely?

"Did Don say anything to you about the boy handing him a USB?" I asked.

Rawson shook his head. 'No, he… There was something in his hand when he came in, though. He looked down at it a couple of times. I didn't pay attention, didn't actually see–"

"Where would he have been likely to put something like that?" I asked.

"He has a laptop in his study."

Rawson led us to the room and my eyes fell on the shiny oblong stick on the desk.

"I haven't seen that before," Rawson said.

Rawson's phone rang and as he took the call his face lit up. "Don! Thank God," he exclaimed, his eyes tearing up with relief as he made eye contact with me. "Where have you been?" He listened for a moment, his features expressing concern.

"What is it, sir," I asked.

Placing his hand over the phone, Rawson said to me, "Says he got distracted and lost all sense of time. He saw that boy again, the one from yesterday. The boy was watching him. When Don approached the boy, the kid ran off and silly old Don – still thinks he's twenty-five sometimes – followed him. He'd already been on his run for a while, so he got all out of breath and had to rest, didn't he?"

I reached for the phone in Rawson's hand. "Let me speak to him."

He handed me the phone.

"Don," I spoke calmly but firmly, "this is Special Agent Ilona Farris. My colleague and I would like to speak to you urgently about the boy you encountered. Could you tell me exactly where you are right now?"

I listened to his response, shooting a glance at Will, and then I spoke again into the phone. "Stay precisely where you are, Don. My partner and I are on the way there and we will escort you back home."

Chapter Sixteen

Will and I jumped in our rented vehicle and screeched down the road toward the riverside.

We were on the Naito Parkway when I said, "Spotted him." Morley was on the opposite side of the street, standing on the corner of a clear patch of grass that was part of the reserve, shaded by a grove of forest green oaks. A group of cyclists sped by.

Will pulled over to the side and I stepped from the vehicle, signaling to the man across the street. "We just spoke on the phone," I called out.

I saw him acknowledge this with a tip of the head.

"I'll escort him over," I called back to Will as I stepped onto the road, watching for a break in the traffic. The sun was strong, and the glare shimmered off the asphalt. I squinted, eyes on Morley again, and shouted, "Wait there, I'm coming across."

Ever since I'd been kidnapped as a teenager, I had been acutely aware of my surroundings, determined to never be caught off-guard again. I'd kept my senses primed for anything, however slight, that might be out of the ordinary. My peripheral vision alerted me to something moving at high speed further along the street. My head whipped in that direction just as an SUV careened from the road and onto the sidewalk, its velocity increasing unnaturally as it sped directly at the man near the corner.

I saw Morley's head turn toward the vehicle as I began to sprint forward, raising my arm and signaling to him again, shouting, "Get back!"

As close as I was, I was still too far away. As fast as Morley might've moved, it was far too late to avoid the vehicle as it slammed into him, the sickening crunch an assault to my ears. Morley's body hurled into the air like a broken doll and crashed back down onto the grassy patch. My eyes followed the SUV, memorizing the license plate as it rejoined the road and roared away.

Reaching Morley, I knelt beside the body, feeling for a pulse. Will appeared beside me. "He's gone," I said, breathing heavily, my voice raspy, strands of hair dropping across my eyes.

"You wait by the body and call it in," Will said, "I'll go after–"

I cut across him. "Will, let me go after that maniac. I got a good view of the SUV; I know the license plate." I was already on my feet.

As I headed back across the road, Will called after me. "Ilona–"

"I'll keep my distance until backup arrives."

I knew how much every single second counted here. The Whistler would be dumping that vehicle at the very first opportunity, a precaution in case anyone had reported the vehicle and its registration number. But I doubted he'd suspect that an FBI agent was on the scene and giving chase.

I spied the SUV several car lengths ahead. I accelerated, ignoring speed limits.

I'll force this lunatic off the road if I have to.

We were moving into a higher-density area where traffic was slowing, and pedestrians were everywhere. The SUV stopped, caught in traffic in the middle of the street. Suddenly, the SUV's doors were thrown open. The man in the hat, a bag slung over his shoulder, exited the car and the boy leaped out from the passenger side. The traffic started moving again. Horns blared and as I watched, stunned, the Whistler and the boy ran into the immediately adjacent laneway, a mere slit between two large buildings.

He'd intended to abandon the car here, I realized. He'd planned every aspect, scouting the area in advance, watching Morley's movements in the morning. The same MO as their escape after the attack on Ken Rossi.

That's the reason he had the boy attract Morley's attention, leading him on a merry chase while the Whistler checked out the area.

Think like the Whistler, I told myself as I pulled the vehicle to the side of the street.

He's going to take to the rooftops again.

I ran along the street and, slowing down, cautiously peered around the corner of the laneway first before charging into it. The lane twisted its way between the two buildings on either side and then opened out onto the street on the far side of the block. I kept my eyes on the walls of the buildings as I navigated the narrow walkway between the older-style brownstone. Had they already scampered over one of the balconies or ledges or into one of the windows, avoiding being seen as much as possible as they made their climb? Reaching the street at the opposite end of the lane I scanned in all directions but there was no sign of the man and the boy.

I craned my neck, looking skyward.

You're up there somewhere.

I wanted to climb. This man and the young boy with him couldn't possibly match my climbing skills.

At the same time, I had to avoid any visible action that might expose me as an urban climber.

Damn that. I have to catch these two.

I ran back along the lane to the main thoroughfare and to the building's entry. I took the elevator to the top floor, from there accessing the stairwell up to the roof. I didn't know whether the Whistler and his companion might have climbed across the walls from one building to another. If so, I wouldn't have the chance to spot them from the inside, but this was the safest and fastest option for now.

The rooftop had two or three levels of scaffolding with pipes and water tanks, partly level and partly sloped. I moved to the edge and scanned the surrounding roofs.

The city's rooftops were like plateaus, separated by canyons of varying widths and depths.

To take parkour seriously as a sport required intense training, a great deal of experience, and properly controlled environments. For the Whistler, it was providing escape routes and hiding places. Were he and his much younger companion practitioners of parkour?

And then I saw them, easing up over the edge of the next building – its roof a little lower than this one, the surface flatter. They'd already crossed to it on their climb up. Sometimes protruding balconies left a short gap to leap between the spaces.

The boy saw me across the way, watching them. He pointed and the hatted man looked up, his face in shadow.

I saw the long, winding rope in his hands. That was what had been in the bag that hung from his shoulder. Unlike serious urban climbers and parkour runners, they were using rope to assist them. He didn't appear at all concerned when he saw me. He and the boy made their way across the roof to the opposite side, and they clambered over its edge.

I assessed the gap from my building to the one alongside. Around six feet. I could do this.

You think I'm some random observer, that there's no chance I'd be coming after you?

Think again.

I retreated from the edge, giving myself plenty of runway, sucked in a deep breath, steeled myself – *get in the zone* – and then ran and leaped.

Chapter Seventeen

It was only a slight drop to the next roof, and it was flat. I knew how to land, tumble, and roll. I hoped the padded lining in my jacket pockets would protect my phone. Back on my feet I sprinted to the edge and peered over.

These two knew how to navigate the urban landscape swiftly and safely. Even the young boy. How?

They were several stories down and, like monkeys, they were swinging from the pipes and the ledges, determining the foot and handholds with natural precision.

I positioned myself and eased over the edge. Like the Whistler I knew to follow the pipes, to visually scout and utilize the cracks or crevasses and ledges and windowsills on this brownstone. The killer had chosen this spot for that reason, the older brick buildings afforded them better climbs with less need for a rope.

I heard a shout from below.

They know I'm following.

I didn't foresee what happened next.

I heard the shattering of glass and, looking down, I saw the Whistler had smashed one of the windows, but he wasn't attempting to go through it. He took hold of a large piece of jagged glass and holding on to the windowsill with one hand he arched his body back, the jagged piece in his other hand, that arm rotating around and around.

No.

And with the force of the propulsion behind his swing, he hurled the glass slab upwards, his aim remarkably precise.

The glass hit my left leg like a piece of shrapnel, slicing into the fabric of my pants.

Almost immediately another one glanced off my lower back.

And then a handful of much smaller but equally sharp pieces flew higher, just past my head, and then showered me as gravity pulled them back.

I climbed back up to get myself beyond the reach of the Whistler's throws. Glancing down again I saw that he had knocked out more of the glass and was angling to the side, allowing the boy to wriggle through.

After which, he followed.

I assessed the situation. If I climbed down intending to follow them through that opening, I couldn't be sure the Whistler wouldn't be poised inside ready to lash out with his foot and knock me off the wall.

Instead, I climbed back to the roof and found the entry point to the building's stairwell. They wouldn't take the elevator; I was certain the man and the boy wouldn't allow the possibility of being entrapped in an enclosed space like that. They would take the stairs.

I flew down those steps as fast as I was able, keeping my focus both on my footing and also on any sign of the Whistler on the stairway immediately beneath me.

I reached the ground level, shoved open the heavy steel door, and burst out onto another laneway around the corner from the previous one, at the rear of the buildings.

There was no sign of the man and the boy. Had they even exited the building this way? Could they have retraced their steps and found a different exit point, or had they returned to the exterior wall, climbing down from there?

I moved stealthily along the laneway, slipping my revolver from my shoulder pouch and negotiating the corner to the next one.

Empty.

I pulled out my phone and called Will.

I wouldn't reveal that I'd attempted the chase across the roofs and the walls; that would raise too many questions about my prowess up there. Instead, I gave the address of the building and reported that the Whistler had fled from his car into the lane, that I'd seen him scaling the walls with the boy, that I'd taken the elevator to the roof and had seen them disappear over the side. Within minutes there would be police on foot and in cars searching this office block and the surrounding buildings and streets.

I took a moment to catch my breath and I bit down on my lip in frustration. I had been so close. A few more minutes and the Whistler would have been within my grasp.

Instead, he'd proven himself to be an experienced climber and athlete with the prowess of a soldier, drawing on his surroundings not just as an escape route but also, in his use of the smashed glass, as a weapon.

And then, even with a young boy beside him, he'd used those same surroundings to vanish, once again like the El Silbón of legend, into thin air.

Chapter Eighteen

Back in Seattle, Will and I joined Zach, Zoe, and Marcia, listening to the USB that Morley had been handed.

We heard the now-familiar seven notes of the whistle, ascending, repeating. And the boy's voice.

> *The years have passed*
> *Your time has come*
> *Listen for the whistling of El Silbón.*

Once again, the hiss that followed raised in me a fear that was potent and visceral, a raw emotion that hadn't been there just a moment earlier but was now unexpectedly drawn out from a place deep within my psyche. It was a fear that spoke to me, something I had come to know only too well from the nightmares I'd had over the years. Just as quickly as that emotion flared, I threw up a mental barrier, pushing it back.

"Rossi's murder was the day before yesterday," I said, "and we know the Whistler and the boy spent that night on the rooftop where they were spotted by other climbers."

"Which means," Will added, "that they have to have traveled to Portland yesterday for the boy to approach Morley yesterday afternoon."

"So how did they travel?" Zach said.

I tapped off the possibilities on my fingers. "It's forty minutes or so by air, three hours by car or bus. We need to ascertain how they're moving across the States given they don't appear to be staying in motels and presumably have no funds."

"We can't assume anything at this point," Will said. "Marcia–"

"Checking airlines and bus companies and car rentals," Marcia preempted him. "And checking on the stolen car, thanks to Ilona memorizing that number."

"And to establish whether or not Rossi and Morley are the same men who were on that plane," Zoe said, "I've got Themis undertaking a deep dive into historical data for dental or medical records, but nothing so far."

Will turned to me. "Your idea – a drone scanning the rooftops – we had no results last night in Seattle obviously, but I'm organizing the same for Portland tonight."

"Good chance they'll still be in the area before moving on again," I said. "Now, if we can pinpoint which of the passengers he'll be targeting next."

* * *

I had no sooner sat down in my office than I saw a familiar figure.

Ross Grande strode in with a broad, triumphant smile. Grande was the agent who'd clasped my hand, pulling me from the deep tunnel after my abduction.

He was now Assistant Director of Special Operations. Based in Washington DC, he headed up various panels devising strategies for the Bureau's development and future direction. One of those panels, which included Will, approved Themis and formed the Unsolvable Crimes Unit.

"I was thrilled you agreed to join the team." He hugged me as I rose from my chair. "Your dad would've been incredibly proud. *I'm* incredibly proud."

At that moment I realized it was A.D. Ross Grande, not the assistant director who'd approached me outside my apartment six weeks ago, who was really behind the effort to persuade me to remain with the UCU after the first case. It seemed obvious to me now and I said as much to him.

His grin broadened but his eyes remained as inscrutable as I'd always found them to be. "That's privileged information, young lady," he said with a hint of mischief.

"Why didn't you approach me yourself, Ross?"

"You and I go back a long way, and your father and I went back even further. I thought that you'd respond to the appeal if it came from one of the other directors instead of an old family friend. I didn't want you influenced by our history."

"You realize you were being deceptive."

He spread his hands sheepishly. "Guilty. But it worked, didn't it?"

"And to what do we owe this visit today, all the way from DC?"

"Important to let you know in person – important to let everyone on this team know – that HQ was more than pleased with the swift resolution to the Piper case. That's obvious, I guess, from the fact we've approved an initial twelve-month trial run for the UCU. There's still a lot of uncertainty about the Themis concept and whether it will ultimately reduce the unsolved crime rate, but it's an excellent start."

"Thank you."

"And this new case" – he gestured approvingly – "once again, highly unusual, and an early solution will play out well with the public and with the media–"

"And with the big bosses," I interjected.

"Indeed."

"Of which you're one," I said cheekily.

"I may seem to be in a high and mighty position, Ilona, but I'm a cog in that much bigger wheel, answerable to the higher-ups, who are ultimately answerable to the president and the public. Obviously, we want it to work, and if the results warrant it, we can start to look at a national rollout. Teams in all States tackling cases that Themis predicts will be unsolvable." He pulled up a chair and fixed me with an inquisitive stare. "So, early days, I know, but what is your take so far on Themis?"

"It's certainly presenting cases that could remain unsolved," I said. "I can see that Zoe's programming has the system 'thinking' as a detective, pulling in related data from multiple sources and highlighting anomalies."

"I don't pretend to understand the algorithms," he admitted. "But artificial intelligence that computes at super speed and 'thinks' like a seasoned investigator? We've got a hell of a lot invested in this."

"No pressure then."

He laughed. "Not what I meant at all."

"I know."

"There's pressure, but believe me it starts with the decision-makers. When it comes to the investigative team, we've got the right mix."

"Actually," my voice rose as I took the opportunity to make a point, "we're not fully staffed for the scale of the investigations needed."

"Will's raised that point, don't you worry." He wagged his finger at me. "It's under consideration."

"This new investigation is a case in point," I pressed. "The bizarre nature of the murder victims' identities means we need to be interviewing not just the families and witnesses to the recent deaths but also the people connected with these men way back when Flight 387 vanished. We need to be doing both simultaneously."

"But you don't have the manpower so it's much slower going."

"We need one team tackling the current murders and another team delving back two decades."

"Where are you currently with the case?" he asked.

I ran him through our most recent inquiries and as I did, Will stuck his head through the doorway. "Ross, I heard you were in town."

Grande was back on his feet and the two men shook hands.

Before anything further was discussed, I spied Marcia striding urgently across the command center area and into the office.

"We have something on the Whistler and the boy," she said.

Chapter Nineteen

"Themis has identified the SUV with the license plates Ilona saw," Marcia told us. "It was reported stolen two days ago, but get this, the car was stolen here in Seattle."

I raised my arms, signaling a breakthrough. "Our Whistler is stealing cars, driving on to the next required location, and then ditching the vehicle."

"And, quite possibly, consistently repeating the process," Will said.

"Can we definitely rule out," Grande ventured, "that someone else stole the vehicle, dumped it in Portland, and coincidentally this Whistler happened upon it?"

"Yes," Marcia responded. "From the roadside traffic cams between Seattle and Portland. Themis accessed footage that showed the license plate. Zoe's getting it blown up to show you on the big screen."

"Excellent," said Grande.

"And it's the same straw-hatted man and young boy that I chased in Portland?" I asked.

Marcia nodded. "The road cam's not clear enough to show the faces through the windshield but Zoe was able to enlarge the image and it's blurry but, yes, you can just make out it's a man and a boy."

The video from the traffic cam played on the screen, and Zoe turned to us. "Themis pulled in stolen car reports from every State for the past three months and there's one, in particular, that resonates." An image of the stolen car report appeared on the screen. "A Mitsubishi sedan reported stolen from LA. It was found abandoned by police here in Seattle less than a week before the Roger Islington parachute incident." Zoe flashed an adrenaline-fueled look of fascination at each of us, raising the palms of both hands to further illustrate a point. "And here's the thing. Neither of the cars used by the Whistler were stolen off the street. There was a break-in at the houses where the cars were garaged. And they were reported stolen by neighbors who became suspicious that something odd was going on."

"Why neighbors?" I asked.

"Because the families who lived in the houses were overseas on vacation. In one of these cases, the neighbor saw the car being driven off when he knew the owners were away."

"That can't be a coincidence," Marcia said.

"I'd already programmed Themis to search for all CCTV from public transport hubs and public buildings. That means bus and train stations, airport terminals, libraries, museums, and information booths, looking for a man in a hat accompanied by a boy. Yes, I know," Zoe rolled her eyes, "that's a hell of a wide parameter—"

"What did you find?" Will cut in.

"*This*," she said, freeze-framing on an airport terminal counter. "A man and a boy fitting the description at the Sea-Tac Airport international departures counter."

I looked at an image of a man in a long coat, his back to the camera and his face partly obscured by the downturned brim of his hat. He was hovering near the line to the counter, the young boy by his side.

"Now watch," Zoe said, unfreezing the shot.

The video played. It was a two-minute sequence, time-stamped 10:05:15 – 10:07:15. The man moved past the waiting line to the counter, animatedly pointing to the boy who was acting in a distressed fashion. With the people lined up at the counter distracted, their attention on the boy, the man leaned in, speaking to the female clerk behind the counter. As she picked up the phone on her desk, placing a call I guessed to her superiors, the man leaned in further.

"Look closely," Zoe instructed.

As the man leaned partly across the counter, he seemed to turn his head towards the computer monitor in front of the clerk, scanning it.

"A family flying out on an overseas vacation," Zoe suggested, "and although we can't hear what is going on, we can see that while the boy creates a minor diversion the Whistler asks for assistance and then flashes a look at the check-in screen. I'm presuming he's noting the family's home address."

"And then he goes to that address, knowing there's no chance the family will be coming back anytime soon, and steals their car," Will stated.

"And maybe even stays there for a night or two," I said, "alternating his and the boy's time between sleeping out on the rooftops and squatting at the unoccupied homes."

"And then moving on before anyone notices," Marcia added.

"Except in these two instances, probably unknown to this Whistler," Zoe surmised, "neighbors sensed or saw something out of the ordinary, discovered the cars missing, and reported it."

Dual green lights began flashing at either end of the horseshoe-shaped console.

"What's that?" Will asked.

Zoe grinned. "Themis has info."

Her fingers flew across the keyboard, opening the 'live' communication channel.

"Hello, Zoe." The Greek-accented voice was disarmingly natural. "You asked for stolen car reports in which the vehicle's owners were away on international vacations." The screen showed a map of the United States with pulsing red dots over several of the States, in the region of the local airports. "I have detected two of these in the past six months."

"Themis, can you cross-reference with where these stolen vehicles were then found?"

"Certainly, Zoe. Overlaying that data now."

On the map, a corresponding blue light pulsed in the appropriate locations. "In each case," Zoe observed, "the stolen vehicle is found in the city from which the next vehicle is stolen."

"Hopping from one stolen car to another," Will noted, "from one murder to the next."

Chapter Twenty

"The Whistler thinks his method is undetectable," I commented. "He stays under the radar by rooftopping and traveling in stolen cars. He uses random methods to kill his victims, with nothing to point to any connection between the deaths. And he taunts his victims in advance with a message delivered by a child." I stabbed the air. "*His. One. Big. Mistake* was using the most recent of the stolen vehicles to run down Don Morley."

"He didn't expect that a federal agent would be on the scene," Zoe said.

My thoughts were tumbling over the known sequence of events, imagining myself joining the Whistler on his journey, thinking as he would think.

"So why this USB message," Marcia wondered, "why this whistling, why this El Silbón persona?"

"The victims all have a connection to Venezuela through their investment firm," Zach outlined, "as well as through family or business associates, so they would know of Venezuela's most famous ghost story." He paused for the briefest of moments, his gaze wandering over each of us. "But is it just a legend?"

"You're not back on that whole ghost meme again?" Will didn't hide the sarcasm in his tone. I saw Will glance at Grande. God knows what the Assistant Director makes of all this, I thought.

"We may not always seem conventional," I said as an aside to Grande, "but that's a good thing if we want to solve the potentially unsolvable. We want traditional thinking mixed in with unconventional ideas, a kind of crazy think tank. It makes certain we think both inside and outside the box."

"Well put," Grande said with a nod.

I could see that Zach was caught up with his own thoughts, barely registering my vision of the UCU. "I don't believe in ghosts per se," he responded, "but when people supposedly *see* ghosts, I believe they are experiencing something. Maybe it's a psychic impression. Many believe we all have some level of psychic ability, dormant in most but greatly enhanced in a very small percentage. Or maybe ghosts and El Silbón sightings are another phenomenon entirely, something the human race doesn't understand or even suspect at this point in our development."

Will was about to comment but Zach barely took a breath, his voice rising and his speech speeding up excitedly. "As I said earlier there have been reports from people over several generations, local to the Venezuelan savannah, who have told of El Silbón sightings. These are poorly educated country people whose claims have been discarded by authorities, but the accounts are consistent with the Whistler resting in treetops or roaming the night roads with his sack of bones."

Take a breath, I silently mouthed the words to Zach.

He half-grinned, barely registering a breath before continuing. "Here in the big cities, this killer doesn't have treetops to rest in but is drawn to the closest equivalent, the rooftops, and he doesn't walk the night freeways, he hits them in stolen cars." He took a step forward, gesticulating expressively to the group. "Decades ago, there was a series of unsolved murders in those savannah communities, the locals reporting a whistling figure seen in the distance before and after the killings. But a story like that isn't, I've discovered, restricted to South America. There are myths from different cultures all over the world that whistling at night attracts evil spirits. There's an old Mexican belief that night whistling beckons a witch called Lechuza. Native Hawaiians have a legend that the whistling invokes ghost warriors known as Hukai'po, and there's dozens more variations on these from all over the world."

"You're inferring this Whistler could be possessed?" Zoe questioned.

"All of those superstitions are just that. Superstitions," Grande pointed out.

"The point," Zach insisted, "is that there is a body of information out there, a history of unexplained phenomena around killers with a connection to whistling. And the reason we can't discount any of that here? Because this case isn't just about a whistling murderer. It's tied in with victims who once vanished over the Bermuda Triangle."

"The most likely scenario," I followed on quickly, stealing Will's thunder whilst flashing him a brief grin, "is that this killer is aware of those histories and has adopted the name and characteristics of the legend. For whatever reason, he sees it as fitting in with his mission of pursuing these Flight 387 passengers. The question is why, and how could they possibly be those same passengers."

"Something else," Marcia offered. "This Whistler is using the international departures point at airports to select families whose houses he'll break into. Who thinks of something like that?"

I saw Marcia's reasoning. "Someone who has been around airports on a regular enough basis and knows how things work," I said.

"Exactly, and it's led to him formulating this idea."

"Themis has addresses for the other business partners who supposedly died on Flight 387," Zoe said, her attention diverted to data that was streaming through to her smartphone. "The closest one to Portland is San Francisco. Sam Garcia in North Beach."

"It's at least a ten-hour drive from Portland to 'Frisco," I said.

"Okay, here's where we're at…" Will was immediately in command mode. "We'll have drones scanning the Portland rooftops tonight, but the chances are the Whistler is already on the move. Zoe, arrange feeds through to us from the International Departure Lounge CCTV at Portland and San Francisco Airports. We'll need to ascertain if the same MO has been used this time and if so, whether the Whistler is staying somewhere in Oregon or whether he has already hit the road." He whirled toward our coordinator. "Marcia, arrange for local police to alert us immediately to any stolen car reports, have Aviation get the G-550 ready, and local state Feds dispatched to both Portland and San Francisco Airports. That immediately gives us plenty of eyes on the ground for when the Whistler plays his diversion game." His gaze settled on the professor. "Zach, let's see what you can put together for a profile on this guy."

He paused for breath. "In the meantime, we're sending local agents to Garcia's home, and we'll have eyes on him 24/7 to ensure The Whistler can't get to him." He turned to me, his eyes brimming with determination. "We've got a plane to catch."

Chapter Twenty-One

Will and I walked with A.D. Grande toward the elevator.

"It seems your Professor Silverstein sees this team as a way to prove his supernatural theories," Grande said to me.

"And that's what makes him unusually valuable."

"I read your strategy on this," he said. "You wrote that the Professor is as determined as you are to find a plausible solution to the cases you take on."

"He isn't just here to prove his theories by vague means. He wants to find that one rare case, the one where there is *no* plausible answer, the one in which our investigation uncovers something that's never been exposed before. Incontrovertible proof of something otherworldly."

"And for authenticity," Grande guessed, "it's important that the FBI is as much a part of that discovery as he is."

"That's his angle," Will said.

Grande nodded. "Makes him an interesting consultant or more to the point, devil's advocate."

"I've been known to call him that." There was a twinkle in my eye.

"There's at least one moment in every day, when I miss being out in the field, so I would've liked to have joined you on your flight south. But I'm afraid I'm due back in DC. More meetings. More verbiage." He laughed. "I wanted to see our newest team in action, and I've certainly accomplished that." He shook hands with both of us. "Keep me updated," he said as he stepped into the elevator.

* * *

As I turned to Will, Marcia came rushing up, brandishing an enlarged photo. "This is from the Portland Airport CCTV. There's been a sighting, just an hour ago. Departures counter. Same MO." She caught her breath. "Themis is accessing the flight bookings right now."

We headed into the Control Center as Zoe ran a stream of data on the screen.

"We've identified the family at the counter during the Whistler's diversion," she said. "I've just arranged for local agents to get around to the address."

"Then we wait," Will said.

We didn't have to wait long. A video call came through on Will's phone. "We're arriving at 210 Heatherbrae Avenue," the local agent said as he and his partner alighted from their vehicle.

We watched as the agents advanced on the house, a single-story Cape Cod. Weapons in hand, the agents checked the exteriors, and then the garage alongside. The garage door had been left partly ajar, the interior empty.

"They've been and gone," the agent reported.

I turned to Will. "We've got the stolen vehicle's license plate, so there's a chance we can nab them en route to the next state."

"I'll put out an APB. In the meantime, we don't take any chances, we hop a flight to 'Frisco." Will grabbed his jacket from just inside his office door.

"I'll see you down in the parking station," I said. "I'm going to make a call to the NTSB."

"Ben Wheeler?"

"Yes." I had my phone out and was tapping the number in. "I know we'll have local agents at the airport before we arrive," I said, "but I'm worried there's more to how the Whistler is going about this."

"You think Wheeler can help?"

"If he has contacts at San Francisco then I'll see if he can line up senior people to look behind the scenes, run patrols around the immediate area. I'm hoping he has a direct line to the people best placed to help." I'd no sooner tapped in the number than my call was answered.

"You must be psychic," Ben Wheeler said.

Holding the phone to my ear, I winced. "What do you mean?"

"I was just about to call you. As you know, we've been interviewing the service providers to SkyLife and the providers' contractors. No one raising our suspicions at this point."

"Okay," I said, sensing more to come.

"But we've been probing further. Unfortunately, as you're aware, no CCTV out there, but…" he paused, clearing his throat, "one of the NTSB investigators here is himself a keen weekend skydiver at SkyLife. He's been talking with the staff out there, trying anything that might jog their memories."

"Go on," I urged.

"There's a contractor they use to look after the grounds, lawn mowing, gardening, that sort of thing. One of the staff remembered that on the day Islington jumped there was a groundskeeper he hadn't seen before."

Another pause. I waited. I expected that he was collecting his thoughts.

"The employee remembered the groundskeeper wandering past the parachute prepping room, looking for a restroom."

"It could have been our man," I said.

"He could've slipped into the prep room when no one was looking."

"And it wouldn't take him long to sabotage the chute," I guessed.

"If he knows what he's doing, literally seconds."

"Brendan Davis told us that regular jumpers like Islington have their own labeled kits, usually put together in advance and then double-checked on the day by the staff."

"Exactly." Wheeler took a deep breath and then added, "It seems this guy knows his way around skydive operations."

"He also knows his way around airports and airline systems." I filled him in on what we'd learned about the Whistler's airport MO. "All of which supports what I was going to ask you. While we have local police keeping a watch in San Francisco, I wondered if you had any contacts from whom you could request extra assistance, just until Will and I are there. The more eyes the better. Especially if they know their way around the lesser-used areas."

"I'll go you one better," Wheeler said. "My dad's back in 'Frisco and he'd leap at the chance to help out. He can be at the airport within the hour, he knows the site, he can be given clearance to access restricted areas." There was the briefest of pauses and I sensed he was recalling something else. "Actually, I can add to that. Let me phone Brendan Davis. One of his franchises operates from a corner of the airfields out there and I know his local guys. They can keep an eye out as well."

"Great."

"And if you're flying out now–"

"We are," I said.

"Then if you can spare a seat, I'll join you."

Chapter Twenty-Two

Later, returning from around the corner to the field office with a pizza box tucked under his arm, Zach was surprised when Brooke Goodman approached him right outside the front lobby doors. "Brooke! Hi. What are you doing here?"

The reporter tossed back her long dark hair and flashed an impish grin. "Oh, you know me, always chasing down the next big story." She tapped her right forefinger to the side of her nose. "Nose for news in a city that may not be NY but also never sleeps."

Zach grinned. "I love it when someone throws out a whole bunch of clichés."

"Then we're on the same page. That's what they're for, right? I was hoping to see Ilona. I was driving by and thought I might drop in on the off chance she's here."

"She's out in the field."

Brooke shrugged. "No problem, I'll call her later. I know it's getting late but is she back in today?"

"Not today, but you can get her on her phone."

"It can wait. I was going to ask if there'd been any headway made on that murder. Or on that strange information about the Whistler and the boy?"

"They're working on it."

"And what about you, Professor?" Brooke asked, her mood lifting. "Are you consulting again?"

"I'm sure you know I can't talk about any involvement I might have with the Bureau."

Brooke gave a gentle smile. "But I'm sure you'd love to, especially if it helps you prove any of your theories about the unknown. I'll let you go, otherwise you'll be eating cold pizza."

"Wouldn't be the first time."

"Late lunch or early dinner?"

Zach shrugged. "A little bit of both most likely."

"Burning the midnight oil on this case, eh?" she called after him as he headed off, waving to her.

As he waited for the elevator, Zach reminded himself that Brooke Goodman was an intrepid reporter. She hadn't just been passing by but had driven here, especially, to subtly troll for classified information. He smiled to himself. *I wasn't born yesterday, Brooke.* He was certain he hadn't given anything away that the UCU would've wanted to be kept under wraps.

* * *

Brooke smiled inwardly, feeling deliciously deceptive in a journalistic kind of way.

I'm sure the Professor thinks he didn't give away anything about the ongoing investigation.

She wasn't about to write anything that would hinder the FBI investigation, she'd learned that much from the Piper case. At the same time, it was her inside scoop on that case that elevated her to her new role at the *Seattle Chronicle*. She was ambitious. And at this time, she wanted nothing more than to use journalism to expose crime and campaign for justice.

Right now, a smart and savvy independent podcaster was breaking more news than any of them and gaining national subscribers by the thousand every hour.

Game on, One Voice.

Although she'd promised Ilona after the Piper case that she wouldn't covertly watch the FBI agents, she'd been staked out in her car further down the street. Earlier, she'd followed when Ilona and McCord had driven off. Making certain she was plenty of car lengths back, she saw them take the turnoff to Sea-Tac Airport.

She hadn't taken the turn herself, just in case they'd noticed the same car further back, following. No, she simply drove on by, and then, having allowed several minutes to pass, she turned back and headed for the airport.

Where were they going? Was this professional or personal?

She located them and watching from afar she saw them being escorted by security to the private aircraft entry point. She knew the FBI's planes flew from there. Another man had joined Ilona and McCord, someone she didn't recognize. Who was he?

She took a photo and then moved away quickly.

And now she knew from Zach's unintentional slip that they were in the field, working this whistling man case and that they weren't going to be back tonight.

This was their second trip to the airport. Yesterday they'd driven here, and she hadn't been able to see them in the terminal. She suspected they'd already gone through to the private aircraft point. If they were using the Bureau's aircraft rather than choppers, then they must be traveling beyond Washington.

The fact they were taking flights to farther destinations implied there were other crimes connected to this one. Did those crimes involve the whistling man and the mysterious boy?

* * *

What am I missing?

It wasn't often that Zach Silverstein thought that question would drive him mad, despite the amount of time he spent searching for elusive facts and missing links. This time, maybe for the first time, he thought it might. He was at his desk in a designated area alongside the UCU command center, his eyes tired from the reams of information that he'd been scrolling through for hour after hour, totally immersed. The cup of coffee he'd made much earlier sat cold and untouched beside him, forgotten.

He'd accessed dozens of archives and scrolled through page after page of police reports and news articles.

Six investment firm partners were on that plane. Three of those murdered in just the past week by someone who appeared to be the mythical, whistling killer.

Three of the partners in that firm were US-born citizens with a Venezuelan connection either through marriage or parental lineage. The others were Venezuelan citizens. The only point of similarity between them was their backgrounds in international finance. Their work brought them into contact with one another and led to them forming their own company, specializing in US investment opportunities for Venezuelans. Their vision was to extend that service to as many people as possible, in a country where economic chaos and poverty were commonplace.

Marcia walked in and pulled up a chair. "You've been uncharacteristically quiet."

"Buried in this material." Zach gestured at the monitor.

"How's it going?"

He adjusted the position of his glasses and ran his hand through his shock of hair. "Feels like I'm going nowhere at breakneck speed," he said with a shrug, "but here's what we do know. Venezuela is a country with economic problems, with a high level of corruption, and an alarming crime rate."

"And this investment firm?"

"A.V. Investments," Zach said. "*A* for America, *V* for Venezuela. A straightforward name for a straightforward company. No history of corruption or unethical practices, no client complaints."

Marcia nodded. "And what happened when the partners went down with Flight 387?"

"A trustee was appointed, and all the clients were given the choice to sell off their stocks or have their portfolio handled by another company if they wished. A few elected to go with a new company being formed out of the old one."

"So, nothing to suggest how those partners have turned up now?"

Zach stood up and stretched. "No."

"And the heirs to each of the six partners?"

"Just one of the beneficiaries, the brother of one of the Venezuelan partners, didn't want to cash in his share. He elected to buy out the other five beneficiaries of the wills and to keep the firm operating under a new name, Investment House, with the clients who stayed."

Marcia frowned, sharing in Zach's frustration. "Dead end, then."

"Not sure." Zach came to life again, pacing to the far wall and back, mind whirling. "Maybe it's a waste of time but I've been digging further into this new firm."

"Okay…"

"Victor Gonzalez is the brother who took over, but he was nothing like his predecessors. Investment House only lasted a few years. Initially, it grew quickly, hundreds of new investors, and then he was exposed as running a Ponzi scheme. A lot of people lost a lot of money. The firm's operations were suspended, and the liquidators moved in."

"But that doesn't have any bearing on the previous firm's six partners?" Marcia asked.

"No."

"So, there's no connection to Flight 387?"

Zach shook his head and lowered himself back into his chair. "But I can't shake this nagging feeling. Is there something else here right in front of me?"

"It's late" – Marcia glanced at her watch – "and you're starting to look like hell."

"Thanks."

They exchanged grins.

"We should call it a night."

Zach turned toward his screen again. "Not just yet, I want to dig a little further." He looked back over his shoulder at her, shrugging and raising his hands. "What am I missing?"

Chapter Twenty-Three

Brooke didn't want to create a problem in her friendship with Ilona.

At the same time, she sensed a bigger story here. Reporters who held back ended up getting 'scooped' by other newspeople. Brooke checked the website on her phone and saw that *One Voice* had a podcast scheduled.

Aiden Sharpe is already leading the way on this.

Maybe there's another way for me to report the developments without Ilona seeing me as the instigator.

If she used the podcast as a front, she could then be seen to be innocently following its lead.

She was sitting in her car, planning to make a live on-air call when her phone rang.

"I thought we were catching up for a coffee?" Louise Carter said.

"Sorry, I got distracted. Following up a lead on a story."

"Anything you want to share with a co-worker?"

Brooke laughed. "Maybe later. Maybe I'll let you share the byline."

"That would be a first."

"Well, I do owe you one."

Brooke and Louise had been fellow junior reporters on the local paper over in Jefferson County. With Brooke's recent move to the city to join the *Seattle Chronicle*, Louise had joined her, a supportive friend sharing the apartment, and wrangled some part-time work with the same paper.

"You were the one that alerted me to the *One Voice* podcasts," Brooke said.

"And this has something to do with that?" Louise asked.

"Got to go, Lou, but I'll fill you in on more later." Brooke hang up and, composing herself, she made the call to the podcaster.

She wrapped a scarf around her mouth so her voice would be muffled, and affected a southern drawl. "I've been listening to your podcasts. I was wondering why the Feds are investigating a local murder but the reason, it seems, is that they've been following up leads in other cities."

"How do you know they're traveling to other cities?" Aiden Sharpe asked his anonymous caller.

"You had a call from someone who saw the killing and who saw the straw-hatted figure and the boy," Brooke said, drawing on the idea she'd formed before placing the call. "That person also sighted the agents who attended that murder scene."

"And?" prompted Sharpe.

"I know that person," Brooke lied. "They told me they recognized the same agents on two successive days taking interstate flights. I'm wondering if there is more than just that one killing. When the unknown boy phoned in and you asked why he'd warned the victim, he answered *they* need to know, not *he* needed to know, *they*." She paused for effect. "Do your listeners know of any other sightings of the whistling man?"

"You've asked the question for me," Sharpe responded. "And I must say you know how to play things close to your chest, don't you? Using the term 'they' when referring to your friend so we wouldn't know whether that eyewitness is male or female."

"I don't want to betray their trust."

"Understood," said Sharpe. "So tell me, can you reveal your own name, or are you another one of the people who prefer the shadows?"

"I think you know the answer."

"So what can I call you?" Sharpe teased.

"Anonymous."

"Common name around here," Sharpe joked. "Maybe you have a nickname?"

"Concerned Citizen," she said, and she ended the call.

Brooke wasn't certain that her ploy would produce results but mere minutes later *One Voice* had another anonymous call, this time from a Portland resident. The caller had sighted a man in a wide-brimmed hat and long coat, with a boy, rushing from an abandoned car on a busy city street. There had been another vehicle in pursuit with a young woman driver. She continued the chase on foot.

Ilona?

Brooke headed into her office at the *Chronicle*. She logged on to her PC and searched for police incident reports from the Portland city area in the last few days. And there it was. A report referring to the car chase. It was a stolen vehicle that had been involved minutes earlier in a fatal hit-and-run accident. Brooke switched over to another database. The victim: Don Morley.

She searched for further information on Morley and anything that might connect him to the other victim, Ken Rossi, in Seattle. Pages and pages of data but nothing with any relevance. There were dozens of Ken Rossis and Don Morleys in the United States.

She looked for Facebook and Instagram pages, Twitter feeds, anything from these two men but found nothing that related to them. In today's online world these two men appeared to be non-existent.

She thought about this killer. A disheveled man in a tattered coat. She thought about the anonymous eyewitness calls to the podcast that revealed this man performed a strange whistle before and after the Seascape Marina murder.

On an impulse she googled 'killer' and 'whistler' and her eyes widened with curiosity with the search results that filled the screen. Hundreds of references to the Venezuelan legend. El Silbón. When the boy had phoned the *One Voice* podcast earlier, this was the name he had given to the whistling man.

Brooke felt a shiver run through her.

She ran a Google search inputting the names 'Ken Rossi', 'Don Morley', and 'Venezuela'. She sat back, shaking her head, her eyes wide in disbelief.

Chapter Twenty-Four

It was just over two hours of flying time from Sea-Tac Airport to San Francisco International. Coming through a private exit gate, Will, Ben, and I were met by the Head of Airport Security, one of the local Special Agents, and Ben Wheeler's father, Robert.

Minutes later we were in the Security control room where the Head – a no-nonsense, middle-aged Hispanic man named Alvarez – waved toward the bank of monitors that lined one whole wall.

"We're the second largest airport in Northern California," he said, "with more than fifty-five million passengers every year, so as you can imagine our security is extensive." He motioned to an area alongside the northern wall. "I've designated desks and PCs for your use while you're here. All my guys are fully briefed. We're patrolling the terminal and the grounds and monitoring all CCTV. We've got the additional backup of local police officers and your local agents" – he gave a nod toward Robert Wheeler – "and of course Robert, an old friend."

"I've toured the staff-only areas and had a word with all the employees back there," Robert Wheeler said. "I'll be looking over the shoulders of the camera guys here, so if anything at all suspicious pops up on these screens" – he made a fist and touched it against the open palm of his other hand – "we've got him. What's more, Brendan Davis's franchise guys are on the lookout for anyone unusual in their area." Glancing at me and Will as he addressed Alvarez, Robert Wheeler added, "As I told the agents on the flight over, Brendan was due to visit his people here later this week, but he's moved that forward and he also caught a flight late this afternoon."

"I heard about the fatality at his Easley Fields site," Alvarez said. "Not good for his business."

"He's determined to help any way he can, as are my son and me."

"Final international departure for today is in an hour," Alvarez said, "and the check-in desk for that is closed. All passengers are accounted for; no incidents involving this guy and the young boy, and no other sightings. Next international flight is early tomorrow."

"I suggest getting some rest and being here again at the crack of dawn," Ben Wheeler said.

I spoke up. "What concerns me is that although media reported on the Ken Rossi drowning, the killer wouldn't have been expecting the *One Voice* podcast. It's publicized his existence nationally and listeners are calling in with descriptions of him and the boy."

"You're worried he'll change his methods," Ben Wheeler said.

"Yes. We don't know how long he's been living off the grid, squatting in other people's homes, stealing cars. He might have used a whole different range of methods to obtain his information from airports."

Will nodded. "If he poses as an employee then he could be here somewhere during the night." He glanced from me to Alvarez and back. "One of us should be here throughout the night. Alvarez, if your people sight this man, or suspect something, either Ilona or I will be on-site to take charge."

"Of course," Alvarez said.

Will turned to me. "I'll take the first shift." He glanced at his watch. "Why don't you get some sleep; we'll switch over around midnight and then I'll be back here by 5 a.m."

"First things first though," I said. "Alvarez, we've got the make and license plate of the vehicle the Whistler stole in Portland. Let's get your people to do a sweep of the parking stations here to make sure he hasn't already arrived. And we'll need to do the sweeps every half hour."

"I'll get that underway."

I glanced at Will. "We need to interview Sam Garcia as well. It's our first chance to speak with one of these Flight 387 passengers."

"Police are watching Garcia's house," Will assured me. "As keen as I am to find out what he's got to say, we need to concentrate on the situation here. We can approach Garcia tomorrow and interview him then."

I let out a breath of frustration. But I knew Will was right. We couldn't be distracted right now from intercepting the Whistler.

"We meet again," came a voice from behind us and we turned as Brendan Davis approached, his eyes firmly on me. "I've just been over at the SkyLife office. Two of my helipad people were on an evening shift and they've agreed to stay on until the early hours so there will be extra sets of eyes over there."

"We've certainly got all the bases covered," Alvarez stated.

"We appreciate the help," Robert Wheeler added.

"Least I can do," Davis said. "I feel I've got a personal investment in seeing this killer brought to justice."

Will's eyes locked briefly with mine and I detected a trace of cynicism. I knew him well enough to know what he was thinking. The image of Davis's skydive business had been compromised by the fatal sabotage of one of his customers. Being seen to play an active role in assisting the investigation was one way of vindicating the business's public image. But I also knew Will well enough to know that he wasn't impressed by breezy, charismatic entrepreneurs. I simply raised a quizzical eyebrow in silent reply.

"I'll be staying at the Marbell Towers," Davis said, "so I'm just minutes away should you need me."

While Alvarez organized the search, Robert Wheeler addressed me and Will. "And rather than be put up in some soulless motel, why don't the two of you join Ben and stay over at my place at Stinson Beach?"

"Dad's house has a four-bedroom, self-contained unit that's on the lower level at the rear of the property," Ben Wheeler told us.

"Plenty of room," his father added, "and the fourth bedroom down there can even function as your on-the-spot office."

* * *

Stinson Beach is one of a string of coastal communities in Marin County, an hour's drive north from the airport along the Panoramic Highway.

Robert Wheeler's home, alongside the dunes off Seadrift Road, was a two-story with both an upper and lower balcony that afforded a view of the Pacific. "My grandfather built this over forty years ago," Wheeler said, leading me and his son through the living area with its polished hardwood flooring to a patio that could also serve as an *alfresco* dining alcove. "Of course, I've done a load of renovations since inheriting the place, and it's worth a mint these days, but hey, I'm retired." He winked. "And Ben's mother and I like it here so we're staying put, for the time being anyway."

Ben Wheeler explained that his mother was away visiting relatives in the far south of the State. His father excused himself after we'd shared a light meal.

As the night fell, I took a glass of white wine down to the lower-level balcony. I gazed out at the shafts of moonlight that illuminated the ceaseless waves on the dark ocean.

Ben Wheeler joined me, and he clinked his wine glass against mine.

"Beautiful view," I said.

"I visit my folks down here for an extended stay two or three times a year." He took a sip of his wine. "Perfect getaway for when some R&R is needed. It's good to have your company and I'm just sorry about the circumstances, certainly not a relaxing time."

I shrugged. "Even so, I would've been holed up tonight in a motel room courtesy of the Bureau, grabbing some cheap Chinese takeaway. So this makes for a welcome change." I waved my free hand toward the ocean and the starry night sky. "Although something tells me I'm not going to get any actual sleep this evening before I head back to the airport. I've never felt so wide awake."

"To be expected I suppose," he said.

"I could just stand here all night, breathing in that incredible sea air and looking at that full moon."

Ben Wheeler extended his hand toward me. "Come with me. I want to show you something."

I placed my hand in his, my curiosity piqued. He led me down the cobbled path, through a steel gate and as we stepped out onto the beach, I kicked off my shoes.

I was enchanted by the moonlit expanse of sand and the sound of the wild ocean. The waves rolled in, crashing against the shore and creating a feeling inside me that was both exhilarating and calming at the same time.

"Where are we going?" I asked. The soft shift of the sand between my toes was heavenly.

"You'll see."

I felt as though I didn't want this glorious evening walk to end. And then he brought us to a halt and pointed out to the headland.

I gasped.

The rusted iron and shattered wood of a shipwreck jutted out from the waves and the rocks. "I had no idea there were any wrecks along here."

"Looks real and it is iron and wood but it's really a sculpture," he said. "It's part of an arts and crafts, music and food festival being held along the beach in a couple of weeks."

"A sculpture?"

"It's made of actual shipwrecked parts, so in fact, I guess it's both," he explained. "It's sometimes only partly visible, and it's not nearly as impressive in daylight. But at night when there's a full moon like this and the tide's just low enough, there's a magic moment when it's absolutely stunning, a sight like no other."

"If they're voting a winner from the sculptures at the festival, then that's got to be the one."

"There will be some spectacular artworks. It's a big event."

"They should leave that one in place after the festival ends."

He shook his head. "That would be great but no, they'll remove the anchor and it'll be taken away."

"It's beautiful," I said, taking in a deep breath of the briny air.

"I've often had the same thought. Sometimes I go across to Mile Rock Beach; there are two wrecks visible from Land's End, the Lyman Stewart and the Frank Buck." He shifted his gaze from the sculpture of the watery ruin and his eyes met mine. "My dad says they remind him of the fragility of our time on this rock, just like all the plane crash sites he investigated over the years. But he also says the shipwrecks speak to him of something else."

"What's that?"

"An example of life in general. He believes they show that we can be broken inside and still be beautiful."

"Your dad said *that*?"

Ben laughed at my surprised tone. "Oh yeah. The crusty ol' man has a hidden sensitive side." He laughed again. "And he actually shows it about once every decade or so."

I joined in the laughter. "Your dad has been an absolute charmer," I chided him.

He raised his hands in mock surrender. "I know, I know. Family joke. Sometimes he's just such a damn gentleman that the rest of us call him an old crust simply to annoy him."

I pulled a face. "Cruel." I suspected that those words were really his own and that he'd quoted them as being his father's as a way of not revealing too much of himself.

"If you ever want to come down here for a few nights, chill out, reflect on life, or whatever it is you FBI agents do," he said, "just let me or my dad know. My mom and he would be more than pleased to have you as a guest and as he said, there's plenty of room in the downstairs unit."

"I really couldn't–"

"You really could," he corrected me. "When this investigation is over and you're ready for a break, why don't you come down then?"

I pursed my lips. "It's a wonderful offer but I don't know…"

He persisted. "I'll join you. You'll be here as *my* guest."

That was when the beam of a flashlight blinded me, and Robert Wheeler could be heard further back along the beach. "Ilona! Ben! Come quickly."

Chapter Twenty-Five

Robert Wheeler drove us to the airport.

As we sped out of the driveway of the Stinson Beach home, I was on my cell with Will.

"The security cams picked up a man in mechanic's gear moving around the airport," Will told me. "He printed off tickets at various kiosks and used a device to scan the barcodes on the tickets."

This was one of the security protocols that Ben Wheeler had spoken of earlier. He'd instructed the airport security team to watch out specifically for this kind of behavior. Criminals with no flight booked had been known to steal credit cards from customers at the airport and scan them at various ticketing kiosks.

Scanning the barcode on the ticket enabled the scanner to view passenger names and flight details. "With this information," he had told us earlier, "the criminal can log on to the airline's website and easily access the passenger's address, itinerary, frequent flyer numbers. It doesn't work at every airport kiosk and it's something that airlines are constantly cracking down on with extra safeguards, but it's something that is still going on."

And it's another method, I thought, for the Whistler to obtain those home addresses.

"This was earlier?" I questioned.

"Yes. It was only after he was seen a few times that security became alerted. He was also seen scanning discarded tickets from bins, and from luggage in the baggage handling areas."

"Posing as a worker and moving around in plain sight," I noted.

"Two of the security guys approached him before we knew what they were doing," Will said, clearly irritated, "and the perp singlehandedly slammed them aside and took off."

"Did they get a good look at him?"

"No. He wore a cap pulled low, and he had his back to them right up until they were close. He spun around, slamming into them simultaneously."

"Where is he now?"

"We're searching every terminal, warehouse, hangar, and office. There's very little activity this time of night, so any movement he makes we should be able to zero in on."

"I'm wondering why he was going through those motions at night," Ben Wheeler said. "Less obvious, surely, during the day."

"The airport still has its busy periods through the evening," Robert Wheeler pointed out as he drove.

"And," I suggested, "now that the Whistler knows we're on to him he's taking precautions. He might've suspected we'd be watching for his actions during daylight."

"The good news," stated the older Wheeler, "is that now you're one step ahead of him instead of the other way around."

I didn't say anything. *Are we?* I wondered.

* * *

"Still no sign of him," Will said to us as we entered the security center.

"You were damn right about this guy knowing his way around airports," Alvarez commented.

The Wheelers conferred with him, and I joined Will looking over the shoulder of one of the officers glued to a security cam.

"Sooner or later, he's got to make a move," Will said.

Yes, I thought, but this is one hell of a big airport, with four terminals, seven concourses, one-hundred-and-fifteen gates, and multiple warehouses, hangars, runways, baggage areas, offices, and an enormous control tower. He could be anywhere and he's smart enough to know how to shift through areas by spotting and avoiding the cameras.

I have to think like you, El Silbón.

I closed my eyes. Willed myself into his headspace.

I opened my eyes again. Glanced around at the bank of video screens showing the concourse areas, the walkways, the building connectors, the now-deserted dining spots, the staff-only warehouse, office, and hangar spaces.

I know where you are.

* * *

No cams were showing the roofs. At least, not those higher parts to which the Whistler would climb.

I was itching to get up there and search those elevated spans. I knew I would be able to locate him. And I needed to do it before the Whistler found a spot from which to climb down to a remote corner and escape the airport grounds undetected. Could I do it without alerting the others to my urban climbing skills?

"You know what," I said to Will. "I was too wired to sleep this evening and I certainly wouldn't sleep now but while we're waiting here–"

Catching my comments, Alvarez interjected, "Why don't you put your feet up in one of the staff rest areas?"

"Do that. There's one just down the corridor from here," Will advised.

I held up my phone. "You alert me the very moment that–"

Will didn't let me finish. "You know I will."

I smiled and gave a wave to Ben Wheeler and his father as I hurried out. I didn't want him speaking up and joining me.

I walked briskly along the corridor but just as I reached the staff rest area, I turned into an exit that ran to an exterior door. Outside, a walkway weaved around the terminal and an adjoining office block and beyond that a row of hangars.

I was formulating my plan as I went.

I couldn't climb the exterior walls of any of the buildings without being seen, nor could the Whistler.

There were still airport workers in and around the area. I smiled at one as I passed him, an older man in aircraft mechanic gear, not the younger man we were looking for. That man smiled back but didn't question me as I held up my badge and said, "FBI."

The man had come from one of the hangars, and I entered that hangar via a side door. There were only a few security lights on and no other staff on the premises. The interior was enormous, and a 737 airliner took up the rear half of the space. A row of offices behind glass walls lined the side of the building immediately adjacent to the side entry point. Further along, there was metal scaffolding and what appeared to be both wood and steel beams embedded in the walls and running up to the vast ceiling.

I saw intermittent loft areas lining the higher levels more than three-quarters of the way up. The powerful aroma of gasoline and oil hung in the air as I craned my neck, sighting the skylights and windows situated at an elevation just below the corrugated ceiling.

I scanned the hangar. Security cams in only a few strategic spots.

The Whistler will have gone up to the top level from a point uncovered by those cams. As I will.

I looked across to the office space. There was a row of lockers along the inside wall. I went through to the office and checked the lockers. They were unlocked, containing only overalls and assorted work gear. Nothing that the staff here expected anyone would ever want to break into and steal.

But tonight you've got two such people.

I pulled on a loose-fitting pair of overalls and a helmet. In the event I was spotted, the outfit and the headgear would protect my identity.

All I needed to do was see exactly where the Whistler was. Chase him off the roof. Then I would call Will and have the teams on the scene within minutes. I'd retreat, lose the outfit, and rejoin my team from another direction.

I'd simply report that I'd stepped outside for some cool air and that I'd spotted the Whistler descending one of the building exteriors.

It should work.

Or maybe I'm crazy.

I ran up the zig-zag staircase to one of the upper lofts from which I could open and squirm through the narrow window. Now I was on a lower rim of roofing, I could step up to the higher, broader expanse.

It was a strange world up here, different from any of the other rooftops I'd explored in the past. I gazed out on the immense sprawl of illuminated buildings, runways, walkways, and streets, and the magnificent control tower in the near distance, a luminous beacon piercing the night.

I moved stealthily across the surface, directing my eyes to every corner of the area and looking across to the surrounding roofs and ledges.

And then I stopped dead in my tracks. No need to be scanning the greater area. I'd guessed the Whistler's movements far more accurately than I could have hoped. It seemed he'd taken the same exit door and nearest hangar as I had, and he also donned a helmet.

There he was.

In a partly covered corner.

In the near darkness.

Right in front of me.

Chapter Twenty-Six

"FBI," I called out, pulling my firearm from its holster and taking aim. Change of plan as I hadn't expected to be confronted like this. The helmet, black clothing, and the pools of darkness meant that he was a shadow. "You need to drop to your knees, hands behind your head."

"Ilona Farris." His voice was a scratchy, ragged whisper but at the same time strangely calm, the tone superior. "Or should I say, maverick urban climber?" He whistled the first few notes of his signature.

I felt a familiar shiver trail my spine like the sharp point of a cold blade.

"On your knees, hands behind your head," I repeated, holding the gun steady and staring him down.

He slowly dropped to his knees, his hands still by his side but even as he did so there was a sudden movement of his right hand. Before it had registered with me, in nothing more than a split second, he slipped a tiny pebble from his pocket and hurled it with deadly precision. It struck me in the left eye, almost blinding me momentarily, the pain so intense that I lowered the gun, raising my hand to my face.

In the next instant, the Whistler had risen and propelled himself forward, crashing into me. I lost my footing and we both hit the roof, rolling over. My gun clattered to the roof and skittered across its surface.

As I desperately pushed myself up, still clutching at my left eye, the Whistler was already on his feet. He'd removed the helmet, drawing on the strings that held the wide-brimmed hat at his back. He pulled it up and onto his head, the brim obscuring his features. He charged forward, swinging the helmet at me. It narrowly missed connecting with my face as I sprang back. At that moment, I was struck with the sickening realization I was perilously close to the edge.

He charged at me again, swinging the helmet once more but this time I ducked and sidestepped in one fluid movement, and then, ignoring the pain in my eye, I ran behind him. As he whirled around, brandishing the helmet, I ran back in his direction and launched into a cartwheel. Swirling through the air, I kicked out my right leg and landed a solid strike below the level of where he held the helmet, smashing my foot directly onto his kneecap.

The Whistler yelled and flung himself back, misjudging his position and toppling over the edge onto the lower level of the hangar's roof.

I breathed heavily, picked up my firearm, and ran to the edge.

The Whistler had clambered over the edge of the lower level and was climbing down the outer wall.

I needed to make that call to Will but I couldn't waste a moment. I couldn't allow even a second for the Whistler to vanish again.

I edged over the side and began the descent, clinging to the piping and rigging and corrugated sheets that made up the hangar's exterior.

It was slow going. This couldn't be rushed. One false move could be fatal.

I had to concentrate on the handholds and although I tried to glance down, I couldn't tell where the Whistler was or how much progress he was making.

Focus.

After what seemed the longest, slowest descent I'd ever made in any of my climbs, my feet touched the earth and my head whipped about, searching for the Whistler. He wasn't that far away.

He had run along the raised asphalt ramp that skirted this side of the hangar and was headed out to the runways.

Why?

Removing the helmet, I raised my hand to my earpiece and activated my comms, my voice hoarse. "Will, the nearest hangar behind the security command, the Whistler climbed down the wall and he's running toward one of the runways!"

"On our way," he replied.

I peeled off the overalls and pushed them with the helmet into a space between the ramp and the wall and then I gave chase.

As I ran, I kept my eyes on the Whistler up ahead. He darted across the runway and turned right, heading across a field toward a small building with an illuminated helipad beside it. The SkyLife building.

I could tell he wasn't running as fast as he otherwise could, he stumbled every now and then, slowed by the knee injury.

I pushed myself to run faster.

I can catch him.

I heard the overhead roar first and then saw the sweeping light. I looked up and gasped at the sight of a Bell 407 helicopter landing.

Despite the drag on his leg, the Whistler was dashing toward that chopper.

I pressed my hand to my comms. "Will, there's a chopper coming in, what's going on?"

"SkyLife's nighttime helicopter flights for couples," Will told me. "I'm told they do moonlit dinners on a beach and they're coming back in."

"For God's sake."

"We see him, Ilona, we're right behind and closing."

The Whistler reached the helipad as the chopper touched down and I cursed as I saw him reach in, pulling both the pilot and a young couple from the craft as he clambered on board.

Got to reach him.

The engine still roared, and the rotor still spun as the Whistler mastered the controls. I ran even harder as the chopper began to rise.

The pilot and the young couple with him stood back and watched, mouths open, as the helicopter was hijacked. I rushed past them and took a running leap into the air, my hands grabbing at the chopper's undersides.

The weight of me pulling down on the landing skids caused the chopper to flounder, rocking back and forth as it hovered, the Whistler struggling to maintain the craft's equilibrium.

I swung my body, pulling down as hard as I could on the skids and attempting to thrust my leg up and over them so that I could leverage myself into the cabin. The chopper spun on the spot but then it began to stabilize. The vertical thrust from the rotor gained power so that my weight no longer affected it, and the machine began to lift higher.

My leg had wrapped around part of the skid but now it slipped off. I realized that hanging on as the craft gained high altitude would be impossible without losing grip and plummeting to my death.

Damn it.

I let go and dropped back down to the ground, watching with burning anger and frustration as the Whistler piloted the stolen chopper across the night sky.

Chapter Twenty-Seven

Flanked by Alvarez and the Wheelers, Will raced across the field, reaching me as I pushed myself to my feet.

Alvarez's hand cupped his earpiece as he barked orders through to the control tower. "We've got a stolen helicopter, helipad, north-west perimeter."

He shot a look at me and Will. "Air Traffic Control is following the chopper on radar," he assured us, "and we've got State Patrol on alert. When this Whistler puts the bird down they'll be ready for him." There was a sudden look of alarm on his face. "Hold on, there's a message coming through." He listened and then updated us. "The chopper touched down briefly at the far end of the airport. The controllers viewed a figure near the perimeter, who boarded the chopper, and now it's airborne again."

"The boy," said Will.

Ben Wheeler placed his hands on my shoulders. "Are you okay?"

"I'm fine," I said.

He nodded, stepping back, relieved. "Thank God."

I sucked in a series of deep breaths, tilting my head reassuringly in Will's direction but there was no mistaking the expression on his face, a mix of relief and anger, and surprise at the affection shown by Ben Wheeler in his concern for me.

"Ilona, you shouldn't have gone after the chopper like that without backup," Will said.

"He came down that wall right in front of me. I couldn't just hold back."

"Yes, you could," he argued. "*For backup.*"

Will held my gaze, and I sensed his confusion at the coincidence of me just happening to be outside and sighting the Whistler. There was a question on his lips, but he didn't ask it, and I guessed that maybe he didn't know what the question should be. Was his mind flashing back to a similar situation that had occurred during the previous case, another moment when unbeknown to Will or any of the others I'd used my urban climbing skills to track down the Pied Piper? I watched as he shrugged off whatever thought was forming.

"When he puts the chopper down, it will be off road. The Whistler and the boy will be gone before the police reach the landing point," I warned. I shot a glance skyward at the disappearing spec in the dark sky and turning back to Will, I said, "*Sam Garcia.*"

"His place is under surveillance."

"It's not enough–"

Will cut across me. "Which is why we're heading there right now."

* * *

It was nearing midnight and Sam Garcia, woken from sleep, sat on his lounge in a bathrobe and stared back in shock at Will, Ben and Robert Wheeler, and me. "I'm in danger from a killer naming himself after one of my country's legends?" he repeated back to us. He was a short, solid slab of a man, with thick black hair and a healthy shadow of stubble. "That explains the message."

"Message? You've been approached by a boy with a USB?" Will said.

"Yes, this morning, at the local store, he came up and handed me a flash drive, said it was important I listen, then he ran off. But how did you–"

"And there was a whistle and then a warning from El Silbón?"

"I just thought it was a practical joke. You know, *kids.*" He was shaking and one of the officers handed him a glass of water. "Why?"

"That's what we're trying to ascertain, Mr. Garcia," Will replied, "and in the meantime, we need to take you into protective custody."

"*Dios mío,*" he said, shaking his head. "This makes no sense. I live a quiet life here…"

"Mr. Garcia, you have the same social security number as someone named Samuel Garcia who was on the missing Ven Air Flight 387," I told him. "Are you that Sam Garcia?"

He stared at me in confusion. "Of course not."

"Can you explain how you have the same SSN?" I asked.

He shrugged. "I have no idea… how can this be? I was born in Venezuela. I have an American mother and when I came to live here, thirteen years ago, I applied for citizenship. Could the authorities have made a mistake, doubled up?"

"It's extremely rare," Will assured him.

"But it could happen," Garcia said. "What about in the case of someone who has died? Do they reassign numbers?"

"No," Will said.

"And the difference here," I elaborated, "is that you're not the only person from that flight with an SSN that this killer is targeting."

"*¿Qué?*" The man put his head in his hands. "What happens now?"

"As I said, we'll need to take you into protective custody," Will said. "A safe house is being arranged and agents will escort you there in the morning. You'll be safe here tonight."

He shrugged and nodded at the same time. "I'll need to let my lady friend know. She lives nearby with her daughter."

"We can take care of that." I pulled out my phone. "Just let me know her name and contact details."

Garcia told me and I entered the data into my cell.

"I can't imagine I'll sleep after this." The man was wringing his hands, clearly anxious.

"Try to rest up as best you can," Will suggested. "There will be both local police and federal agents inside and outside, watching from all angles."

After conferring with the police officers inside the house, I stepped out the front door with the others.

Indicating the watch on his wrist, Robert Wheeler said to me and Will, "I suggest the two of you come back to my place and at least try for a few hours shut-eye before you're racing headlong at this thing again."

"This time I think I'll sleep," I said.

In Wheeler's vehicle on the way back, I said, "The other two Flight 387 victims lived comfortably off investments. If we track how they got started with this 'new' money…?"

"I'll talk to Zoe about it first thing," Will said. His phone rang. "The chopper was abandoned in a clearing further along the coast. The local field office is searching the area–"

"But they won't find any sign of them," I said through clenched teeth. "It's dark, and the Whistler will have stolen another car."

We arrived at the Wheelers' residence.

"We join the hunt at first light. He'll be headed for Garcia's place without knowing that we've got agents staked out there. We'll get him, but right now we all need some rest." Will headed to the room allotted to him, bleary-eyed.

As I moved across the lower-level living area to one of the other rooms, I stopped for a moment in front of a mural of photos that adorned a corner wall. I hadn't paid it any attention before. There were photos from different points of the Wheeler family's life, a couple of shots of a much younger Ben Wheeler with his parents and a variety of other shots of Robert Wheeler, which must have been taken during the time of the Ven Air 387 investigation.

One of these was a photo of the younger Robert Wheeler with a couple of other men, and one of those was the younger Ross Grande, in his agenting days long before he became an Assistant Director. The other man in the photo wasn't anyone I knew but he wore an airline uniform with the name 'Sun Air' emblazoned on it.

Ben Wheeler ambled up alongside me. "There are plenty of old photos in our family albums upstairs," he said, smiling conspiratorially, "if you're fascinated enough to want to look through them some time."

"You were a good-looking kid, weren't you?" I said with a laugh.

"Probably looked better in photos than I did in real life," he joked.

I pointed to the photo that had caught my eye. Something about the picture of the three men bothered me but I wasn't sure what it was. Perhaps I should take another look or give it further thought in the morning when I was fresh. *If* I was fresh. "I didn't know your father knew our A.D., Ross Grande."

"Sometimes I think my dad knows just about everyone there is to know. He certainly knew plenty of police officers and federal agents during those investigative years." He turned to face me. "You know, Will was right when he said you shouldn't have gone after the Whistler on your own like that."

I gave a churlish shrug. "What can I tell you? I'm one of those mavericks that don't follow protocols all the time."

"Like one of those edgy TV law enforcement characters."

"Nothing like those." I shot him a mock look of offense.

"Get some rest, eh?" His face was close to mine now.

"That's the plan."

Right now, I needed to be as rested as I could be for the day ahead.

Once in my room, I lay my head down on the pillow, closed my eyes, and willed my mind to switch off and my body to relax.

Thoughts of the day came rushing in, unbidden, as they often do in the quiet moments. The grief I witnessed in both Rossi's and Morley's partners and Islington's widow was like a whirlpool, drawing me back to the death of my mother. I felt an old familiar heaviness of heart as I thought of the deep loss, not just for myself but for my father.

One of the last times I'd had with my mother, in the hospital, had stayed alive deep in my memory.

I'd been just seven years old and my mother had held me and spoken with great openness and tenderness about the disease. "I don't want to leave you and Daddy, darling, but sometimes God calls for us, so I have to go."

"I want to go with you."

She gave the gentlest of smiles as she hugged me. Tears welled in the corners of her eyes. "I need you to stay here with your daddy. I want you to grow up and have a happy life and for you and your dad to always look out for each other. Could you do that for me, my precious?"

I had stared back, my eyes smarting. "But Daddy and I will miss you."

My mother's right forefinger touched my forehead. "I'll always be with you in *here*, darling, talking to you, filling you up with all my love, so much love. Say it with me. So much love."

"So much love." I began to sob, not fully comprehending why this had to be.

Was I living the life my mother would've wished for me? I sometimes pondered this but how could you ever really know the answer to such a question? I was certain my mom wouldn't have wanted me to pursue my secret – and dangerous – obsession, I hoped she would at least be able to understand it.

Often, when the adrenalin kicked in and my exhilaration was soaring, I felt my mother's spirit more than at any other time.

Good night, Mom, sleep tight.

I tried to still my mind but my brain was buzzing and the thoughts kept coming. Strangely, it wasn't the other details of this case or the threat posed by the Whistler, or the maddening mystery of the passengers that was angling for my attention.

It was the photo on the wall outside my room.

Chapter Twenty-Eight

It wasn't unusual for a field office like Seattle to have lights blazing into the night and agents at their desks burning the midnight oil.

With a husband at home and having raised three boys – now three young men – Marcia Kendall had always made a point of keeping regular hours as much as possible.

Tonight was not one of those nights.

When the UCU tackled a case that Themis predicted would remain unsolved, it required the early intervention of their specialized team in collecting evidence, analyzing the crime scenes, determining which leads were relevant, and all in a condensed time frame.

The UCU's mission, Marcia knew, was to beat the Themis prediction and to solve the unsolvable, focusing where possible on the UCU's base, Washington State.

Like Zach and Zoe, Marcia had been following up intensely on specific lines of inquiry.

Late evening. She was going to have to call it quits and look at her search results with fresh eyes in the morning.

She wandered back through the office and across to where Zach was still glued to his monitor. "Go home."

"I think I'm too tired to go anywhere," he quipped without looking up.

Marcia was insistent. "The process is complete. You now look like a zombie."

"I feel like one."

"How did you go looking for a profile for this Whistler guy?" Marcia asked, reminding him of McCord's request.

"Got some input from the Behavioral Analysis Unit," Zach said, "and we're on the same page about that. For starters, we're looking for someone with a background that would give them a reason to identify strongly with this legend."

Marcia couldn't resist a jibe. "If he, or *it*, isn't the original nineteenth-century ghost."

Zach shot her an exasperated look. "Even I don't think that's the case here, though I'd love to get up Will's nose by proving otherwise."

"But to do that you first have to eliminate every other possibility," Marcia said, knowing Zach's thought process on that.

He nodded. "As I pointed out earlier, the El Silbón legend is well-known throughout Venezuela. It's much less known everywhere else except for Columbia, which has its own version. Our best guess is that the killer is from Venezuela. The legend originated in the savannah lands where many of the locals still believe in it. So, it's the best and first place to focus our efforts."

"It's already sounding like one hell of a needle in a haystack."

Zach nodded his agreement but pressed on. "What is different though is that this Whistler has a constant companion."

"The boy."

"If we can figure out who he is *first* then that might lead us to the Whistler."

"We start by looking at the savannah lands," Marcia prompted.

Zach began gesticulating excitedly, adrenaline kicking back in. "Which is what Zoe now has Themis doing. Maybe this boy is related in some way to the Whistler. Maybe that's why the Whistler is dragging him through all this."

"What did the BAU have to say about the Whistler's young companion?"

"They're working up an additional profile, factoring in the boy's role in delivering the messages," Zach replied.

"All we can be certain of right now is that there is a very strong bond there, something out of the ordinary—"

"You think it's something other than family?"

"Maybe," Zach said. The history, science, and criminology professor was in his criminologist mode. "What we can be sure of, is the Whistler isn't someone with a thirst to kill just for the fun of it. As Will said, these victims have been identified and tracked down specifically. This is someone with a grudge, and perhaps the boy shares that same grudge."

Zach's voice rose and fell and rose again at various points, caught up in the complexity of the profiling. "Perhaps because the Whistler's background is on those savannah lands, or at least the poorer districts of Venezuela, he is someone who's lived an itinerant lifestyle, a traveler who is familiar with living rough and squatting and has sharpened those skills to survive. But not just that. He's also a chameleon. We've seen how he's adopted roles to deceive and obtain information in airport terminals, and to gain access to the parachutes at the skydiving center. This killer is more likely to have brought along the boy due to a common bond. He identifies with him."

"Okay," said Marcia, "but why this murderous grudge against the partners of A.V. Investments? You've established their operation was all above board, unlike the firm it later evolved into."

Zach let out a deep breath of frustration. "Tell me something I don't know."

"So Zoe is linking Themis with Venezuelan police systems?" Marcia said.

Zoe was approaching from the main command area, overhearing this as she reached them. Marcia peered over her glasses at her. "Here's another crazy person who thinks they don't need sleep."

Zoe didn't appear to have heard this, responding instead to Marcia's previous statement. "We're searching for any incident reports involving a tall man wearing a wide-brimmed hat traveling with a young boy," she offered. "And we're looking for reports of boys missing from the savannah lands in the last few years. Kids who would be around twelve years old now."

"Find him—" Marcia began.

"And we find the Whistler," Zach said.

Chapter Twenty-Nine

The past

The boy always woke in the middle of the night, unnerved by bad dreams but calmed by the cool breeze that wafted through the narrow window slit.

This time was different. This time he woke to searing heat, to flickering light and smoke wafting through that opening, to the sounds of chaos outside his room, of shouts and cries and running feet and crashing wooden beams.

He was wide awake instantly, swinging his legs over the side of the bed when the door was flung open.

"Follow me!" Even in the near darkness with the deafening sounds beyond the room, the boy couldn't mistake that voice.

He went to grab clothes, but the tall man said, "No time, I've got clothes for you."

As he ran out into the corridor, he saw that the man was dressed in fireman's gear.

"You're a fireman?" the boy asked breathlessly as other children were led away by groups of rescuers.

Firefighters entered the building with hoses gushing water into the air.

"I'm what I need to be," he shouted back.

The boy could hardly recognize the area outside. The buildings were alight, the flames soaring through the blackened structures and licking the night sky. Fire crews streamed out across the grounds, walls of water shooting high and forming a shimmering arc over the devastation.

Children were being herded into groups beyond the fire perimeter. There were police vehicles and emergency service vans everywhere, sirens blaring from the vehicles still arriving.

"This way," the man commanded, leading the boy away from the others. The rescue workers were oblivious to their movement amidst the chaos.

They ran into the heavier patches of darkness, to the far northern aspect of the grounds.

"Where are we going?" the boy asked, his eyes darting from the carnage behind them to the surrounding swathes of forest.

"Keep moving," the man instructed as he led the way. "This is the time."

"What time?" the boy called out, maintaining the pace.

"The time I promised you would come."

PART TWO

Chapter Thirty

Day three

The agents guarding Garcia's house were watching the surrounding grounds. Sam Garcia was in his room, dressed in darkly colored casual gear and running shoes. The doors were locked, the windows latched, and his car was in the garage.

This was the very situation for which he'd been told to be prepared.

Be prepared. What am I, a boy scout?

He had never thought there was any need, certainly not now after all this time. And yet here he was in exactly that kind of situation.

His only preparation, if you could even call it that, was simple but he believed it would be effective. Now he was going to find out if he was right.

It was the limbo between dark and light, the quietest minutes, and the most effective ones for making a silent, stealthy, and unexpected escape. It was also the moment of the changeover in shifts between the police officers outside. He sensed that the federal agents inside, their eyes on the windows, would also be momentarily distracted by the arrival and departures at the front and rear points around the house.

He quietly opened the door to his room and moved along the hallway to the interior door that led to his garage. From the garage, there was a side door that opened onto a section of the pathway that ran along the length of the house. There was a thick hedge here and on the other side of that was the fence between his property and that of his neighbors. The path was narrow, shielded by the house and the hedge, and Garcia pushed his way through the thick shrubbery. There was a half-sized gate cut into the fence, obscured by the vegetation on either side known only to him. He opened the gate just enough to scramble through, pushing it flush behind him, and emerged through the corresponding shrubbery on the other side. His neighbors were elderly, and even if he made a sound, which he didn't, they would sleep through a hurricane. Their motion lights were only in the front of their property, not the rear, and from this point, Garcia was able to climb over their back fence and into the darkness of the woods that skirted this exclusive housing estate.

He had nothing with him but the clothes on his back and his wallet. He simply had to slip away.

Behind him, he knew the officers on watch were geared for anyone trying to sneak onto his property.

They weren't expecting a hidden exit point hidden right beside the house. They weren't anticipating that the man they were guarding would break out right under their noses.

Chapter Thirty-One

The moment Will had sat down on the bed several hours earlier, in the middle of the night, he'd felt the bone-weariness descend on him. He'd pulled off his shoes and laid-back. He'd undress in a moment, but he needed just a minute to let his body relax, to allow himself to sink in and enjoy the velvety touch of the sheets.

He'd glanced around the room. The décor was spare and whilst he had never been one for filling up an area with photos, he visualized the two pictures that sat atop the wooden bureau in his apartment back in Seattle. One was of himself as a boy, posing with his parents, and in the other he was of a similar age, sitting with his uncle. There was a chair in the corner of this guest room, adjacent to the bed and for a moment he thought he saw a figure seated there, acknowledging his efforts with a tip of the head and an easy smile.

His role at the FBI wasn't just a job or even a career to him, it was a mission. He'd been just ten years old when that favorite uncle – an easy-going, genial, simple and hardworking man who had always made him laugh – was gunned down in his store in a robbery gone wrong.

Young Will McCord had wept, his whole family had been traumatized, and in the weeks after the funeral, he'd eavesdropped whenever the police were updating his parents on their progress. He had searched for the local press reports relating to the crime and felt a sense of closure – though he didn't know that term at that young age – when the killer was apprehended.

He knew then what he wanted to do with the rest of his life. It wasn't even his choice, he sometimes thought later on, and he'd said as much to Ilona. It was more like a calling, reaching out and welcoming him to the greater cause, embracing him like a second skin that was a perfect fit.

On every case, every investigation, there was a moment, just a moment, when he sensed his Uncle Thomas standing or sitting off to the side, a quiet observer, his smile as warm as ever, giving a slight tilt of the head that showed how impressed he was with his nephew's journey in life.

As his eyes drooped, Will thought of Ilona, and his mind backtracked to the airfield earlier in the night, his heart in his mouth as he'd watched her leap and grab hold of the undersides of the helicopter, just seconds away from being whisked skyward before releasing her grip and dropping back to the ground. Reaching her, he expelled a deep breath of relief when he saw she was okay, and the face that had stared up at him filled his mind now as he lay in the bed. Slender and fine-boned, the light olive skin of her face was framed by waves of chestnut brown hair that might have dominated her features if it wasn't for those deep, intense hazel eyes. Eyes that were constantly brimming with curiosity, determination, and… something else. Something Will had never been able to fathom and which she certainly didn't speak of.

Will knew that everyone had a side to them that they kept just out of view – hell, he was no different – an internal voice coupled with imagined, alternate lives we all live in tandem with our real ones. He sometimes wondered what kind of whole other life Ilona might have inside her head, and whether she ever let it intrude into the real world. Was that the reason for her reckless attempt to single-handedly bring down a chopper as it lifted off the earth?

In their time together as a couple, she'd spoken of her teenage ordeal, kidnapped and held for ransom in a dark, dank place, but she'd only ever covered the surface details. She'd never revealed her deeper-set feelings, hopes, and fears, and he understood that. But he was often reminded of it as he had been earlier on the airfield, by the fervent stare from those eyes. He'd wondered about the secret inner realm that passed like a shadow behind her irises.

He prided himself on how well he'd suppressed his true feelings since he and Ilona had started working together again. But in his innermost thoughts, he imagined a moment when he could tell her that he was falling in love with her all over again.

When his phone buzzed, waking him, Will thought at first he must have dozed off for just a minute or two while reliving that earlier moment, when in fact he'd been out cold for several hours. He was instantly alert when he heard the voice on the other end of the line.

* * *

I woke to my name being called.

I was out of bed in seconds, and I pulled a gown around my shoulders as I flung the door open.

Will was there, his clothes rumpled, phone to his ear. "Garcia's gone," he said.

"What? How?"

"Vanished from his room," Will said. "We need to go."

Ben Wheeler was standing further back. "I'll drive you," he said.

Robert Wheeler walked with us to the garage and watched as his son drove Will and me out of the long driveway.

As the car turned onto the street there was a moment when the line of the coast could be seen over the bluff. "I would've liked you to have been able to see that shipwreck sculpture again," Ben Wheeler said, his eyes meeting mine. I smiled but remained silent, sensing that Will had picked up on the intimacy between us, although he said nothing.

"Any idea what's happened?" Wheeler asked.

"It's not entirely certain how he did it, but Garcia slipped out of the house in the early hours," Will told him. "The police stationed there are certain he wasn't taken by force as there's no forced entry."

"If that's the case, then Garcia's got something to hide," I said. "He said he didn't know why the Whistler was after him but at the same time, it seems he didn't want our protection. He wanted to get as far away from us as possible before we grilled him any further."

My phone pinged and I read through a text from Zach, his snapshot of the profile on the Whistler.

We were met at the door to Garcia's house by the San Francisco agent-in-charge. "Our guys have uncovered a hidden gate in the fence beside the house," the senior man said, leading us around the side toward it. "Most likely he crept through there. It's out of view of any of the surveillance we've had going on, and from there he could have vaulted over his neighbor's back fence. There's a trail running by a creek in the woods behind these houses."

We pushed through the hedge and scanned the area beyond.

"The other thing," said the local agent, "is that you wanted to know about cars stolen in the area where the chopper was abandoned. There's a report just in, a Mazda stolen near there in the middle of the night, noticed by the owner earlier this morning, and officers have located it—"

"Abandoned in a street close to here," I finished the sentence for him.

"Yeah."

"He came here after this Garcia guy." Ben Wheeler was incredulous. "But with this place surrounded, and Garcia scarpering in the middle of the night, at least the Whistler can't—"

"None of that will matter," I cut across him. "He is smarter than that. The fact that the boy approached Garcia at a local mall yesterday morning means they were already here, watching the house before they went to the airport to line up a home to use as a base."

"That's how they knew when he went to the stores," Will added, "so that the boy could get the USB to him."

"The Whistler will have scouted the surrounding area," I said. "Which means he knows about the woodlands behind these houses and the trail that runs by the creek. When he came here in the middle of the night and saw the police, he'll have retreated to a spot from which he could survey the scene." I took a breath, mentally placing myself in the Whistler's shoes, seeing what he would have seen. "He expected Garcia to run. He knows as we do now, that the last thing Garcia wants is to be in the FBI's protective custody."

"So what would this Whistler do?" Wheeler wondered.

I was picturing the Whistler and the boy, travelers, itinerants, just as in Zach's profile, roaming the rooftops just as I'd observed them doing, seeking out homes to break into. I remembered the images from the Venezuelan myth, of the Whistler on the tree branches in the night. He was a chameleon who'd become adept at assuming a disguise, blending into his surroundings, and at using whatever items could be obtained to assist his covert lifestyle. He was an elaborate planner but also an opportunist, his agenda evolving on the spot to meet unexpected circumstances.

"The Whistler already knows where the trail runs," I said, "and the points at which it leads out onto surrounding streets or areas of the riverbed. He'll be somewhere further afield, watching for Garcia, ready to pounce."

Wheeler shook his head in amazement. "Good God. Then he could've already got to Garcia."

"Not necessarily," I said. "Garcia might have fled the area before the Whistler was on the scene."

Will was on his phone to Zoe, thankful she and the others were in the office early. "Zoe, I need an aerial grid of this area downloaded to my phone. Can Themis pinpoint entry and exit points to the trail that runs behind the properties by the river?"

"Sending it now and I'm putting you on speaker. Marcia's here and she's signaling frantically… she's got something for you."

"Will" – it was Marcia's voice – "I'm dredging through the info we've collected on Garcia. Very little as you'd expect, but he did purchase a small boat several years back, and there's a ramp nearby. Locals can moor their boats there for a small council fee."

With Will directing as he analyzed the grid on his phone display, we drove to the secluded point from which the river trail could be accessed. This was an area away from houses, close to a spot with an amenities block and from which boats could be launched from the council ramp.

"You think this was his plan B getaway all along?" Wheeler asked.

Will nodded. "It's the perfect spot."

"In which case," I warned, "the Whistler already knows about it."

Chapter Thirty-Two

The trail was heavy with shadow, overhanging limbs from the tree trunks created a portal-like effect, the spectral dawn light breaking through the thick canopy of leaves. Despite the cool morning air, Garcia's brow was lined with sweat and his heart thumped like a drum. But if he could make the remaining distance to his boat then surely he could be gone before this mysterious Whistler found him. Even so, his eyes darted frantically over the trail ahead and the surrounding woodland.

A crow squeaked, a shrill, threatening sound, and his pulse quickened further in fear. A smell of earthy decay was strong in his nostrils.

He heard the sound of someone behind him, jumping down from a tree. He turned and his eyes widened in fright at the sight of the tall, gangly, hatted man in the long overcoat.

"Sam Garcia." The hatted-man's voice was guttural.

Garcia turned back again and broke into a run, but he struggled for breath and his legs felt as though they were weighed down by iron.

Before he had run far, he was grabbed from behind, pushed to the ground, and he felt the cold steel of a wire around his neck, slicing into his throat.

He twitched, rolling over, his fingers clutching his throat where a fountain of blood gushed. And then, as his consciousness faded, he heard the short, sharp refrain of a whistle.

He felt a hand remove the boat's ignition keys from his pocket, and then the ghostly figure was gone, his repetitive whistle fading into the forest.

Chapter Thirty-Three

Ben Wheeler brought the car to a screeching halt at the boat ramp and alighting from the vehicle, Will and I heard an outboard motor. Racing to the riverbank I saw the dinghy speeding downriver. I caught a glimpse of a man in a hat and a boyish figure beside him. "He's taken Garcia's boat."

"No sign of Garcia," Will observed.

I moved closer to the waterline. "God, no…"

"You're thinking he's drowned him?" Will said.

"Wait." I raised my head, listening. "Can you hear…"

"I can't hear anything," said Will.

I heard it again, the low strains of a groan, coming from the trail. I ran toward the sound, Will directly behind me and on his phone to Marcia. "We need satellite surveillance of the river here," he barked. "The Whistler and the boy have taken a boat. Mobilize patrols ready to meet it when they beach it."

Seconds later we came upon Garcia's inert form on the ground.

I knelt beside him, searching his eyes and there was a glimmer of recognition there. He wasn't moving, his lacerated neck and upper torso wet with blood.

Will stepped back, now speaking quietly into the phone. "And we need an ambulance…"

"Sam, do you know why the Whistler came after you?" I asked Garcia. "Is it because of the missing plane?"

His eyes were boring into mine, and the fear of death I saw in them unsettled me as much as the blood and the deep, razor-thin gash across his throat.

His lips moved, an attempt to speak, but no words came.

"What is it, Sam?" I said, taking his hand in mine. "Can you tell me what this is all about?"

His body shook, a violent spasm, and then he managed to croak just one word. "*Hermanos…*"

"What do you mean?" I asked gently.

"*Mon… tesi…*"

I squeezed his hand reassuringly as Will looked on.

"Go on," I urged him.

Garcia coughed up blood, and another convulsion shook his body. He lay motionless, his dead eyes staring at nothing.

* * *

As the paramedics removed Garcia's body, Will had his phone on speaker. "The dinghy was abandoned further downriver and there's a shopping mall across the other side of the parkland, just off the main road," Marcia advised. "There's a stolen car report from that mall, it just came up on the system. Zoe's feeding road cam footage from the area into Themis, searching for the car by the license plates."

"Keep us posted," Will said. "And, Marcia, something else you can help with. Garcia said something before he died… in Spanish."

"What was it?"

Will glanced at me.

"He said *hermanos… montesi*," I told Marcia.

"*Hermanos* means brothers in Spanish," Marcia advised. "*Montesi*… sounds like a name."

"Thanks, Marcia," Will said. "We'll be visiting Garcia's lady friend next."

"Understood."

"And Marcia, remind me, where does the next on our list of remaining passengers live?"

"Southern California. Joan Miguel."

"We'll head there to interview her as soon as we can. And we need to arrange for her and the last on that list to be taken into protective custody."

"Underway," Marcia confirmed.

Zoe came on the line. "Themis has been digging for anything in recent years on Sam Garcia."

"What have you got?" I asked.

"Once again there's practically no digital trail. Like the others, he's been living a comfortable, fairly secluded lifestyle, almost entirely off the grid."

My phone rang. I didn't recognize the number on the display but when I answered, Brendan Davis said, "Agent Farris, my staff brought me up to date about the stolen helicopter. They're retrieving it now. Were you injured?"

"I'm fine. I can't talk right now–"

"Have you got him?"

"The authorities are in pursuit."

"Where?"

"He was last seen on a boat on the river, close to where the chopper was abandoned."

"I've canceled this morning's joy flights," Davis said. "I'll speak with the police and see if I can assist them by having our chopper fly over the area. Another set of eyes in the sky."

"You've got their contact details?"

"Yes."

"Then I'll leave you to it."

I rang off and glanced at Will.

"The sky cowboy?" he asked.

"Maybe his chopper will come in handy."

Will lifted his eyes skyward, shaking his head. "Let's move."

* * *

Maria Arcido was a middle-aged woman with hair as thick and dark and lustrous as any I had ever seen. Striking eyes, a professional demeanor, she sat forward in her chair, hands clasped in front of her, clearly distressed but suppressing her grief.

"We'd been close for a couple of years," she said, her voice strained, her eyes red. "We are both Venezuelan born with a United States parent, living in the same area here. We met at a Spanish club in San Francisco, and although he kept very much to himself, just a few local friends, Sam was very good to me and my daughter."

The teenage girl beside her reached across and held her hand tightly. "*Mamá…*"

Maria cupped her daughter's chin in her hand. "It's alright, *querida.*"

"I know this is an incredibly difficult time, Ms. Arcido," I said, "but if you could answer just a few questions, it might make all the difference in finding out who did this, and why."

The woman nodded her understanding and stifled a deep sob.

"Sam said just a few words to us." I chose my words carefully. "He said the brothers Montesi… does that mean anything to you?"

She thought for a moment. "Montesi?" She shook her head. "No."

"If you could cast your mind back," Will said, "for anyone or anything that might relate to those words."

146

"*Por supuesto*," she said, and she hung her head lower, eyes closed, one hand still firmly holding that of her daughter's.

After what seemed a long time, Maria Arcido raised her head, and looking from Will to me, shrugging, she said, "Perhaps he was trying to say, Montesino. Once, a year or so ago, I was with Sam at the Spanish club, and he met with a man by that name."

"Just the one man?" I asked.

"*Sí*. Sam said this man was an old friend from his youth in Caracas. They went to the private executive bar for a few drinks while I was with some of my friends. It was just the once, I didn't see him again, and Sam never mentioned him, in fact, he never spoke of his early days or his family. He was such a private man."

"Did this man say whether he still lived in Caracas?" I asked. "Was he on a visit to California?"

Maria gave it some more thought. "I remember... I did ask him if he still lived in Venezuela. He said no, he was US born, and he lived in the States." She was tearing up and she looked pleadingly at me. "I want to help, but this is no use to you..."

"It may be more helpful than you could possibly imagine," I said.

Chapter Thirty-Four

As we left the house, Will was on the phone with the UCU team. He instructed Marcia and Zoe to run a search on an American Venezuelan man, or brothers, named Montesino.

My brow furrowed.

Montesino.

Where had I seen or heard that name just recently?

Will noticed my look of concern. "What is it?"

"That name. It's ringing a bell."

"Can't place it?"

"No."

"It's likely a reasonably common South American name, Ilona," he pointed out.

"I know." But I also knew that wasn't the reason for the familiarity. So what was it?

Ben Wheeler had been waiting in the car.

As we opened the doors, my phone pinged, and I saw it was one of the alerts I'd arranged. It meant that a new *One Voice* podcast had been uploaded. "Aiden Sharpe's put out a new post," I said to the others.

"I've got a mini-tablet in the glove compartment," Wheeler said. "Easier than the phone for watching it. We can take a look if–"

"Yes," I interrupted, "let's see if there's anything more on the Whistler."

He retrieved the tablet and fired it up. Will and I, leaning across from our seats, watched as Aiden Sharpe appeared on the screen, earphones on, addressing his subscribers. "Breaking news," he said with his trademark conspiratorial twinkle in the eye. "Coming not from the great all-powerful traditional mass media but from little ol' me. We have the young lad, the apparent messenger for the Seascape Marina killer, on the phone for a second time. Hello?"

"I'm calling because I have a message for one of your viewers," the boy said, his voice cold, icier than any child should ever sound.

"Okay," said Aiden Sharpe with a tentative air. "And who is this viewer of mine?"

"She knows who she is."

"How do you know she's one of my viewers?"

"Because she's been following El Silbón, so she will be listening to anything from him or about him."

"And this podcast has become something of a flashpoint for that," Sharpe suggested proudly.

"The lady followed us to one of our secret places," the young voice on the line said. "It means she knows one of our secrets, but it also means El Silbón knows one of hers. Something she doesn't want others to know."

"Why wouldn't she want others to know?" the podcaster queried.

"El Silbón recognized her from the news, so he knows who she is," the boy revealed. "And he knows why she must keep it from those around her."

"And what is your message for this mystery lady?"

"She must stop pursuing us and never pass on what she's discovered." The boy's voice was calm and dispassionate, no doubt simply reiterating what his older companion had instructed him to say. "Otherwise, El Silbón himself will call and expose her name, her role, and her secret to the world. And then El Silbón will kill her."

The boy ended the call before Aiden Sharpe was able to utter a response.

The on-air pause was only brief. The podcast's signature theme started up and Sharpe's voice came in over it like a sweeping bird of prey. "So, there you have it, heard here for the first time. It seems there is a mystery woman out there, someone we might know from the news, whom this killer and this young boy have sighted following them. And there can be no question this woman's life is in danger. Who is she? What is this secret the boy refers to? As always, if anyone out there has seen or heard anything that might relate, however remotely, to El Silbón, the Whistler, and this murder, you can place a call or send a message anytime 24/7 and *One Voice* will be ready to take it live."

"A woman who's followed the Whistler," Will stated, looking at me. "You followed him, in Portland and again at the airport here. And the boy says they know who she is because they've seen her on the news."

My heart was beating rapidly. The best way to deflect this from me, I told myself, is not to be defensive, but instead to agree and go with the flow. And then lead the trail of thought somewhere else. Will knew I'd chased the Whistler but he had no idea the chase was across the rooftops.

"And I've been interviewed on the news," I said. "First with a suicidal rooftop jumper and later during the Piper investigation." I allowed a beat to pass, for my comments to settle. "But the boy said the lady followed them to secret places, that she knows their secret and that the Whistler also knows hers."

"And you chased them but you didn't see any secret places," Ben said.

"No," I said, but I pictured the Whistler on the roof in Portland and the hangar roof at the San Francisco Airport. I glanced at Will. "We need to find out who this woman is and what she knows."

"We'll get the team on it," he responded, "it could be important. But it's also possible this Whistler is simply trying to divert our attention."

"Agreed." I felt a surge of relief that Will wasn't seeing any more of a connection with me. I was cursing myself that I'd chased the Whistler on that first occasion without any form of disguise. I hadn't anticipated the killer would recognize me, from afar, as the federal agent seen in media interviews.

Mistake. Big mistake.

"Any updates on the Whistler's position?" I asked.

Will made a call to the local field office chief and then relayed what he'd been told. "No sightings."

I nodded and I turned my face skyward for just a moment, the movement of the clouds, driven by brisk air currents, capturing my attention. "He's vanished again."

Chapter Thirty-Five

Marcia ambled across to where Zach was at his desk, scooping breakfast cereal from a bowl and munching down.

"Don't tell me you never went home," she said.

"Okay, I won't tell you."

"You slept at that desk?" She furrowed her brow, her voice stern. "*Not* good, Zach…"

He looked back at her sheepishly. "Got in a few hours' sleep. You'd think I'd be wrecked but I feel… energized…"

"You look exhausted," she scolded. "Did you unearth anything further about this guy who took over the investment firm?"

The professor swiveled in his chair, tapping his keyboard, then faced her again. "Victor Gonzalez and his Ponzi scheme were all over the front pages in Caracas. He scammed a lot of people, small-time regular folk as well as big banks."

"You already told me that last night," Marcia reminded him.

"He might have got away with it but there was a financial crash, one of his clients went bankrupt and the ensuing audit exposed his practices before he'd had time to cover them up."

"They didn't find the money?"

Zach's tired eyes met hers. "The money was moved offshore, laundered through dozens of shell companies in various countries. Never traced. Stashed away somewhere by Gonzalez."

"He was indicted?" Marcia asked.

"He never made it to trial," Zach told her. "He was on bail; the trial was due to commence but Gonzalez never turned up."

"What happened to him?"

Zach rolled his eyes and raised his hands, palms upturned. "A warrant was issued for his arrest. His lawyer, his family, no one knew his whereabouts." His voice rose, his sleepy eyes firing up with a newfound intensity. "They never found him. No clues. No trail. There's a theory that he had hidden partners, organized crime guys, and that they bumped him off and kept the stolen millions for themselves."

"He should never have been out on bail," Marcia said.

Zach rubbed his thumb and index fingers together as though counting off notes. "Corrupt officials."

"What has any of this got to do with Flight 387?"

Zach turned back to his computer, tapping the keyboard again. "Maybe nothing, but..." As an image came up on the screen, he motioned for Marcia to come forward. "Take a look at this," he said.

Chapter Thirty-Six

Ben Wheeler pulled the car into the airport parking station. In the back seat, phone to my ear, I listened to a voicemail that had been left earlier by Brooke Goodman.

"There are several other reporters hot on this trail," she said, "and with anonymous calls revealing more and more to *One Voice*, if my paper doesn't run with this we'll be scooped. So my report on this is going live on our news sites within thirty minutes. It would be great, Ilona, if you could call me back before that, I'd like your confirmation that there's more than one murder and that they're linked to Ven Air 387 passengers."

I turned to Will in the seat alongside me. "Brooke has uncovered that we're investigating more than one murder victim who was on Ven Air 387."

"How the hell did she piece that together?" Will said.

"She's one smart cookie."

"Can we get the paper to hold off?"

"This voicemail was left a while back; I hadn't seen it. The news will already be live."

"Damn."

"Let's hope we can get to the other two passengers before they've seen it." I didn't need to voice any more of my fear to Will, the fear that the other two would disappear before they'd been reached. I knew he was thinking the same thing.

* * *

A half-hour later the flight to our Southern Californian destination was being called.

Ben Wheeler was returning to Seattle on a later flight, and he embraced me as I readied to leave. I felt uncomfortable with the embrace in front of Will and wondered if Ben noticed that I wasn't overly receptive.

As Will and I headed through the passenger boarding bridge I noticed Will regarding me with a sullen expression, although he didn't say anything. "Penny for them?" I said.

"Can't help wondering," he shared, "that if the Whistler, apart from the kid being with him, is otherwise a lone wolf, with no transport, no base, no apparent resources, then how the hell is he always one step ahead?"

I shrugged. The same thought had been nagging at me.

It was an hour and a half flight to the Southern Californian city of San Diego, where Joan Miguel, the female partner of the investment firm resided. We had been in the air for half an hour when I checked my phone and saw that the *Chronicle*'s website had run the story about the connection between the murders and the Ven Air flight. Social media was lighting up with speculation. Follow-up articles were already appearing on other news sites.

Coming out of the arrivals gate at San Diego International we were met by the local FBI man. The expression on his face told me my fears had been well and truly realized. "Our guys called me from Joan Miguel's home," he informed us. "The place was locked. They broke in, no sign of her but there were signs of someone having hastily packed and fled. Neighbors confirmed they saw the woman getting into a black SUV just minutes before our men arrived."

"I don't suppose anyone saw the plate number?" Will asked him.

"No."

Will's phone rang and after a brief confer, he turned to me. "Agents arriving at the other address, for Paul Ramsay, in Tijuana, have the same report."

I fixed him with an intense stare. "The moment news of the other murders broke, these last two have flown the coop."

"And they've had help," Will said.

I flicked back a strand of hair, biting down on my bottom lip. "This isn't just about the Whistler's lone vendetta and those six passengers," I said. "Someone else is involved. Something else is going on."

* * *

Will and I were frustrated that after more than two days of intense investigation across two states and having had the Whistler within our grasp twice, we'd reached a stone-cold dead end. So whatever the team in Seattle had learned was crucial to the next steps taken. It was late in the day when we walked back into the UCU command center but despite our near-exhaustion, we both wanted a full briefing on the team's findings.

We entered Zach's area and reconvened with Zach and Zoe at the command center, where Marcia joined us.

Zach filled us in on the background of Victor Gonzalez, the man who'd taken over the investment firm after the demise of the original partners, his subsequent arrest for fraud, and his disappearance before his trial. He pulled up an image on the Themis screen, showing us a photo of Gonzalez from fifteen years earlier at the time of his arrest. The likeness was immediately obvious to all of us.

"He looks very much like the younger Ken Rossi," Zach said.

Will stepped forward, squinting. "They're one and the same?"

"Zoe had Themis run aging software on this photo and the result" – the photo on the screen changed to show the edited image – "is pretty damn close to the morgue pictures of Rossi," Zach said.

"Gonzalez's fingerprints were taken at the time of his arrest in Venezuela," Marcia chimed in. "I'll get Themis to access them and have IAFIS run them against Rossi's."

IAFIS was the FBI's Integrated Automated Fingerprint Identification System.

"*If* it's the same man," Zach elaborated, "and if the Whistler knew Rossi was really Gonzalez, then his vendetta against him might be because his family was a victim of Gonzalez's financial fraud. Hundreds of Venezuelan investors were wiped out financially by Gonzalez's actions."

"That doesn't explain his killing crusade against the others," Will pointed out.

Zach shrugged. "No…"

"Okay, so, Zoe," Will said, narrowing his gaze on her, "did Themis dig up anything on the Montesino name?"

"There's just one connection that fits," Zoe said. She motioned to the screens as she tapped her keyboard, summoning her AI software, almost as though it was her alter ego.

My eyebrow raised in anticipation of this new data, even as Zach caught my eye. His finger was pointed to his own eyebrow, a grin spreading across his rubbery face. I shook my head with a look of exasperation, rebuffing his attempt at humor, and diverting my focus back to the screen.

"Background on Carlos and Dio Montesino," said Themis in its distinctive Greek-accented female tones. A slideshow of images began rolling across the screens. "The sons of a Venezuelan diplomat and oil executive, they were born in the United States and spent their youth living between the two countries. With their father's help, they worked in government and oil company executive roles before setting up as private consultants. It was widely reported but never proven that Venezuelan officials steered millions of the state-owned oil company's cash reserves into their financial consultancy. It is believed those officials received a share of future profits." Business profile photos of the two men were among the images that scrolled by. My focus intensified and I cocked my head. Something about one of those photos… What was it?

"Their consultancy was suspected of being a cover for drug-running operations and Ponzi financial schemes," Themis continued. "However, despite several investigations, the brothers were never charged. They returned to the United States over twenty years ago and created a new enterprise, purchasing residential and commercial real estate as well as a private airline, for VIPs, special charters and cargo runs. Their base is in Seattle, with offices in Caracas, Florida, and Los Angeles."

"Themis, is there anything specifically linking the Montesinos to any aspect of this case?" Will asked.

"Before their relocation, they owned the offices in Caracas which were leased to Victor Gonzalez's Investment House company."

Will glanced around the faces of the team. "That's not enough to sanction a raid of the Montesino offices." He focused on Zoe again. "We need Themis to find something that enables us to search their offices. We need to find out why Sam Garcia gave us their name."

"I'll broaden the search parameters," Zoe said.

Looking to me, Will said, "None of this brings us any closer to the Whistler."

I nodded grimly. "Now that the killer knows the FBI is on to him, it's unlikely he'd attempt the same MO at the airports. And with the remaining investment firm partners vanished, we're robbed of the chance to catch him in the act of going after them."

"If he knew how to find them in the first place," Zoe said, "then we don't know for sure that he won't be able to track them down again."

"Which brings us back to having to learn who the Whistler is." Will glanced at Zach. "Where are we with that?"

"We've got Themis checking on missing children from the Los Llanos region in Venezuela," the professor replied. "Profiling points to this whole thing starting there. I figured it would be easier to find data on missing kids from there and if that helps us learn the identity of the boy traveling with the Whistler–"

Zoe jumped in. "It could lead us to the killer himself."

Chapter Thirty-Seven

A suite of offices was set back from the UCU command center and one of these had been designated for me. I hadn't yet begun to use it, so the shelves were bare and the walls unadorned. A window gave me a view of downtown Seattle.

Before heading home for the day, I was standing just inside the doorway, assessing the space – it was as good a time as any and the first real chance I'd had to consider the personal touches I might bring, when Will slipped in behind me.

"Got a minute?"

"Of course." I stepped aside, enabling him to move further in, and he closed the glass door behind him. I noticed he seemed a little awkward which was unusual for him. Even when there'd been awkwardness between us in the past, Will had always been able to emotionally disengage while on the job and present an assured front. Always the consummate professional. It was one of the things that impressed me the most in our early days together. And the thing that infuriated me the most in the latter stages of our personal relationship.

"As you're aware, we've had agents sifting through the Piper's home, collecting anything relevant to the case for the Bureau's files."

The Piped Piper case, the first UCU case we had worked on, was the last thing I wanted to be thinking about right now.

"Yes. And?"

"The Piper compiled background on each member of the UCU and various other operatives."

"I know that, Will," I said impatiently.

"His file on you was a great deal more comprehensive than anyone else's."

"Hardly surprising."

"Not just on you personally, but on others close to you. There's quite a bit on your kidnap as a teenager and on your father's career and retirement."

I chewed on my bottom lip, mulling this over. I didn't need to be dragged back through all of that. At the age of fourteen, I'd been placed in a box at the bottom of a deep shaft. The box was fitted with a camera that transmitted my image to my father's computer. The blackmailer had demanded my father, an Assistant Director at the Bureau, release classified documents to the media.

Those documents had publicly exposed a corrupt FBI agent.

Although the blackmailer had never been officially identified, it was believed he'd been the husband of a woman whose life was ruined by the corrupt agent. The husband committed suicide before the case against him was proven. The FBI believed that the petty criminals who'd carried out the actual kidnap had been hired by this man. Those kidnappers had never been caught.

Perhaps I had been mentally blocking it out but the Piper had said something to me, during the final hours of our conflict, that had made no sense at the time.

I suspect your abduction was part of a plan with a very different agenda.

What had he meant by that? The Piper had not had any inside knowledge of my kidnap, which had been a cold case now for fourteen years. But he had a brilliant mind. He'd been analyzing the material. Why? To taunt me with it, I expected.

If the Piper's suspicions were correct then what was the very different agenda he alluded to?

I closed off the memories and my eyes met Will's. "Given the Piper's extreme interest in me and my family, I want to take a look at his notebook on me."

"I expected you would. They're currently down with Records."

"I know we don't normally remove items from the building–"

"You want to take the material home with you?" Will guessed.

"Yes."

"Records have photographed the pages for a digitized file. I can have that put on a USB. But Ilona–"

"Just give me some time to read through and assess his notebook," I insisted. "It's something I need to do."

Chapter Thirty-Eight

The Piper's notes, speculating about my teenage kidnap, had the unwanted effect of drawing me back to those memories.

I was fourteen years old and had been on the way to a friend's place when I sensed someone right behind me. Before I could react, a hand covered my mouth with a cloth. The smell was overwhelming and later I was told it had been chloroform. The cloth was held against my mouth, causing my body to slacken, as I was pulled into a van. I began to feel sleepiness descend and then I felt the prick of a needle in my neck. I slipped into unconsciousness even as I tried to force my eyes to stay open.

I woke in a dark, confined space. It was a box with very little wriggle room. From the smell and the feel of it, it was heavy timber. A crate? Had I been buried alive? I breathed heavily but I was screaming on the inside. My hands were tied but not tightly enough and I managed to slowly free them. It was my mother's voice – the mother I missed so much – that I heard in my head, calming me, emboldening me to shift my position, to trace my fingers along the inside lid of the box I was in, searching for anything that helped with leverage, and to push up.

And keep pushing.

The lid was heavy, but it was loose.

Lying in a confined area made it impossible to budge it from underneath. Or so the kidnappers thought. And so I would have believed.

My mother's voice told me otherwise.

You can do it, Ilona. I'm here. I'm with you. I'm always with you. Keep pushing. Shift the position of the lid. Just a little. And then just a little more. Eventually, it will be in a position from which you can edge it aside. Just enough to squeeze through.

Push.

* * *

This was the sequence of events that I was told about afterward: the video feed from the box was routed via multiple servers all over the US, masking its location, and sent to my father's laptop. But special agent-in-charge Ross Grande, heading up a crack cyber team, had pinpointed its source. It was housed in an abandoned, half-built nuclear plant in a sparsely populated area of the state.

Grande and his team converged on the building and found the deep shaft at the same time that, free of the box, I had climbed halfway up the narrow, uneven brick walls, clinging to the thin crevasses and ridges in the rock like a spider.

It was believed the kidnappers, alerted to the FBI's arrival on the extensive site, had fled before being detected.

"Ilona, we're getting a rope and pulley down to you," Ross Grande had bellowed through a loudspeaker.

I was exhausted and in danger of falling.

They had to act fast. Powerful lights directed down into the blackness showed the speck that was my body spread out spider-like against the steep side of one of the walls.

I'd called up to him, my voice faint. "I can't… hold…"

"Hold on, Ilona. Just a little longer. We're coming."

Grande, a colleague of my father's, was the first face I saw as I was pulled up. I grabbed his hand at the top, leaping away from the gaping hole with its seemingly endless drop to oblivion. Was I mad, brave, or desperate to have attempted that climb? Maybe all three.

Grande was around forty, a strong, determined, and reliable type with soulful eyes and a never-say-die attitude.

"We've got you," he said, holding me close. After a reassuring moment, he released his grip, standing back and appraising me. "I don't know how you managed to shimmy up so far and hang on but thank God you did."

I swallowed hard, still gasping for every breath. "Who did this?"

* * *

I snapped out of my reverie. How many times had I relived that moment?

I hated the memory of being in that box and, after freeing myself from it, of looking up at that seemingly endless shaft from its base. But as I'd walked away, flanked by Ross Grande and the other agents, I'd glanced back and felt a glimmer, just a glimmer of satisfaction that I'd managed part of that climb, that I'd taken my fate in my hands and struck out for freedom. I felt a sense of achievement that I'd made it out. As we exited the abandoned site, the sky above, always endless, seemed even more so to me than it ever had before.

Later, as I'd sat in the back of the FBI vehicle, I'd looked out on the buildings of DC and imagined scaling them, taking control, reaching forever for that sky and the freedom it represented.

Snapping from those memories back to the present, I scrolled through the digitized pages from the Piper's scrapbook. Newspaper clippings. Copies of FBI reports covertly obtained.

In the margins of the pages, the Piper had made handwritten notes. He listed all the people involved in the corrupt agent case as well as in my kidnapping ordeal.

'Who benefited?' he'd scrawled.

My eyes roamed over the list of names. The Piper's obsessed mind wanted to know everything about everyone, and then use that against them.

I'd always wanted to solve the case of my kidnapping. Find those petty criminals. And prove that the man who'd committed suicide had been behind the entire plot.

The Piper's scribbled musings seem to be pointing somewhere else. But where? And was he right?

I suspect your abduction was part of a plan with a very different agenda.

Could these scrapbooks hold the clue to solving my kidnap of fourteen years ago?

* * *

It was mid-evening and I'd only been reading for a short while when my phone rang. It was Will. "How are you going with that material?"

"You don't need to check up on me," I said, exasperated.

"I know, but–"

"But nothing, Will."

His response took on a strong authoritarian tone. "Ilona, you know damn well when an agent has a close, personal connection to a case, they are supposed to be kept at a distance from that case. I'm cutting you some slack here, so you need to cut me some as well."

"Okay."

"What you were going through mentally after your kidnap as a kid," Will said, "it's not something you ever really opened up about."

"I opened up as much I needed to, Will." Involuntarily, I felt my lips tighten as I drew in a sharp breath through my nose, instantly regretting the abrasive tone I'd adopted. Every time I thought my past with Will was yesterday's news, yesteryear's emotions, I unexpectedly reacted in this way. I was reminded yet again that there were still unresolved tensions there. *Still.*

"If you ever want to talk about it with me, Ilona, one agent to another, one friend to another..." I couldn't mistake the natural air of concern in his voice. "I'm here, I'd like to think we could do that."

"I don't need to talk about it," I insisted.

"If you're sure."

"I'm sure," I said. "But…" I hesitated, my thoughts unclear.

"*But*…?" he prompted.

"Maybe we could talk, but not about my kidnapping."

"Okay."

"About the Bureau. About the Piper's insinuation there was something else to it all."

"What about it?"

"I want to see the Bureau's files on my kidnap and those specifically concerning my father."

"Those files are classified and require a higher clearance than you or I–"

"I need to see everything that's in those files," I said.

A silence, born of my frustration, hung between us.

I didn't expect what came next. The intent in Will's reply. "I can't promise anything but let me make a few calls."

I heard a sound – movement – from my balcony. And from the corner of my eye, a shadow, a blur. It could have been something shifted by the wind except there was no wind.

"Just a moment, Will," I said.

I slipped the phone into my jacket pocket and slid the balcony door open enabling just enough space to step out and survey the area. The warning from the boy on the podcast was on my mind. Had I unknowingly been stalked by the Whistler? Did he know where I lived?

Nothing. Once again, my overactive imagination…

I turned, stepping back into the apartment when I caught another rush of sound, and whipping my head around, I reeled in surprise as a man swung onto the balcony from the overhang above. He'd climbed the outside of the building. But in that same moment, he was upon me, there was a needle prick to my neck and I felt the same fear I'd known as a fourteen-year-old when I'd succumbed to the darkness.

Chapter Thirty-Nine

I opened my eyes drowsily and everything around me was a haze. I sat up, I was on a hard floor, and as I regained full consciousness my surroundings took shape. Metal bars. I was in a cage. There were more cages alongside. And beyond that, brick walls. Was this a prison?

My hands were tied firmly behind my back and my jacket, blouse, and pants had been removed. I'd been stripped down to my underwear, and I saw my clothing beyond the cage, crumpled in a heap on the floor.

I heard the sound of a door opening and shutting, footsteps, and then three men appeared from the far side of the room. I steeled myself for whatever was to come. Watch, listen, observe, I reminded myself. Becoming aware of the rigging around the edges of the large area – conveyor belts and hard machinery – I deduced I was in an industrial warehouse, and the cages were lock-up storage units for products. Not a prison though it might just as well have been.

All three men wore ski masks and dark, nondescript shirts and pants. They were toned and muscled, and the tall man in the center appeared to be the leader, stepping forward ahead of the other two and addressing me. "And so we meet again."

I shot him a perplexed look. What did he mean by that?

"Our employer has an offer to make to you, Agent Farris," he said. "But first, I have some video, recorded here earlier, that you're going to watch." The man had a satchel swinging from his shoulder and he removed a tablet from it and held it up, moving closer for me to view.

The image on the screen was of another area like this one, with Brooke Goodman in one cage and Aiden Sharpe in another. And just as the three men had entered this room, so they had entered the room in the video, the lead man addressing the two prisoners. "And so here we are," he'd said to Brooke and Sharpe in a tone that was as uninterested as it was menacing. "The wannabe Lois Lane and the coward who thinks he's a hero when he's in his podcast studio. I don't know which one of you is more despicable."

The two men on either side of him were brandishing sawn-off shotguns and they shifted into a stance, clutching the firearms, primed for trouble despite the fact Brooke and Sharpe were locked behind metal bars. I noticed that the tall man was holding the same tablet. He held it up for the two of them to see. "This was recorded earlier," he announced.

An inset appeared on the screen I was viewing, showing me the images that Brooke and Sharpe had been shown earlier. I held my breath as I looked at footage of Brooke's work colleague and friend, leaving her home, slipping behind the wheel of her car. "Louise, your reporter friend," said the tall man.

Brooke gasped.

The image changed. Now it was of an elderly woman lifting shopping bags from the trunk of her car. "Even *One Voice* has an easy-to-find mother, eh?" the man said smugly to Sharpe. He paused the video.

Sharpe didn't speak but his breaths were coming in deep, rapid bursts.

"This is the offer," the tall man said matter-of-factly. "Ms. Goodman, your meddling has alerted the public to the Whistler's multiple killings, and you've drawn a connection between those and the plane crash victims from long ago. You are to cease all reporting of this nature, and in fact, you're to advise your readers that those connections were merely coincidental."

"And if I don't?" Brooke fired back.

"You will be released unharmed," the man said. "But your colleague will suffer a violent and painful death. And she will only be the first of your colleagues and friends to suffer the same for as long as you continue to refuse our request."

Brooke didn't respond. She simply stared at him, eyes wide with fright as though not comprehending.

The tall man turned to Aiden Sharpe. "Let's go back to this video. Shot earlier, just before we brought you here." The footage on the tablet screen resumed. A hooded man came from seemingly nowhere, barreling into the aged woman and knocking her to the ground. The man sprinted away, and the camera zoomed in on Sharpe's mother. Her head had hit the asphalt, and blood smeared her forehead. The video ended.

Sharpe shot forward to the bars, his fists clenched. "What have you done?"

"Your mother was taken to the hospital by others in the parking station. She is fine. This time."

Sharpe's shoulders slumped but his fists remained clenched.

"You've drawn far too much attention to this case. You're not to podcast anything on these killings ever again and you're to ignore any incoming calls on the subject. And if you refuse, then your life becomes a living hell, starting with the filthy, degrading death of your mother. But it won't end there, not if you do not do as we ask."

Sharpe's voice was barely a whisper. "You can't… be serious…"

"You'd do all this," Brooke said, "just to kill this story?"

The abductor stared back at her. His silence was all that was needed to answer her question.

"But the story is out there now," Brooke protested. "The wider media and the public already know–"

"Believe me, with no further reporting from you two," the man cut across her, "and the trail on the Whistler going cold, the media and the public, fickle as they are, will soon move on, their attention on the next big story, the next big crime." He paused for effect, allowing the weight of his words to sink in.

Watching this replay, I did not doubt that Brooke and Sharpe would know only too well the truth of those words. Another set of unsolved crimes slowly being buried in the news archives as time marched on.

The man resumed his warning to them. "You might think you can leave here and contact the FBI and your friend Agent Farris, but let me assure you, she will not be there to help. You will never be able to contact her, let alone find her. And if you think the FBI can protect all of your loved ones, and that they can then discover who we are and come after us, *think again*. You have absolutely no idea who and what you are dealing with, nor do they. No concept of our power, no inkling of our reach. Your loved ones will die. Your lives and your careers will be destroyed. And despite all of their attempts, neither the FBI nor the media will ever identify us. The alternative: do as we ask, let this investigation fade into the annals of the unsolved, and you have nothing to fear. It's an easy choice, really."

A silence hung in the air. Neither Brooke nor Sharpe spoke or even twitched.

And then the tall man spoke again. "I need your answers."

"Yes." Brooke's voice was a croak, and tears were streaming down her cheeks.

"You leave me no choice," Sharpe said through gritted teeth.

The video ended and I looked away from the screen, my eyes locking with those of the man in the mask.

"Goodman and Sharpe were drugged and returned to their homes," he said. "And just as when we took you from your home, we know how to avoid onlookers and CCTV spots."

"What are you going to do now?" I demanded.

"We're the ones asking the questions. And that is partly what this is about. Questions. You have been tracking this nutter who calls himself El Silbón, the Whistler. We need to know what you have uncovered so far."

"You must know I won't reveal anything about our investigation."

"Perhaps you need the same motivation as your reporter and podcaster friends?" He tapped the tablet, and another video came to life on the screen. I felt a screaming need to close my eyes. I didn't want to see this but there it was. Clara, my Washington DC friend who'd been like a sister to me when we'd been growing up and with whom I'd stayed in contact. The video showed her on her way to her job, completely unaware she was being followed and filmed.

"Refuse to answer our questions and your good friend will meet a dreadful accident."

"The FBI does not give in to criminal and terrorist demands," I said, my eyes blazing with defiance.

"And yet your father did," the man said, his voice cold.

Nothing could match the ice-like shiver that engulfed me at hearing those words. I stared at him, wondering what was coming next.

"Refuse and not only your old school buddy but also your consultants, the quirky professor with the outlandish ideas, and the dashing young aviation expert, will meet horrific ends." He paused for effect.

I didn't need to see this man's face to see that he was enjoying his power over me. How did he know about Brooke's colleague, Louise, how to find Sharpe's mother, and who the UCU's consultants were? Who was this man's employer?

"They will, of course, appear to be completely unrelated accidents," he continued. "Nothing to arouse suspicion."

"If you want the Whistler story killed, and you say the trail's already gone cold, then why do you need to know where our investigation is at? Why are you protecting this killer?"

"You won't stop with the questions, will you?"

"Maybe I'll trade one of your answers for one of mine," I said stubbornly.

"Maybe I'll indulge you," the masked man said. "We're not protecting this Whistler. If anything, the opposite."

"The opposite? You want him stopped? Then let the FBI do its job. Let me do my job."

"The FBI won't be stopping this killer," came the reply, "because *we will.* The Whistler is our problem, and we will deal with it. Now, one last time, Agent Farris, answer me or we'll proceed right now with the deaths of your friend and your colleagues while you're watching. Believe me when I say that there is nothing that can stand in our way. What does the FBI know about the Whistler?"

I sucked in a deep breath. Who were these people?

Our team knew very little about the Whistler. Even if I told them what I did know I doubted it would be of any use to them. It wasn't worth withholding and causing the deaths of my friend and the team members, but did I even have enough information to satisfy these monsters?

"The Whistler stakes out airports for details on people heading overseas and then breaks into their homes and squats there for a night or two before moving on," I said. "He and the boy travel from one place to the next in stolen vehicles, and when they're on foot, they move via places where they can't be seen."

"What places?"

"Rooftops."

"Rooftops?" the masked man repeated disbelievingly.

"There are no witnesses or CCTV cameras up there," I explained.

"He thinks he's some kind of urban Tarzan?" said the man.

"Like his ghostly namesake, he knows how to move about mostly unseen." I felt the bile rising in my throat.

"How did you make the connection with the Ven Air passengers he'd targeted?"

"We identified them by their social security numbers."

"Which of course would never have happened if it wasn't for this series of murders," the tall man said, for the first time slipping and showing emotion. Frustration. "And you were tracking the killer by knowing his next victim and planning to intercept him?"

"Yes." I wasn't going to reveal any more than that. Why did these mysterious men want to apprehend him in advance of the FBI?

"What else have you learned?"

"That's all," I said.

One of the other men spoke for the first time. "She's lying."

"No," said the leader, "I think perhaps Agent Farris has told us all she can." His eyes were still boring into me. "As I'm sure you realize, Agent, we cannot allow you to leave here alive. You know far too much about us."

"I don't know *anything* about you," I protested.

"You know we exist and that we're after the Whistler. That's enough. And no matter what further threats we might make, you would not be able to keep your mouth closed, not forever, and you would always pose a threat."

"It doesn't matter what happens to me, the FBI won't stop, they won't let this go."

"Our employer believes they will," he responded. "They'll be distracted by your disappearance and their search for you, and they'll be stymied by the Whistler's lack of activity. There'll be no clues to follow, but there'll be new cases, new orders – time moves on and so, reluctantly, will your colleagues." He turned to the other men. "Take her."

The two men moved toward the cage and one of them unlocked the door.

"We're on the top floor of a building in a mostly disused area of the waterfront," he said.

Why was he telling me that?

The other two manhandled me across the room and onto a stairway, following his lead, and they pushed me up the stairs and out onto a broad expanse of roof. I didn't know what time it was, and I didn't know how long I'd been unconscious after they'd brought me here, but it was still night. There was one nightlight positioned at one edge, casting a glow across the roof.

"We're seven levels up and it's a sheer drop over the side," the tall man said.

"You're giving give me a commentary on how I'll be killed?" I spat the words at him.

"Perks of the job." There was no emotion in his voice. The sharp, raw edge was still there but otherwise, it was as though he and his two associates were simply going through the motions. This murder was just another task before finishing their shift.

I strained against the two men as they pushed me toward the edge. Still groggy from before and with my hands tied tightly, I was powerless against the brute strength of my assailants.

Their leader continued his commentary. "We'll remove your body from the ground below to a small boat and deposit you in the ocean. Most likely you'll be washed further out and never be found. In case the sharks don't finish what's left and you are either fished out or washed back in, you'll be a broken, crumpled corpse, with no clothing, no ID." His voice rose, an inflection that seemed to indicate a sense of completion and triumph. "If and when you're identified, the FBI will have nothing to go on, no murder weapon, no way to conclusively discern the cause of your injuries, no signs as to where you'd been or how you ended up in the water."

He wants me to know, even in these last moments, I thought, that they are the winners.

"And you will never know this, Agent, but long before any of that occurs, we will have silenced the Whistler. The FBI case will remain open but unsolved. We won't allow either Brooke Goodman or Aiden Sharpe to remain alive for too long, of course. The story becomes yesterday's news, and the world moves on."

Chapter Forty

The men in the ski masks dragged me to the rooftop's edge. I caught a glimpse of the yard far below and the dock areas beyond with pockets of the ground illuminated by faint lights. I'd been pulling against the men but now I allowed my body to go limp, feeling like giving up, exhausted, but my thoughts were spinning as though they had rotors. *What can I do?*

I felt a slight loosening of the iron grip the men had on me, an unintended natural reaction to my body going limp and offering no resistance. Now I would have to make one swift and awkward move, catch them unawares. I allowed my legs to buckle. As I sagged downwards, I tipped forward while simultaneously snapping my head back, violently slamming the back of my skull against the groin of one of the men.

He cried out and lost his hold on me as he reeled back in agony, instinctively moving his hands to the sensitive area.

In one continuous movement, I rolled my body away from the edge. I pulled the other man with me, but he quickly maintained his equilibrium and strengthened his grip on me, shoving me back to the edge.

I was on my back, pushing against him, my feet jammed in the raised ridge that ran the length of the roof's edge. The tall man rushed over, gripping my other side, and adding his weight.

None of us could have anticipated the sudden roar of sound, the rush of wind, or the blinding light that swept across the rooftop. An FBI Bell 407 chopper swooped overhead. From behind the men, spilling out of the stairway entry, Will led a group of agents, their guns trained on the three masked attackers.

One of the men, determined to finish the job, ignored this incursion and heaved his body against me, edging me over the ridge.

Will fired. Blood erupted from the man's neck, and he was flung back and over the side, his body falling away even as Will lunged, grabbing hold of my shoulder and grappling back with me.

The tall man and the other stood back, hands raised, as agents surrounded and handcuffed them.

Will untied my hands and I rubbed my wrists and stretched my arms out.

"Are you okay?"

"Yeah." I breathed deeply. "Thanks for coming but what took the cavalry so long?"

He nodded but only managed a half-smile. "I never did understand how you can joke in moments like this."

"Self-taught." I watched as my two remaining abductors were led away. "How did you find me, Will?"

"Your phone."

I nodded. "Yeah…" And then realization dawned on me. "It was in my jacket pocket."

"We were in the middle of a call, so the line was still open."

"Enabling you to trace it." I hugged my knees to my chest, shivering, the full extent of my ordeal beginning to take its toll.

"Let's get you into those clothes," Will said, holding out his hand to pull me up.

I rose to my feet, steadied myself, and crossed my arms over my bra. "Will, what the hell have we stumbled onto here?"

Chapter Forty-One

Zach was wide awake lying in bed when his cell rang.

If he might have expected a call from anyone at this late hour then it certainly wasn't from Zoe Marshall.

"Zoe?"

"You sound like you were still awake?" she said.

"I was."

"Good, I didn't want to wake you–"

"You don't call someone at 11 p.m. if you don't want to wake them," he observed. "Where are you?"

"I'm still at the office."

"Do you ever sleep?"

"No, but I'm working on it."

He sat up, suddenly concerned. "What's up?"

"I know it's crazy late, but Themis has found something, and I thought–"

He didn't let her finish. "I'm on my way in."

* * *

"You wanted Themis focused on children reported missing from the flat plains around central Venezuela." Zoe stood up and stretched, trying to suppress a yawn.

"Yes. Los Llanos," Zach said.

"The state of Portuguesa is in the northwest there," she advised, taking her seat once more at the main Themis console. "There was an orphanage in its capital, Guanare. It was the scene of numerous escape attempts and protests and came under investigation for abuse and corruption. A fire gutted the orphanage several years ago and it's an unusual case. The cause of the fire was never discovered; eyewitnesses claim they saw a strange straw-hatted figure that looked like the legendary El Silbón, on the grounds before and after the disaster. All the children were rescued except for one whose body was never found."

Zach ran his fingers through his springy dark curls. "That's why Themis has zeroed in on that one, because some of the legends say the Whistler came from Portuguesa, one of the other towns there, Guanarito. It's where the legend may have originated."

"Yes, Themis will have curated the information on missing children based on age, circumstance, and location. And matching with the Venezuelan folklore she will have highlighted that connection."

"What do we know about the missing boy?" Zach asked.

Zoe's eyes were flitting across the on-screen data. "Okay, here's where it gets crazy."

"You think it's only getting crazy now?"

"The boy's name was Dantes Otero. Records were destroyed so his age at the time is unknown, but judging by newspaper reports he would have only been a toddler. He was orphaned when his parents died in a car crash, not long after they'd lost their meager savings in a financial scam, similar in some ways to the one Gonzalez once ran." She paused, her eyes locking on Zach as the two of them absorbed the unexpected similarity. "The child wasn't in the car, but whoever was looking after him at that moment, left him at the door of a childcare center." She rubbed her temples. "Sadly, that sort of thing is not uncommon in the poverty-stricken areas of the country, and it's been exacerbated by the political turmoil."

"Did the boy have any other relatives?"

"None that we can find any reference to."

Zach mulled all of this over. "Do we know what happened immediately after he was left at that center?"

Zoe scrolled through reams of data. "He was fostered for a brief time by a single woman." Her eyes widened as she read the details. "Wow."

"What?"

"That foster parent lived in Guanarito." She took a deep breath.

"What about other victims of financial scams, including Gonzalez's victims? Any that have any link whatsoever to this boy by way of jobs, schools, anything at all?"

Zoe was glued to the data as Themis brought it forth, reams of information scrolling by, many points of reference highlighted, none of them significantly relevant… and then…

"Here," Zoe said excitedly, turning to Zach.

"What have we got?"

"Another one of the Gonzalez victims… this one once lived next door to the woman who fostered Dantes, and had a son who was also orphaned."

"What do we know about this victim?"

Zoe's fingers raced across the keyboard. "A single parent. He committed suicide after being financially ruined by Gonzalez. He had a son, a thirteen-year-old, and the system's brought up a rap sheet on him for violence and petty crimes. Ran with a gang, but they were more like a bunch of street punks…"

"Can Themis find out any more about him?"

"Already has. I'll let her tell you. Themis, what have you got on Sebastian Rivera?"

"Sebastian Rivera," Themis repeated. "When his father was bankrupted, Sebastian and his father went to live with the boy's uncle and aunt in Guanarito, next door to the woman who some years later would foster Dantes Otero. After the death of his father and on charges of robbery and violence, still a minor, Sebastian served time in a youth detention center. Later he was sent for a brief time to the same orphanage as Dantes Otero, although they were not there at the same time. Sebastian was released from the orphanage when he came of age," Themis concluded, "several years before the fire that your previous inquiry uncovered, Zoe."

Zoe stretched. She was tired but her voice was bubbling over with the excitement of a breakthrough. "There's a good chance the missing child, Dantes Otero, is the boy…"

"And that Sebastian Rivera is the Whistler," Zach said. He scrunched up his face in confusion. "They lived in neighboring houses but not at the same time. They spent time in the same orphanage, but it was many years apart, and there is a sixteen-year age gap between them. None of that makes sense." He directed his attention to the machine. "Themis, where did Sebastian and his father live before being bankrupted by Gonzalez's scheme and before moving in with the uncle and aunt?"

"An exclusive enclave in Caracas. It contains the homes of American expats and Venezuelans with strong US ties," Themis advised.

"Thanks, Themis," Zoe said. Her eyes scanned the streams of related data that the AI was processing and then she turned to Zach. "It appears the enclave was not one of those for the super-wealthy but for mid-level to senior executives, small business owners, private school teachers, and so on."

"Which explains why Sebastian Rivera would speak English," Zach remarked.

"Yes. The kids of those parents are schooled in English as their second language. I expect it was Sebastian who then taught English to Dantes."

"What did Sebastian's father do?"

Zoe navigated to another series of documents – a company profile of the father, and school assessments and police reports on Sebastian. "His father was in cyber systems. He schooled his son in computers and Sebastian, being highly intelligent, self-taught himself a great deal more but he got into hacking and–" she paused for a moment as her eyes scanned the information "–as that rap sheet showed, he was a troubled kid. He had a vicious, vindictive side, often getting into trouble, even before the tragedy that befell his family." She took a moment, reading through one of the counselor reports from the youth detention center where Sebastian had served time. "He exhibited deep anger at the fact that his mother had deserted him and his father. According to the report here, Sebastian's mother had an affair and left the family."

"Was Sebastian hard to handle in the detention center?"

"No," Zoe replied. "Quite the opposite. According to the report here, while on the inside the kid withdrew into himself."

"The El Silbón folk tale began with a boy who murdered his father, after learning his father had killed the boy's unfaithful mother," Zach reminded Zoe. "The boy's grandfather punished him by whipping him and then casting him out, condemning the boy to wander for eternity, carrying his father's bones in a sack. There are various versions of this, but they all end the same way." He leaned in closer to the screen as though he could step into it and discover more. "So, when Sebastian's father was bankrupted and then committed suicide, it seems Sebastian's vicious side manifested further. If we're on the right track, then this all started with Sebastian finding out where Victor Gonzalez was. And then going after him. But before that, in Guanarito, he formed a bond with young Dantes."

"If we're right, it would seem that several years after he'd left the orphanage, he became determined to get Dantes out of there, take him under his wing," Zoe surmised. "But there's no evidence he'd ever met Dantes before that."

They looked at each other, mystified.

"Are there any photos of Sebastian and Dantes?"

"Nothing documented," Zoe said.

Zach shrugged. "Sebastian began his long journey to track down the man responsible for his father's death."

Zoe's eyes were still locked on Zach's. "But why take the boy with him? And why go after the others as well?"

Chapter Forty-Two

"Agents will check on Brooke Goodman and Aiden Sharpe," Will told me as we headed to the vehicles outside the warehouse.

"I want to check on them myself."

"You're still shaken, you need rest."

I ignored him. "Brooke moved into an apartment in the city when she started her new job. We can be there in fifteen minutes."

Will was behind the wheel and switched on the ignition. We watched as the other agents led the handcuffed men, now shorn of their ski masks, to the other waiting vehicles. FBI forensic vans were pulling up and lights swathed the area. "It's the middle of the night…"

"I don't need to have that pointed out, Will."

He sighed in frustration. "Okay, but only if you promise to let me drop you back at your place afterward and you go in and you rest up."

"Deal."

"I'll keep you to it."

I shrugged cheekily. "You can try," I said in a lowered voice, suppressing a smile.

Fifteen minutes later I breathed a sigh of relief when I knocked on Brooke's door and the young reporter opened it, sleepy-eyed, disheveled, and relieved to see me and Will standing there.

"Thank God those men returned you here as they said they would," I said. Will and I entered the apartment, leading Brooke to the sofa and seating her there.

"I've been lying on my bed… half-awake, at least it felt like I was half-awake…" Brooke said, staring wide-eyed at the two agents.

"You were coming out of a chloroform-induced sleep," I explained.

"You know… what happened…?"

"Yes. I was also a captive of those men. They showed me a video of the ultimatum they made to you."

"But you're here?"

"Thanks to Agent McCord," I said.

"I know those men sedated me but…" Brooke took a deep breath. "I wasn't totally knocked out."

"You were in and out of consciousness," Will guessed, "partially aware of what was going on around you?"

"Yes."

"You're safe now," I assured her, "and there's no threat to your colleague and flatmate. Just to be certain, we'll ensure Louise is placed under police protection while we clear all of this up. Two of those men are in custody and one of them is dead."

"I was crumpled in the back seat of a car, being brought back here," Brooke said. "They didn't know I was listening. They… had strong accents. They spoke English but they dropped foreign words here and there."

"What were they saying?" Will asked.

"Something about how well they'd performed their roles, and that they deserved more. One of them said he was going to have a word with… and I think he said… *los hermanos*…"

"It's Spanish for 'the brothers,'" I said.

"Does that mean something to you?"

I nodded. "I'm beginning to think it means everything."

* * *

Fearing I was too wired to sleep, I stripped out of my gear and stood under a steaming hot shower, allowing the rush of water to drain the tension from my body.

Toweling myself dry I slipped into a light negligee and crawled into bed, just a sheet draping my lower half, hoping that if I propped myself on my pillow and read something light then I would be calmed enough to drift away.

It didn't work.

I rose from the bed, went to the window, and gazed out at the Seattle night skyline.

Damn, I needed to climb. Clear my head.

I glanced at the clock on the wall. Just a brief climb, I thought.

Fifteen minutes later I was several streets away, on a narrow road that twisted behind the high-rises on the main street. In my blue tracksuit and hood, I climbed up the side of a building, focusing on the handholds and footholds, the ledges, the windowsills, the balcony edges, onto the wide expanses of the rooftops – a wild spirit breathing in the sights and sounds of the unseen world above.

I perched on the edge of a roof, like a bird of prey surveying its kingdom. Every other time I had ever done this, it had cleared my head while intoxicating me with adrenaline.

This time, the jumble of thoughts wasn't clearing.

Why hadn't the FBI ever solved the mystery of my kidnap and my father's blackmail? That question had always been in the back of my mind, under the surface.

When my head hit the pillow an hour later, I was asleep before I knew it.

Chapter Forty-Three

Day four

Thank God for the coffee guy further up the street who was open at 6 a.m. for the city's early starters, thought Zach.

Having laid his head on the desk and slept for a short while, as Zoe had alongside him, Zach was red-eyed and rumpled when he walked back in.

He placed a coffee on the bench beside her. She was just waking. He stood for a moment watching as she yawned. He enjoyed their camaraderie and wondered if there was more to it. He certainly felt drawn to her.

She sipped at the steaming liquid in the cardboard cup, giving a long, grateful sigh. "Giver of life."

Zach leaned back in the leather chair, feet propped against the console, cradling his coffee cup. "Where were we before we passed out?"

"Before we slept," Zoe corrected.

He shrugged. "Slept."

"Sebastian Rivera," Zoe reminded him.

"Because his father was an American expat–"

Zoe overtook him, the coffee and her adrenaline kicking in, her speech matching Zach's for speed. "It meant Sebastian had a passport and must have managed to obtain one for the young boy. I'd say he's done that by stealing papers from someone he knew at the enclave."

They were interrupted by Marcia as she entered the command center, raising her eyebrows at the sight of Zach and Zoe at the console.

"Silly me," she said, "I thought I'd get an early start and be the first one in. You two look like you've been here all night."

"Not *all* night," Zach protested, raising the takeaway coffee cup to illustrate he'd been out.

Marcia shook her head, raising her eyebrows. "You sound like one of my sons."

Zoe mimicked a zipping of her lips. "I'm pleading the Fifth."

"You look like a woman on a mission," Zach said to Marcia.

"Gonzalez's fingerprints came in and Themis had AIFIS run them against Rossi's. I'm about to send an email to everyone on the team. The prints are a match."

"So, Gonzalez has been masquerading as Rossi all along, which means the others are also likely to be impostors." Zoe exchanged a glance with Zach.

"And you two look like you're on to something," Marcia noted.

"We believe we know who the Whistler is," Zoe said.

She and Zach took turns in bringing Marcia up to speed on their discoveries from the night before.

"We believe that Sebastian Rivera came here to the US to track down Victor Gonzalez and the others who, it now appears certain, are all using those Ven Air passenger SS numbers," Zach said, concluding the update. A deep line furrowed his brow as he frowned, steeped deeper in thought. "But what we don't know is *how* he knew where to find them all."

"Look at this." Zoe gestured to various documents she'd called up on the screen. "Sebastian took a job as a cleaner with a contract company, and one of that company's clients was the liquidator dealing with Gonzalez's investment firm. The liquidator had the Gonzalez computers. Working there both during and after hours, Sebastian could have found out what the passwords were, logged on to those computers, hacked his way wherever he wanted, and then erased any sign of his activity."

Zach nodded. "Of course. He found something that the liquidators weren't looking for because it wasn't finance-related; documents linking Gonzalez to the people who knew Gonzalez was using the Rossi identity. The instigators behind what now seems to be a whole network of impostors."

"How do we find the link to those people?" Marcia wondered.

"We tread the same path Sebastian did." Zoe's eyes scanned the documents. "Coming to the US, he contracted to a cleaning company here in Seattle."

"He found a firm that cleans for the instigators," Zach said, his anticipation rising. "We find that company and we find the people behind these impostors."

Zoe winked at him. "We'll make an operative of you yet."

He frowned. "I already am a kind of operative."

"So once again" – Zoe ignored Zach's mock sulkiness – "Sebastian goes in as a cleaner to this other firm, hacks their software, and this time gets the SS numbers and names he's after."

"Right under their noses," Zach added.

"Next step, I'll get Themis to gain access to that cleaning contractor's client files."

Zach expressed his frustration. "And for that, warrants which will delay us."

"Maybe not. A lot of these firms have websites that list their client base as an endorsement. Let me get on that."

Marcia had been quietly absorbing the information. "Armed with that list, Sebastian goes after Gonzalez – who is posing as Rossi – and then tracks down the others who are masquerading as the business partners on that flight. But why is he after them?"

"Some twisted idea of justice," Zach suggested. "But mostly because he expects it to get him closer to the owners of the firm that created this impostors' network. He wants to bring *them* down."

Zoe gave a nod as she checked the cleaning company website, simultaneously scanning for more data on Rivero. "Sebastian rented a cabin in a trailer park here in Seattle. Seems he's spent a year there, planning this."

"And I'm guessing," Zach took up the narrative, "that during that time he's also taken a job at an airport."

Zoe scrolled further through the data. "Sea-Tac. He worked there as a casual cleaner."

"Gaining his inside knowledge on an airport's operations," Zach said.

"I'm surprised he was using his own name," Marcia stated.

"Actually, it makes perfect sense," Zoe pointed out. "He and the boy weren't illegal aliens at risk of being caught by authorities. They had what would appear to others as legit documentation. His airport job was legit. It was only when he went on the road to commit these murders that he went totally off the grid so none of it could be traced back to his real identity. He became El Silbón, the Whistler, in every possible way – in appearance, by squatting in other people's houses, and by traveling in stolen vehicles."

"Planning to wipe out each of the Ven Air impostors, step by step," Zach said. "His way of sending a signal to the kingpins behind all of this, an omen of their impending deaths."

"Okay, here are the cleaning company's clients…" Zoe paused, her breath catching in her throat, her eyes widening. Her voice rose. "And there's the connection we've been looking for. The Montesino brothers' real estate company is a client." She swiveled in her chair, her gaze on Zach and Marcia intense. "The instigators."

Zach arched his back and then straightened. "The remaining Ven Air impostors vanished before Sebastian reached them, but he'll simply change his plan."

"What are you thinking?" Marcia asked.

"He'll skip to the endgame he'd always intended. Going for the Montesinos themselves."

* * *

Dio Montesino woke and his eyes flashed on the time. 7 a.m. He pulled on jeans and a loose shirt and walked out onto the wide, wraparound hardwood balcony, looking on the panoramic view. His body was lean and muscular as though sculpted, his arms folded across his broad chest. A morning ritual. The sky was clear, the reflection of early morning light rippling across the waters of Puget Sound, the vista offering up glimpses of the distant ranges.

That vista served as a confirmation of his and his brother's success, of their importance and relevance.

These years now were meant to be the easy time, the reward after all the hard work. He had never felt, not for a moment, that he wasn't in total control. And he knew Carlos had always felt the same.

Until now. This past week. First, the murders. Then the media and the FBI making the connection with Ven Air 387, a connection that should never have been possible to make.

Carlos had been certain they could clean this mess up and maintain the status quo.

So why do I not feel it?

He glanced at his six-thousand-dollar limited edition crystal wristwatch, another reminder of his power and achievement. The previous evening, his most trusted operative had phoned in, on schedule, to report that the first phase of the night's plan – abducting, threatening, and then returning the podcaster and the reporter to their homes – was complete.

That same operative was late for the follow-up check-in, to confirm completion of the next phase – the silencing of the FBI agent.

Damn.

He slid his cell phone from his pocket and called his brother. Although Carlos was in the house alongside his, it was only partially visible, separated by a lush expanse of gardens and a grove of trees. He wondered if Carlos was with one of his many women. He and his brother had both been married and divorced but Carlos was the one who was making the most of his bachelor status.

His brother answered the call. "Dio, what is it?"

"I haven't received the confirmation."

"But the first phase went as planned," Carlos stated.

"Yes."

"Then give it time."

"There should have been a call sometime through the night."

"Dio," said his brother, "you're reverting to your old nervous ways." He chuckled. "We have this under control, *hermano*. We have a small army out there scouting for this El Silbón fraud, whoever he is. And our best men were handling last night's mission."

"I'm concerned."

"Dio, I've seen our surveillance photos of this Agent Farris. She's an attractive woman, no?"

"What's that got to do with it?"

"So our men are taking a little longer, having a little fun with her. Weren't we guilty of the same thing in our younger days? They will call when they're done. *¿De acuerdo?*"

"Agree," Dio said with reluctance.

He allowed himself another admiring glance at the magnificent view and then he walked into the main living area. He had not phoned the men to check on them. It was the protocol that they never made calls that would distract or disrupt a job in progress.

And then his phone rang, startling him even though he was waiting for it.

"What delayed you?" he shouted into the mouthpiece.

He could never have anticipated what he heard on the other end of the line.

In place of an answer, he listened to a short, unsettling whistle, followed by a boy's voice.

The years have passed
Your time has come
Listen for the whistling of El Silbón.

The man's whistle began again and then abruptly the line went dead.

His phone rang, this time it was his brother. "You just received the same call as I did?" Dio anticipated.

"What the hell is this?" Carlos roared down the phone, no longer the calm presence of just minutes earlier.

"He's coming for us," Dio said.

And then the quiet of the early morning was shattered by the shrill screech of the house alarms.

Chapter Forty-Four

I knew that Ben Wheeler was an early riser so an early call to him wouldn't be out of the ordinary. I wanted to let him know I believed we were making headway on the case.

"Good to hear," he said. "That means it shouldn't be too long before we get you back down to my father's place in 'Frisco for that break."

I smiled to myself as I ended the call. It was a generous offer but a vacation was the last thing on my mind as I worked with the other members of the team to build the UCU.

I walked into the office and across the open layout of the command area. Zoe, Zach, and Marcia were at the console. I brought them up to date on the night's events.

They were stunned but, regaining their focus, they reported their most recent finding on the Whistler's identity, and his trail to the Montesino Brothers.

I glanced at the first of the three wall-mounted screens on which Zoe had navigated to a photo of the brothers.

I stared at the image of Dio Montesino, the face that had previously brought a spark of familiarity.

Even as I stared at it, my thoughts shifted, strangely returning to Ben Wheeler and those few magical hours of solace on the San Franciscan coast.

Why did my mind keep snapping back to that? Yes, I'd liked it, I liked Ben, but I wasn't some love-struck teenager and, what's more, the team and I had a long, hard, busy day ahead. This wasn't remotely like me. And in the next instant, my memories moved to the photograph on the wall outside my room there. Robert Wheeler and the younger Ross Grande with another man. A man in a flying outfit.

Something inside crystallized, my memory fusing with the image in front of me.

The third man in that photograph, taken all those years ago, was a twenty-years-younger Dio Montesino.

Zoe was watching me closely. "You've got that seeing-something-stranger-than-Hogwarts look on your face."

"That's a look?"

"It is now."

I moved closer to the console. "One of the Montesino companies is a private airline."

"Yeah."

"What is it called?" I asked.

Zoe pulled up the profile on her desk monitor. "Sun Air."

"It *is* him," I muttered.

"Who are you talking about?"

"There's a photograph on a wall in Robert Wheeler's home. One of the men in the photo had a name tag with the Sun Air logo on it." The man's name had also been on that tag. That was why the name Montesino rang a bell with me when I'd first heard it.

"Ilona, you're not making any sense."

"I know."

Zoe frowned as she exchanged glances with Marcia and Zach. "Maybe explain?"

"The photo is of Robert Wheeler in his aviation investigator days, twenty years ago. A.D. Grande *and* Dio Montesino are in that photo."

The other three took a moment to process my words. Marcia looked into my eyes as though she might find the answers to the avalanche of questions erupting inside her mind. "Still not sure it's making sense," Marcia said on behalf of all three of them.

"No, it doesn't, and it's about time we find out exactly what it does mean," I said.

Zach swiveled in his chair to face Zoe, his expression revealing a sudden thought. "We learned earlier that Sebastian served time in a juvenile detention center and some years after that, he was running with a street gang."

"Yes."

"What happened then?"

"He was picked up by *policía* and sent to the orphanage until he was of legal age."

"If he was released from the detention center, the authorities would have transferred him to the orphanage then. If that didn't happen, then why didn't it? How did he come to spend a couple of years on the streets? Perhaps we can find out more about him, from those in-between years?"

Zoe tilted her head, absorbing the possibility. She exchanged glances with me and Marcia, and I nodded. When Zoe spoke, her words were directed to her AI. "Themis, set a parameter from the time of Sebastian Rivera's release from the detention facility and his entry to the orphanage two years later. Bring up all docs relating to

Sebastian and the detention and orphanage establishments."

The documents appeared on the screen in a gallery format. Scrutinizing them, Zach said, "There's nothing specific to the detention release."

"Themis, scan for all documents showing the detention center's history from that period until now."

A newly created gallery with an outline of documents appeared. "The detention center was severely damaged by fire," Themis reported, "and all boys were temporarily moved to another location until repairs were complete. Eyewitness accounts claim that a tall man in a tattered coat and a wide-brimmed hat was seen lurking in the area as the emergency services fought the fire. News reports from the time recount that suspicious locals believed it was the ghost of El Silbón. Detention center staff believed it was the same man who had previously visited a boy. They suspected that he took the child away. Sebastian Rivera was listed as unaccounted for until apprehended by *policía* two years later."

"It seems the Whistler started a fire at the detention center," Zoe surmised, "using its cover to free Sebastian, the same as Sebastian did at the orphanage when he came for Dantes Otero several years later."

"But we believe Sebastian *is* the Whistler," Marcia said, pursing her lips in confusion.

I was carefully considering Zach's line of thought. "I'm certain it was Sebastian who started the orphanage fire and took Dantes," I said. "But several years before that back when he was in juvie, there was *another* El Silbón. A man that visited him there, who later lit the fire at the detention center and freed him."

"Themis," said Zoe, "do the detention center records show who young Sebastian's visitor was in the months leading up to the fire?"

"Listed as a friend of the boy's uncle," the machine advised. "The name given does not respond to traces."

"A false name." Zach rose, paced, hands gesticulating. "For over one-hundred-and-fifty years there have been eyewitness accounts of a straw-hatted whistling figure, sighted at the scene of vicious crimes throughout Venezuela. And it's happened again, at a deliberately lit fire at a juvie center. Perhaps there *is* more to this than Sebastian simply adopting that persona when it suited him. There *is* or *was* someone, or something else, before that."

"CCTV?" Zoe asked.

"Nothing available," said Themis.

"Official records are scarce from that region at that time," Marcia commented. "It's a wonder we've learned as much as we have."

Zach looked at Zoe, raising his finger and indicating the bank of monitors. "Can I make requests of Themis?"

Zoe grinned. "Yes. She's programmed to respond to your voice."

"You haven't mentioned that before."

"You haven't asked."

They shot each other looks of friendly mock defiance, and I sensed from their camaraderie that there was an undercurrent, a spark between the professor and his former student who, as his colleague, was in every way now his intellectual equal.

"Themis," Zach said, leaning back, hands clasped, enjoying the act of communicating directly with the machine. "Can you access all government, medical, and legal data that has the names Sebastian Rivera and Dantes Otero in both Venezuela *and* the United States?"

"We've already scanned for every bit of data on Sebastian that we can," Zoe pointed out.

"In Venezuela, yes, but in the US that search has focused on his movements, his accommodation, and his jobs," Zach said, "and it hasn't included Dantes. Maybe a deeper dig will give us a clue as to who this earlier El Silbón was?"

"This might take a little while," Marcia said, rising from her chair, "perhaps this ragged-looking group could use some refreshments."

"I wouldn't say no," Zach said.

There was the familiar ping of Themis displaying newly sourced material, and Zoe said, "Maybe not so long, after all."

Marcia sat back down as the facsimile of another document appeared. I quietly marveled at the machine's super speed, made possible by the razor-sharp algorithms designed by Zoe.

"Sebastian was the beneficiary of a trust fund, set up in the US a few years after his father's death," Themis announced. "He was able to claim the inheritance held there, of several hundred thousand dollars, when he turned twenty-one."

"Themis, who set up the fund?" I asked.

"The name of Sebastian's benefactor was never listed on the documents at the benefactor's request. The trust was managed by a US law firm until Sebastian came of age, traveled to the US, and collected the funds."

"If Sebastian has that kind of money," Marcia wondered, "then why was he living in a trailer with Dantes, and why does he live on the streets, using other people's homes for shelter and stolen cars for travel?"

"All part of the Whistler persona," Zach offered.

"It keeps his Whistler activities completely removed from his real self," I speculated, "so that a connection would never be found. At least, he believed that a connection wouldn't be uncovered."

"What happened to the money, Themis?" Zach asked.

"There is no corresponding amount in Sebastian's account, no other financial accounts in his name, nor any accounts belonging to Dantes Otero."

"He's used it for something else," Zach speculated. "Themis, before Sebastian's time in the detention center, he lived briefly with his uncle and aunt in Guanarito. His uncle died soon after, but what about his wife – Sebastian's aunt – what happened to her?"

A moment later they heard the ping of a newly sourced document being displayed. "Elena Rivera. Sixty-two years of age. Current location on screen." An address in Guanarito appeared.

Zoe glanced at her watch as she checked another data stream on her PC. "Guanarito is three hours ahead of us."

"We need to talk with her," I said. As Zoe set it up, I phoned Will, rapidly bringing him up to date. Zoe put the call to Guanarito on loudspeaker, and we listened expectantly to the drone of the dial tone. I turned in Marcia's direction. "She'll speak Spanish, most likely without any English."

The woman who came on the line sounded frail. "*¿Hola?*"

Marcia introduced herself in Spanish and explained that she would be translating for her colleague.

"Mrs. Rivera," I said, "my name is Ilona Farris, I'm a US federal agent and I wonder if I could take a moment of your time. I am trying to be of help to your nephew, Sebastian Rivera."

Marcia translated my words.

The woman was naturally confused. "*¿Eh? ¿Por qué?*" The mention of the boy's name had unsettled her. "Sebastian? *¿Por qué?*"

My gaze settled on Marcia. "Maybe we're going about this the wrong way."

"Might be less confusing if my voice is the only one she hears," she said.

I agreed. "Ask her to tell you anything she remembers about Sebastian and his family and the events that led to the tragedy. Fill us in on what she's saying as you go along so that Zach, Zoe, and I can have some input."

"Okay. I'll start by asking her what led to Sebastian's mother abandoning the family."

Zoe whispered, "Themis is recording the exchange, so we can go back over the conversation if need be."

Chapter Forty-Five

Will strode in at 8 a.m. to find me standing alongside Zoe, Zach, and Marcia at the Themis console. He shot me a quizzical look. "We had a deal."

He hadn't raised my promise to get plenty of sleep when we'd spoken earlier on the phone. He'd waited until we were face to face. "And I've had a full two-hours' sleep," I countered, quickly adding, "You never designated the length of time."

He was silent, stroking his chin disapprovingly.

"What's more," I said, "for some reason I've never felt so fully rested."

He frowned, waving his hand in acceptance. "You've spoken with Sebastian Rivera's aunt?"

"We've had a long conversation, or at least Marcia has, and Señora Rivera – Elena – filled in a few of the gaps."

"What have we got?"

"The aunt told us that Victor Gonzalez had been a neighbor and a friend of the Riveras for many years," I said. "As we've learned, Sebastian's father entrusted his finances to him. And the aunt tells us that Gonzalez employed Sebastian's mother Selena, part-time, at his firm. But what Sebastian's aunt also revealed is that Gonzalez and Selena had a long-term affair. And known only to them, Gonzalez is Sebastian's biological father."

Will showed his surprise and took a moment to absorb this. "Sebastian didn't know?"

"The aunt says he didn't," I said. "And as we know, Investment House crashed, Gonzalez was arrested for fraud and vanished. Never seen again because he started a new life in the US using Ken Rossi's ID. Sebastian's dad – whom we now know was his stepfather – committed suicide. The aunt believes he'd discovered the affair and that it was both his financial ruin and his wife's betrayal that led him to hang himself."

"And Sebastian's mother?"

"Selena abandoned the family before her husband's suicide, devastated by their financial ruin and Gonzalez's disappearance. She maintained some occasional contact with her sister, Elena. Elena told us that Selena took up with another man in another town and for whatever reason, probably shame and pure selfishness, she asked her sister to care for Sebastian while she embraced her new life. However, it didn't go well. Selena and her new man lost everything they had saved to another financial scammer. But there's also something else." I took a breath.

"Go on," said Will.

"She had another child." Marcia took up the narrative.

"I didn't see that one coming." Will pulled up a chair and eased himself into it. "Sebastian has a sibling he doesn't know about?"

"The aunt told us Sebastian wouldn't have known about his mother's pregnancy," I said. "And Selena and her new lover died in a car accident a couple of years later, so there was never going to be a chance of a reunion with Sebastian down the years."

"Okay," said Will, "and do we know anything about this other child?"

"Elena Rivera became distressed dredging up these memories of her sister," Marcia said, "and she ended the call. I'll give her a little time to compose herself and I'll phone again and see if I can learn anything further."

"As for Sebastian, he later discovered Gonzalez was living in the US as Ken Rossi," Zach added, "seeing him solely as the man who caused his family's ruin. Which means Sebastian doesn't know that when he murdered Rossi—"

Zoe cut in, unnerved by the irony. "He murdered his real father."

Silence engulfed the five of us as we reflected on the revelation.

It was Will who broke the silence, asking, "Anyone have any further thoughts on the mystery woman whom the boy claimed was following the Whistler?"

"I've spoken with some of Detective Radner's colleagues at the SPD, and with a few news outlets," Marcia said, "dredging for any clues on who such a person might be, but no one had any information that fit."

No one said anything further and I breathed an inner sigh of relief.

Zach changed the subject with a comment directed at Will. "Ilona brought us up to date on last night's abduction."

I narrowed my gaze on Will. "What's the update on those men?"

"The warehouse is owned by the Montesino real estate investment company," he said.

Will listened intently as Zoe and I brought him up to date further on the team's findings on the Montesino brothers. He nodded. "All of which fits in with the two surviving men who abducted Ilona. I've had them under interrogation through the night. One will say nothing, the other admits to being employed as a security man for the Montesinos. He said that, amongst other tasks, he and his partners undertook thousands of domestic and commercial robberies for them."

"Robberies?" Marcia's heightened tone was like a snap. "I've been following up on the robbery that took place at the Rossi home not long after the Ven Air 387 disappearance." She paused, gathering her thoughts. She had the attention of all of us. "I spoke with the families of two of the other A.V. Investments passengers. Both recalled there were break-ins at their homes within a month of the plane's disappearance and as you can imagine, it sent off alert signals up here." She tapped her forehead. "I programmed Themis to search for burglaries at the homes of all the families of the 387 passengers. There were robberies within a month or two, at every single address of the American passengers on that plane."

"Every passenger?" I challenged.

"Yes."

"What was taken?"

"Petty cash, jewelry, but as each report is an isolated event they are not seen as anything more than a regular break-in. A minor crime, forgotten over time."

"So what *is* the connection?" Zach wondered. "What were the thieves after?"

I locked eyes with Will. "We've got more than enough probable cause for search warrants of the Montesino properties."

"The request is before a magistrate this morning," Will said. "An urgent request delivered to his home."

Marcia's phone pinged and she checked the message display. "Warrants are issued," she said. "What's more, he's approved the special request for Themis to conduct searches without waiting for the hardware, by remote connection to their networks."

Will put his palm up to bring the meeting to a halt as he made a call. Ending the call he said, "We're all set up with the other field officers. One hour. Simultaneous raids on the Montesino properties in Washington, Florida, and California."

"What about Caracas?" Zach asked.

"We're negotiating with the Venezuelan Attorney General," Will replied. "That will take longer, but regardless, I expect we'll find everything we need here in the US." He returned his attention to me. "You and I will be part of the raid on their Seattle HQ."

"What about their home addresses?" I pushed.

"They don't have physical home addresses listed anywhere," Zoe pointed out.

"Then they're living in one of the hundreds of domestic properties they own and rent."

Zach didn't hide his contempt. "No doubt luxurious enough to befit their million-dollar status."

"Themis," Zoe instructed the machine. "Which of the Montesino properties are closest to their office HQ?"

"Let me know the minute you have a result," Will instructed as he moved toward the exit. He glanced at me. "We're due at a raid."

Chapter Forty-Six

The past

Sometimes, when he cast his mind back, before the fire, before he'd gone to the rescue of the boy, the young man's memory replayed the nights when, still just a boy himself, he'd gone out with the others, running wild on the streets of Guanarito – strolling the alleys and the parks, jumping rooftop to rooftop, and climbing the buildings, the monuments, and the trees. They'd broken into storefronts and offices causing chaos and damage.

One night, fleeing the *policía*, he'd taken a dusty coat from one of the city's homeless men and a wide-brimmed hat from another. This disguise gave him an older appearance, and he sauntered confidently through the darker shadows. One of the homeless, waking from a drunken stupor and sighting him, pointed and called out, "El Silbón."

The boy laughed. It hadn't occurred to him but, yes, with his lanky frame and disheveled clothing, he did resemble the figure from the ghostly tale. The tall, friendly man who had called on him at the juvenile detention center had also used that disguise, as well as that of a firefighter. He'd often wondered about the identity of that man – the man who had set the fire and freed him from that dark, miserable place of imprisonment.

That mysterious man had left him with a group of trusted adults, friends, assuring him that he would be looked after. But soon after those people fled their residence during a time of great political unrest. The boy joined a group of wild youths who lived on the streets, and enjoyed the danger and the thrill. But it wasn't to last.

Two years later he'd been caught.

A magistrate ruled that due to detention overcrowding, and because he was only a short time away from being declared an adult, he'd be taken to an orphanage where he would be watched closely.

Lying awake at night, he thought of the mystery man who'd rescued him, and of the homeless man's call in the night. He decided that when he exacted his revenge on those that destroyed his family, that was who he would become.

That figure of legend.

He did not know it that night, but he would return to the orphanage several years later, creating a firestorm in the same fashion that the mystery man had done.

Only this time, Sebastian re-enacted that event to destroy a different place of evil, and to take young Dantes, his half-brother, under his wing.

He would always remember that night, the night he became El Silbón, the Whistler.

PART THREE

Chapter Forty-Seven

I stepped from the vehicle as it pulled up across the street, my attention riveted to the sight of a dozen men, the agency's insignia emblazoned on their jackets, rushing into the office block, shouting, "FBI." Will and I followed, the thunderous sound of the boots on the stairs ringing in my ears.

Entering the Montesino offices, Will ordered the three employees there to return to their workstations as the FBI team began confiscating the computers and filing cabinets.

As the offices exploded with activity, we questioned the three workers – two young women, and a young man.

"Where do we find Carlos and Dio Montesino?" Will asked them.

"They're rarely in the office," one of the young women replied in a wavering voice. "They work remotely."

"Do you have their home addresses on file?" Will questioned.

The three employees stared back vacantly. It was clear to me they knew very little.

As the field agents checked the premises and continued removing the confiscated items, Will stepped into the corridor, and with me beside him, he made a video call to Zoe. "Any joy with those home addresses?"

"The Montesinos have dozens of properties close to the city," Zoe replied, "but we're sifting through them as fast as we can. In the meantime, there's a report in from your interrogation team. One of the men being questioned has confirmed that those robberies of deceased accident victims were the ones he and his group carried out. The thefts were mostly a cover, what the Montesinos wanted were wallets and personal papers and files."

I exchanged a glance with Will. "IDs," I said.

Marcia came into view. "Yes. Original IDs belonging to the missing passengers were what they were really after. For example, a recent, out-of-date driver's license, stashed in a drawer or an old wallet, still in the house, not needed by the passenger on that trip but not yet thrown out with the garbage."

"But used, after some time, by the impostors," Will said, "as IDs for renewing a license or opening an account."

"If those robberies were a front for getting the legitimate IDs of deceased persons," I said, "then an op like that could have been going on for years, for thousands of accident fatalities."

"We need Themis to go nova on this, Zoe," said Will. "Check for correlations between *all* deaths by accident where a deceased person's home was burgled within, say, two months."

"There could be hundreds, maybe thousands more impostors." I shook my head. "All the impostors needed was to have a similar-enough appearance to the deceased person. Not difficult given that most people's appearance changes just enough after ten years, let alone twenty."

"What's more," said Zoe, "we've also learned from the men being interrogated that the Montesinos had developed their own facial recognition technology. They used it to search through photos of the deceased people, looking for matches with the physical characteristics of the criminals they were creating new lives for." She took a breath. "Even so, I hardly think the Montesinos could have pulled off something on this scale, though, without..." she left the rest unspoken as though grappling herself with the concept.

"There's something else," Marcia said, adding, "I managed to get in touch with Elena Rivera again, and while we didn't talk for long, I did discover that part of the reason for her distress earlier was due to shame."

"Shame?" I echoed.

"Yes. She's always felt guilt that her neighbor was unable to keep fostering her sister's child – a boy – and for health reasons Elena was unable to care for him. He was sent to an orphanage and his name, I've learned, was Dantes."

"Good Lord," said Will. "Dantes Otero."

"And given Sebastian's ingenuity, it's no surprise once he was older he would've tracked down what became of his mother. I'm guessing he was around sixteen when Dantes was born, which explains the age difference. Sebastian discovered he had a half-brother who was in the same cruel orphanage and when he was old enough, he took matters into his own hands," I added.

I looked out the corridor's window at the street below. A crowd of onlookers had gathered, and the first news van pulled up. "What's going on here will be all over the media very quickly. So, the brothers will know we're on to them."

It was always best to have the element of surprise on your side but that wasn't likely to be the case now.

"Maybe we can beat the news reports." Will glanced at his wristwatch and then focused again on the phone display, directing his comments to Zoe. "We need to know where to find the Montesinos before they run."

Chapter Forty-Eight

Receiving an alert on her phone, Marcia motioned for Zoe to bring up the cable news channel on the main monitor as Zach looked on.

A voice-over accompanied images of the action on the screen. "Armed with search warrants issued just hours ago, FBI agents have raided the Seattle HQ of the real estate and investment behemoth Montesino Brothers and conducted simultaneous raids on the company's offices in Florida and Los Angeles. While the exact nature of the raids is unknown at this time, the speed and the scale of the operation makes it clear that the American Venezuelan entrepreneurs Carlos and Dio Montesino and their senior staff are under suspicion of a major crime in a rapidly accelerating investigation."

Zoe reacted to a signal on her phone and browsed the display screen. "Hmm. Not surprising."

Zach shot her a questioning glance. "What is it?"

"Mr. *One Voice* didn't waste any time with a follow-up podcast."

She brought it up on the monitor and the other two gathered closer behind her, eyes fixed on the screen.

The familiar intro and then the fade-in showed Aiden Sharpe in his studio. "Something a little different today. I'm joined by *Seattle Chronicle* journalist, Brooke Goodman." The cam pulled back to reveal Brooke sitting beside Sharpe in his studio. "I have to report that both Brooke and I were last night locked up and later released. Our abductors issued warnings and threats, demanding we shut down our reports on the Whistler killings and the links we've suggested with the missing Ven Air 387 passengers."

"It was a harrowing experience," Brooke added, "but we will not be shut down from reporting on this or any other investigation."

Sharpe chimed back in. "We know that a certain FBI agent was also targeted by these men, and we suspect that this morning's raids on the Montesino companies are linked to this. If anyone out there knows anything about the Montesinos and would like to share, you can phone or text me now. In the meantime, for those who don't know of the entrepreneur brothers, here's a brief bio…"

* * *

Zach and Marcia had taken up spots on either side of Zoe around the horseshoe-shaped console. Turning away from the podcast, they each refocused on analyzing separate streams of data. The files that Zoe was studying had been mined from the Montesino computer network. "Elaborate firewalls in place," she commented as much to herself as the others.

"I'm guessing they're nothing that Themis can't make mincemeat of," Marcia said.

Zoe grinned, her eyes never leaving the monitor. "She's cracking these security shields faster than even I expected."

"More of your exquisite programming." Marcia glanced across at the figures churning across the screen. "Social security numbers?"

"Thousands," Zoe confirmed, "all held in the Montesino network. There are a hundred just from a decade-old train disaster in the southeast. There are bus crashes, sunken ferries, a bridge collapse from over fifteen years ago."

"And the robberies?" Zach wondered.

"Themis has so far linked a thousand of these tragedies with house break-ins, and she's finding more and more by the minute."

"All petty burglaries?"

"Yeah. Same MO. Nothing huge. A cover for what they really wanted. IDs."

Chapter Forty-Nine

Will McCord gathered the team around on our return to the UCU. "Here's what we know," he said. "The Montesinos use the stolen SS numbers to set up wealthy criminals, like Victor Gonzalez, with new lives in new locations. All made possible through the use of their private aircraft and real estate holdings."

"Why not use completely new, fake IDs?" Zach wondered. "And why use one from a high-profile missing plane victim?"

"For that very reason," I suggested. "No one imagines for a minute that a person in front of them is someone who died years earlier on a famously lost flight. Even then, for any of those names, there are hundreds, maybe thousands of others with the same name."

"There would have to be some instances, surely," Marcia said, "where law enforcement does call up a person's social security and sees the connection."

"These impostors will have stories lined up to talk their way around it," Zoe suggested, "or in a more extreme situation, simply disappear again."

"The question, then," said Marcia, "is how did they know the addresses of so many accident victims of all kinds, so quickly?"

"I think the answer lies in the photo I saw at Robert Wheeler's home," I announced, "the one in which he poses with A.D. Grande and Dio Montesino." I turned to Zoe. "Have Themis dig through those Montesino computers and the mainstream media. We're looking for every photo where one or both of the brothers appear, every article of reported business news about them."

"That won't take Themis long. Sit tight."

We watched as images and media items were listed on the screen.

"We need Themis's face recognition on all the people posing with the brothers in those photos," I instructed.

The ID software kicked in, spinning circles around the heads in one photo after another, the word 'Verifying' appearing in a corresponding circle. I anticipated that all the men and women in those photos would have an online business presence, making identification relatively simple. And I was right.

Profile photos of the various faces began assembling in a vertical column with that person's bio in an accompanying box.

Zoe, making the mental connection to what I was looking for, zeroed in on certain profiles, reading aloud, "Image from 2010. The man with whom the brothers are shaking hands was the lead accident investigator at the Federal Government Special Crash Investigations Program." The vertical column of data continued to scroll, Zoe highlighting another entry. "The woman alongside them here is a senior official with the Transportation Board." She followed this with another highlighted entry. "The man seen here is a senior investigator with the country's premier accident insurance company."

"Each of whom was able to deliver confidential, private addresses of accident victims," I pointed out, "just as Robert Wheeler was able to do with Ven Air 387 and other disasters."

"You think all those officials were blackmailed?" Zach asked.

"Blackmailed and probably financially rewarded as well." I couldn't imagine the horrific impact such a revelation about his father would have on Ben.

Will had been watching and listening intently, standing a little further back. "We need to keep this highly confidential, while we investigate each of these connections."

We all nodded.

"Of course," said Zach.

Will's gaze turned to me. "A.D. Grande was with the brothers in a few of those photos."

"As he was in the photo I saw at Robert Wheeler's house," I said.

"You and I will dig deeper but it could be mere coincidence, Ilona."

My eyes bore back into his. The words from the Piper's scrapbook were like an echo at the back of my mind.

Ross Grande, Special Agent in Charge at the time, led the team that rescued Ilona and gained the most from her father's forced retirement.

"It's no coincidence," I said without emotion. "We need to find out how the Assistant Director figures in all this."

I noticed that Zoe had gone quiet, her eyes glued to the monitor. "We're not holding your attention," I said to her half-jokingly.

"Sebastian has to have done something with that money," she said. "But the results have come through from Themis on the search that Zach asked for. It hasn't turned up Sebastian's name anywhere other than for the trust fund."

"When you think about it, though, that very fact makes perfect sense. When Sebastian came here from Venezuela, he would've kept his next move under the radar," said Will.

Zoe's eyes brightened, another surge of adrenaline overcoming her tiredness. "He could've used an alias so that he couldn't be linked with the money. Themis, compile a list of every US business started or purchased for an amount similar to Sebastian's trust fund amount. Initial focus on the twelve months after he accessed his inheritance."

"Commencing search."

"Whew, that will be one hell of a list, more than I requested," Zach commented. "And one hell of a long shot."

Zoe smiled at him. "I specialize in them."

"We still haven't established just how the Whistler could be sighted at the detention center's fire, at a time when Sebastian was just a small boy," Marcia said.

"Someone else adopted the persona long before Sebastian." My eyes fixed on the various columns of data on the large screen. "And I think I've got a good idea who it was."

Chapter Fifty

I shifted my weight from one foot to the other as I outlined my suspicion. "Victor Gonzalez is Sebastian's biological father, and this was never revealed to the boy. But Gonzalez would have kept tabs on the boy's progress, from afar."

I could see that Will had guessed where I was going with this. "You think Gonzalez made trips to the country and visited Sebastian at the detention center."

I tilted my head in acknowledgment. Our old team spirit was as strong as ever. "He could've adopted a simple disguise and told the boy that he was a friend of the family.

Or maybe he never gave the boy an explanation for his visits. It makes perfect sense that in addition to destroying the center and freeing Sebastian, Gonzalez would set up the trust fund for when his son came of age."

"But he didn't take Sebastian with him when he returned to the US," Marcia said.

"He couldn't stay in Venezuela and risk exposure," Will stated, "and he couldn't take the boy without creating a trail that might compromise his new ID. I don't expect he wanted the boy with him, anyway. He never did. He was purely looking after Sebastian's interests without any further personal involvement–"

"Themis has something on the Montesinos' home addresses." The sudden urgency in Zoe's voice diverted our attention back to the large screen.

On the monitor behind Zoe was an aerial view of large coastal properties. "Two properties, side by side, that fit the bill," she said.

"Montesino Investments have two hobby-farm compounds on Whidbey Island, each of which has three-hundred feet of waterfront," Themis announced, "each with a double-level five-bedroom main residence, a private, deep-water marina, and several outbuildings including guest cottages and garages. Neither is listed as currently being rented nor used for business purposes."

"That's where they're living," I stated. The island was thirty miles north of Seattle. "Zoe, find out as much as you can about the history of those two properties." My eyes met with Will's. "We need to get out there."

"We don't know what to expect on approach," he cautioned, "whether they're on the premises, and whether their security guys are in place and armed. And the Whistler could already be out there so we're taking every precaution." He directed his gaze at Marcia. "I want Ilona, myself, and the men with us fully weaponized," he instructed. "Short-barreled shotguns with breaching rounds, tasers, Kevlar vests."

"They'll be ready in ten," she responded.

* * *

Detective Paul Radner strode into his office and eased himself into the chair behind his desk. He took a minute, as he always did, settling his gaze lovingly on the framed photo beside his PC. His daughter, Sarah. There wasn't a moment of the day he didn't miss her but his work kept him well and truly preoccupied most of the time.

He didn't dwell on her final moments, falling from a great height after being drawn in by those urban climbers – fools who thought they were brave; amateurs who considered themselves untouchable daredevils. For just a few moments he allowed his memories to wander through the years of her childhood and he smiled inwardly at the sound of her cheeky laugh and the sight of her blonde curls.

The station lieutenant poked his head through the open doorway, interrupting Radner's reverie. "Detective," said the younger man, "you remember that investigation a few years back, an employee blowing the whistle on supposed money laundering at that real estate investment firm?"

"Of course, I remember." It was one of those cases that had been a sore point with Radner. "I got a call from the Feds telling us to drop it, that we would be interfering with an overarching investigation of their own."

"And then nothing ever came of that."

Radner huffed. "Yeah."

"And a few months after that the ex-employee was fished out of the Puget Sound. Supposedly an accidental drowning."

Radner showed his impatience. "What about it?"

"The FBI just conducted snap raids on all the offices of that firm."

Radner switched on the television in his office and watched the news flash. The team behind the raids was Ilona's unit.

He placed a call to her and when she came on the line, he told her of his investigation three years earlier, when he'd been shut down before he'd ever got to interview the brothers. "I can fill you in on the details later but right now I'm offering the services of the SPD. If you'd like some extra manpower as backup–" He paused mid-sentence as she gave him the addresses and suggested a rendezvous at the brothers' homes.

Ending the call, Radner looked at the younger man. "Grab a couple of the officers," he said, "we're paying a visit to those brothers."

* * *

It was a little over an hour's drive along Interstate 5 to Whidbey Island. We were in two cars, Will and I in one, two field agents in the vehicle following. Radner and the SPD officers would meet with us at the scene.

As we sped along the Interstate, Will was on his phone, arranging for one of the Navy's Seahawk helicopters to be on standby at the Naval Airfield which was located on the island at Oak Harbor.

When the cars pulled up in the expansive driveway that fronted the first of the two palatial houses, the police officers spread out, securing the perimeter, while Radner joined me and Will at the front door. Seeing there was no reaction to the door chimes, Will and Radner applied force and kicked the door in.

The lieutenant and his officers followed us in, one remaining on watch at the door while the others checked all rooms on the two levels. "No sign of the occupants," the senior field agent reported back to Will via his comms.

"Maintain your watch on both levels," Will instructed. He had an incoming video call from Zoe and motioned for me and Radner to move in closer to his phone.

"We've discovered something incredible about those houses," Zoe said.

Chapter Fifty-One

"Sixteen years ago," Zoe told us, "the brothers used a renovation firm that builds panic rooms and escape passages for the very wealthy."

"Go on," I said.

"Buried twenty feet under both those houses is a connecting tunnel, a panic room, and a soundproof exit passageway, all carved out of the ground and encased in concrete and natural rock. There's a fifteen-thousand-square-foot bunker housing cars and small boats. It leads to an exit portal complete with a boat ramp." After a beat, she added, "Not what you wanted to hear."

"No," I responded. "How do we find the entry?"

"It's hidden behind a staircase on the lower level. The staircase will lift automatically when you press the wall switch, which just looks like a regular light switch panel."

"Found it," I said.

Will, Radner, and I watched as the staircase lifted, revealing a sloped passageway. With Radner remaining on watch, Will and I raced in, sighting on the left the connecting passageway to the neighboring house and on the right, the door to the panic room.

We followed the subterranean tunnel, which was brightly lit, illuminating rough-hewn stone walls and ceiling. We moved quickly but cautiously along its winding passageway – hearing a sudden rumble of noise from ahead – and we emerged a minute later into the large hangar-shaped area that Zoe had described.

I marveled at what had been built here. On the one hand, it made sense that a criminal operation like that of the Montesinos would have elaborate firewalls embedded in their cyber network, just as it made sense they had unlisted addresses and that their fabulous homes were out of town.

But the panic room, the underground tunnel, and the escape route to the nearby shore, complete with a motorboat – this was something else. Paranoia on steroids.

And yet it made a peculiar kind of sense. The Montesinos' clients were the super-wealthy elite who had been arrested and arraigned for trial. Ahead of their court appearances, they had elected to disappear, starting new lives under stolen identities. So the brothers knew it could happen to anyone – they'd seen it time and time again. That was what their multi-million-dollar empire had been built on.

The enormous exit doors were open, revealing the boat ramp, and as we sprang forward we saw the compact, covered motorboat thundering away from the shore on the choppy swell of the waves, as a strong wind blew from the south.

"Damn it," I exclaimed.

Will was on his phone, giving the order for the Seahawk helicopter to fly in and pick us up. I knew he was certain that the last thing the Montesinos would expect was to be pursued from the air.

As the Seahawk flew toward the beach, Will and I raced across the sand to meet it.

The chopper hovered, churning up the surf directly beneath it, its ladder swinging. Will moved forward, waving for me to clamber up and board first.

But I held back, my mind buzzing.

The sight of the motorboat speeding away from the shore reminded me of that moment just days before, a smaller motorboat spiriting the Whistler and the boy away from the ramp near Sam Garcia's home in California. The Whistler had made his escape along the bush trail that led to the river. The boy had been in the boat, waiting.

From that point, my mind flashed to the Whistler climbing down from the hangar roof at San Francisco Airport, the boy waiting for him across the field.

Though he was always with him, the Whistler never took the boy directly into any of the scenes of his murders. The boy was always nearby – as he'd been at the Seascape Marina when all this began – always waiting, and in some cases waiting with the escape vehicle or craft.

Will threw a hurried glance at me. "Ilona!" he shouted, to be heard over the roar of the rotor blades.

I stared back, unmoving. The memories from those previous incidents were like a movie playing in my head. Why? "Something isn't right," I shouted back.

I glanced across the wide strip of sandy shore. A grove of trees and bushes skirted the edges, shaking under the force of the wind. I returned my gaze to Will, his eyes smarting, squinting against the wind from the rotors. "If we dart for those trees we'll be shielded from sight."

He glared at me. "Whose sight?"

Ignoring the question, I shouted back, "Tell the pilot to retract the ladder and take off. Anyone watching from afar should be fooled into believing we're on board."

"You're not making any sense," Will shouted.

"I don't think the Montesinos are on that boat."

"Then who is?"

"The boy."

"Ilona, we need to go now."

"Trust me on this, Will." The helicopter needed to take off before it was obvious they were hesitating. I knew, as did the whole team, that the Whistler was ultimately after these crime lord brothers.

"The Montesinos must be on that boat," Will insisted.

"I think the Montesinos are back there," I said, tossing my head in the direction of the houses. "I think they're inside their panic room, and I think the Whistler is hidden on the premises, waiting."

For a split second, Will's eyes searched mine. He didn't respond straight away. If there was one thing I knew about him, it was that he could remain calm and mentally sharp, weighing up the odds and making decisive moves when under pressure. Like now. All agents were trained to do this. Will McCord excelled at it.

His hand cupped the comms at his ear, and he shouted an order for the chopper to leave without them and follow the boat.

Then he and I ran across the sand to the trees.

* * *

We crouched there, catching our breaths, our throats hoarse from the shouting. I could have downed a liter of water in a single gulp.

"You think the speeding boat was a ruse?" Will said.

I nodded, still breathing heavily. "Think about it. The Whistler will have known about the raids, if not from breaking news reports, then maybe from an informer on the scene. He's always had contingency plans to keep him one step ahead."

"True."

"He'd expect the FBI to raid these homes. So how could he get to the brothers first if he knew we were closing in?" I took a deep breath, glancing across to the point where we'd exited the tunnel, then looked to Will again. "I think he'd already done his homework about the underground passage, Will. Think about his MO. He teases his victims with an early warning that he's coming for them. I believe he'd already contacted the brothers, spooked them and then he's made his way here to the properties and set off their alarms—"

"Knowing they'd retreat to their panic room."

"Yes. And he's expecting us to arrive, see the boat speeding off and give chase. It's no mental leap we'd believe it was the brothers, but I think it was Dantes, intending to lead us away."

Will followed my line of reasoning. "The brothers assume it's the Whistler in the boat because the FBI's moving in."

"Yes. And they emerge from their safe room unaware the Whistler is lying in wait."

"That's a hell of a hunch." Will's eyes wandered to the ramp and the tunnel entry. "But you might've nailed it." He shot me an alarmed look. "It means the agents in the house are in danger." He activated his comms, and his eyes widened. "No answer."

Chapter Fifty-Two

As we re-entered the bunker, we heard voices. The Montesinos. The heavy wooden door of the panic room opened in the passageway on the other side of the bunker. Venturing out, both Carlos and Dio Montesino sighted us, and turning rapidly, they retreated into the room, attempting to close the door behind them. Racing into the passageway, I leaped forward, swinging the muzzle of my shotgun into a position to jam the door open. Will was not far behind, his pistol drawn.

I quickly adjusted my grip and aimed the shotgun in front of me, stepping through the doorway. It wasn't a large room and the brothers were at its opposite wall, Carlos furiously inputting a code into another door positioned there.

"Step away from that door, hands in the air," I ordered.

Dio glanced back at me fearfully, but Carlos ignored the order, cussing and re-entering the code. That door wasn't responding. In that instant, it struck me that this room was not just small, but strangely bare of any items of furniture, anything at all. Something wasn't right. And then there was a sudden ear-piercing screech, the lights blacked out, and in the split second before they came back on there was a grinding sound and a rush of air, and the wooden door banged shut. As it did, a hidden metal door slid across behind it. All in a matter of seconds.

What the hell just happened?

I'd been cut off from the passageway, and from Will.

* * *

Reactively, Will was forced to step back at the unexpected force of the door that slid by less than a hair's breadth in front of his face, propelled from a narrow partition between the side walls. Just before this sliding metal panel clanged shut, he glimpsed the Montesinos in the room, saw the inner wooden door slam closed and heard its locking mechanism click into place.

He took a deep, ragged breath. There was more to this than your average panic room, but even so, this double-door composition wasn't something any of them would have anticipated.

He shouted Ilona's name but heard nothing in response, no sounds at all, and he remembered Zoe's comment that the whole area was soundproofed. He activated his comms but got back nothing but static.

His cell rang and he answered it. "Zoe?"

"Will, I've uncovered something else," she said urgently, "something very strange. There was another panic room blueprint in the files."

"What do you mean?"

"There's a hidden escape door – that's a common feature of these rooms – but this one leads to a larger area, the *real* panic room. The first room appears to be some sort of trick, to fool anyone pursuing the brothers, or perhaps to lure their enemies and trap them."

Will gulped in air, his throat dry, his voice a hard-edged rasp. "Go on."

219

"Seems it's been designed so that the Montesinos, from the second room, can seal an enemy in by remotely relocking the inner door and activating a hidden, outer metal sliding panel."

Will cursed out loud. It was like some real-world set of firewalls.

"What's more, they can pump in lethal gas."

"No…"

"The SafeRooms company informed us, also, that their internal systems were hacked several weeks ago."

"Which means the Whistler knew all about those mechanisms," Will realized with horror.

"Will, what's happening there now? Where's Ilona?"

"She's trapped in that first room."

"What?" Zoe shrugged off her surprise in an instant. "Okay, but the Montesinos won't be hanging around in their second room," she sounded hopeful, "so Ilona should be okay. There's an escape shaft and they'll have taken that; it leads to the foot of the hills."

"The Montesinos aren't in that second room," Will responded gravely. "They're trapped with Ilona."

"God, no. The second room…?"

"The Whistler's the one in control," Will said.

Chapter Fifty-Three

"What is this?" I said, my gaze fixed on the two brothers, setting the shotgun aside and drawing my pistol. They stared back at me, silent, defenseless, stunned.

There was a speaker above the rear door and a voice crackled over it. "Perhaps the all-mighty Montesino brothers would like me to answer."

I looked at the speaker as though it held a picture of the man speaking. "El Silbón, the Whistler?"

"Two so-called panic rooms," the Whistler said. "One of them a fake."

I glanced at the brothers. Still silent. Both men were fit, muscled, could be considered dangerous-looking, and yet at that moment, they were like animals caught in a trap, wide-eyed, and squirming. Dio gave me the impression he might start shaking and shivering at any second while Carlos, the larger and broader of the two, was like a pit bull, alert, searching for a way out, ready to pounce.

They knew something I didn't. What was it?

And then the Whistler's odd and unsettling whistle, those seven notes in a rising scale, came over the speaker. Repeated several times and morphing into the frightening, reptilian-like hiss that made my blood run cold.

When the Whistler spoke next, it was with a bitter edge. "You might be wondering why all this is happening, why now, and how I tracked you down? And I might have explained, but perhaps it's just as fitting for the Montesinos to take their final breaths without knowing, stripped of the control they thought they would always have."

"But I can tell them," I said. I wished I could see his face, observe if he was gripped by surprise at how much I could reveal. "I know who you are and what you know, Sebastian Rivera. That those missing plane passengers are impostors. Rich criminals who evaded the law, and that one of them, Victor Gonzalez, caused the suicides of your father and also that of young Dantes Otero's father."

I allowed a moment for him to absorb the full weight of my knowledge. "I get that you wanted revenge against Gonzalez and your own brand of justice for the Montesinos, who made his escape possible. But why go after all the other impostors?" If I could engage him in conversation, draw him out further, maybe I could give Will the time to find a way in.

There was no emotion in his response. "The Montesinos have their fingers in every pie imaginable, every level of law enforcement and government. That is their great power. On my own, I could not bring them down. So I attacked their business, the one place I could cause real harm. Their secret network of clients."

I saw his reasoning. "With their clients being murdered systematically, the Montesinos would notice straight away."

"Yes," he said, with a lift in his voice. He was excited by the audacity of his plan, one man against a machine, David vs. Goliath. "The word would have spread quickly throughout the underworld. With their false identity scheme compromised, there would be no new takers, the money would dry up. I wanted them to experience their empire crashing."

"Like all the victims of the criminals they protected."

"Yes. And eventually, I'd move in for the kill."

"But the FBI's investigation robbed you of all that."

"It does not matter. The end result is the same and justice for my father and the other victims is complete."

"Brilliant," I conceded. "But it has to end now, Sebastian."

The brothers had been motionless, listening intently, but now Carlos Montesino shouted, his lips curled in anger, sweat bristling on his brow, "You're a coward, Sebastian Rivera!"

"Then you are calling yourself a coward," the Whistler shot back, "because I am simply sitting here, in the control room you built, doing exactly what you were prepared to do to anyone who came for you. What you *did* do to the employee who tried to rat you out recently."

"You hide behind the mask of some mythical ghost" — Carlos spat the words — "but you are no more than a weak and pathetic man."

"And so the great and mighty Montesinos, architects of a multi-million-dollar criminal protection plan, meet their end at the hands of a weak and pathetic lone individual. How ironic."

Carlos smashed his fist against the stone wall and blood spurted from the wound it opened up across his knuckles.

"You don't have to do this, Sebastian," I called out. "You've accomplished your mission. There are agents and police officers out there on the premises. Let us out and we take the brothers into custody."

"They have the riches to conduct a lengthy legal fight. And the contacts to instigate an escape. No, it's not a chance that can be taken. They must end here."

"And me?"

"In war, there is always collateral damage." There was a sudden churning sound, the grueling hum of machinery, vents slid open in the ceiling, then, a whooshing sound.

Gas.

"Sebastian!" I shouted. But I guessed he'd already taken another escape route as the gas began to seep through.

Dio Montesino dropped to a sitting position. "When the murders began it was clear our network was compromised… but we didn't act quickly enough, we believed we could win as we always had."

"Shut up, Dio," Carlos commanded. "Let me think."

"Why bother? The one thing we didn't plan for was being trapped in here ourselves." He began coughing, his face reddening.

The gas permeated the air, its odor overwhelming. Carlos and I began coughing with each breath.

I glanced around at our natural rock prison.

For the team outside the room, there was no way to break in.

And for me, there was no way out.

I sat down, back against the wall, knees drawn up.

Restrict movement.

Take long, slow breaths and hold each one in as long as possible to delay the effect of the gas.

Dio Montesino was doing the opposite. Panicking. Breathing rapidly, coughing, spluttering.

Carlos was still on his feet. He smashed his fist in fury a second time against the wall. Breathing in too much of the gas too quickly.

For all their power, intelligence, and arrogance, they had no idea.

"Breathe slowly," I instructed. "Long, slow breaths."

They weren't listening.

I glanced at my phone. No signal. The room was sealed off in every way possible. And for just a moment, in that instant, I was my kidnapped fourteen-year-old self again, back in that box, imprisoned, at the base of a deep shaft in an unfinished, deserted nuclear power plant.

Against all odds, I had escaped.

But this was very different.

Very final.

I coughed, tried to suppress it, breathed, coughed again, my vision starting to waver, my mind foggy, my eyes feeling the weight of sleepiness.

A voice in the distance. Getting closer.

My mother.

Keep your eyes open, Ilona. Fight.

Stay awake.

Think of the panic room as an escape room.

How do you escape?

Fight.

Think.

I was certain I felt the touch of my mother's hand on mine.

I'd managed to start climbing out of that shaft years ago but there was no opening above me here.

I've missed you so much all these years, Mom.

Maybe it's time to be with you again.

Chapter Fifty-Four

Think of the panic room as an escape room.

Fight.

Think.

I couldn't let the memory and the voice of my mother down. I needed to keep thinking this through.

I forced myself to my feet, moved forward, and examined the inner door. It was thick, solid wood with a deadbolt and steel hinges. I glanced at the brothers. "Why is this door wooden?"

"We only needed the outer door to be impenetrable steel," Carlos explained. "This one was primarily used by us to come and go when the room wasn't being used as a trap."

"This door uses a key?"

Carlos pointed toward the second safe room. "We keep it in there."

"And does the outer steel door have an electronic keypad in case you need to activate it manually?"

"Yes."

"Is the panel for the code on both sides of that outer door?"

He grunted.

I had expected as much. The outer door had a double-sided panel as a fail-safe for the brothers but just a regular lock and key for the inner door.

"What's the code?"

"What's the point?" he shot back in anger and frustration. "We can't get through *this* door." His fury at being trapped by his own ingenuity was palpable.

I glared at him, coughing, shouting. *"Carlos, what is the code?"*

He glared back and then, dismissively, told me the numbers.

I closed my eyes and imagined I was the Whistler, and once again I willed myself to think as he would think. He knew the brothers wouldn't have any weapons on them, not that pistols would be of any use in this situation. He knew the inner door didn't use a keypad and that its actual key was with him, in the control point.

But the Whistler wasn't expecting *me* to be trapped in the room with the brothers.

Wars have collateral damage.

But I'm no ordinary collateral damage.

Unlike the brothers, I had my weapons. Including my short-barreled shotgun.

I drew on my Bureau training. At Quantico, I'd been schooled in the act of door breaching, the tactical process by which police and military services broke through doors of all kinds.

Whether it was a regular door, a cell door, or a safe room entry point like this one, there was one common feature of wooden doors that didn't rely on a security keypad – the bolts inside the framework that both closed and released the locking mechanism. The only ballistic method that could be used on a door like this was firing the shotgun – not the most reliable but, I now realized through the haze of my thoughts, the one course of action open to me.

Carlos had dropped to his knees beside his brother; both were struggling to breathe, eyes bulging.

I holstered my pistol and retrieved my shotgun from where it lay. "Move further back," I ordered.

"What are you doing?" Dio sounded as though he was being physically choked.

I ignored the question and raised the shotgun. The room was beginning to spin, it was as though I had extreme vertigo, and the edges of my vision were darkening. There wasn't much time left. The strength was draining from my limbs, my knees were buckling, the gas fumes thick throughout the confined space.

I focused on the door, on the area between the doorjamb and the lock. I aimed the muzzle of the weapon to a point between the handle and the locking mechanism, tilted the gun to a 45-degree angle, and reached further into my memory, recalling my trainer's instructions. "Get the directional placement right and the shot will blow the lock so that the door breaks free."

I was doing this from the opposite side of the door from which it would usually be executed. Trying to break *out*, not in. Holding still, forcing myself not to cough, I fired, and the wood splintered. I lowered the gun, dug my fingers into the gauge the round had made and attempted to pull it. No movement. I repositioned the shotgun and fired a second time; this time the lock shattered, and the door shifted. I pushed my fingers into the widened gap and opened it toward me, revealing the outer door. I lunged forward, my fingers touching the keypad. Before I could input the numerals, I fell away, my vision completely blurred, and slid down to the floor.

I struggled to find one last reserve of strength but felt myself fading away. I'd already spent too much energy. I became conscious of a shadow looming above me. Carlos. He was pushing forward and reaching out for the panel. He punched in the number but even as he touched the final numeral, his body crashed down on top of mine.

Chapter Fifty-Five

I woke with a start, coughing violently and then gulping in lungfuls of pure air.

"Thank God you're okay," Will said.

I was on the ground just outside the panic room, looking up at him. I shifted into a sitting position, my breathing more regular now, and I glanced about. There were two bodies, covered in sheets, lying on the other side of the bunker.

"We tried to revive them, but they didn't make it."

"I told them to restrict their movements, take slow breaths, they wouldn't listen."

His hand covered mine. "Just take it easy."

"If it hadn't been for Carlos, he somehow punched in the code…"

"Nothing more you could have done," Will assured me.

"The Whistler?"

"The second room, the real panic room, has an escape passage that runs through to the forest," Will said. "Radner and his men found the tunnel and went through to the room. As we expected, the Whistler was gone so now they're searching the forest." He held up the display on his phone, showing me the blueprints that Zoe had sent through.

I held his phone for a moment as scrolled through them. "The men stationed upstairs were all okay?"

"The Whistler knocked them unconscious, tied them up, but they're all fine."

I took a moment, taking deep, measured breaths. My head was clear and my body was rapidly returning to normal.

"We cleared all your vitals," Will told me. "And there are medics on the way."

I nodded. "So the Whistler waited for the Montesinos to exit the main panic room once they thought we were gone…"

"He then entered that room from the forest tunnel."

I nodded again, taking it all in. "The Whistler must have had another scare lined up so that the brothers would rush back in and be trapped."

"Whatever it was, he didn't need to execute it. They raced back in, anyway, when they saw us return. But now" – he squeezed my hand reassuringly – "we're on his tail."

"But he'd expect that." I stared at him with unblinking intensity. "We're on a long stretch of coast, plenty of hiding spots. And Dantes will be waiting somewhere on the other side of the water."

"So how does the Whistler get to him?" Will, like me, still didn't think of the killer as a young man named Sebastian Rivera.

"Once he emerges into the forest he'll move through the trees."

"Our guys know that."

"He'll be practically impossible to spot; those trees are over a hundred feet high, and the canopy is perfect camouflage. We know he'll have staked out the area, with something in mind. We need a map of boathouses along the coast."

Will was on his phone straight away, briefing Zoe.

I was on my feet. "We need to join the search."

"You're not going anywhere," Will insisted. "You need to rest up until we can get you to a hospital."

"For what? I'm fine."

"Radner and his men are out there with our agents," Will said. "Let them take it from here."

"We need to search the coastline and the boathouses, not just the forest."

"Yes, and I can get a couple of the men to join me and follow that up. Zoe's sending through a map," he said.

I locked eyes with him. I knew that look on his face and thought better of arguing the point. "Fair enough. You go, then."

"I'm waiting with you until the medics are here."

"For God's sake, Will, I'm fine and you know damn well you can't lose any time. Grab those men and go and I'll rest up."

He stared back, considering my words. "Okay."

* * *

Will instructed the naval chopper to fly back over and then made another call, arranging navy motorboats to be deployed. They'd reach Whidbey Island within twenty minutes. And then he was gone.

I would go upstairs to the main house in a little while but for now, I sat back down on the bunker floor, cross-legged, and willed myself to leave the chase to the rest of the team while I re-energized.

My mind rolled through the events leading up to this point.

Why hadn't the Whistler fled earlier once he knew the raids were underway? Why put himself at this level of risk? It wasn't hard for me to imagine his mental state and that gave me the answer – he was too close to his endgame to abandon it and arrogant enough to believe he would, as always, outsmart his pursuers and beat the odds.

So, what was he thinking now?

I closed my eyes, pushing all other thoughts from my mind. I needed to become the Whistler again.

Think as he does.

How do I deceive those who are bearing down on me?

Every step of the way, the Whistler had been the great deceiver.

He'd fled through the hidden escape passage which exited out in the forest. That exit, I'd noted on the plans shown by Will, was disguised as a rusty old disused drain hole partially covered by shrubs.

From there, he would climb to the treetops and stealthily make his way across the branches to a point near the shoreline, close to one of the boathouses. He steals a boat but where does he go? Out on the Sound he's exposed. The boy, Dantes, is waiting…

I opened my eyes, thoughts whirling. A kaleidoscope of alternative possibilities. The Whistler. A phantom. Leading us on a desperate chase through the trees.

A *phantom* chase because that's not what he's done at all, I realized.

I imagined an impromptu plan, the same plan I was sure the Whistler had devised. Fleeing through the escape passage, lifting the old drain cover, casting it aside, tramping the surrounding grounds. Signaling his movements. Then hiding close by.

Once Radner and the agents had been to the tunnel and then gone out into the woods, the Whistler would do the unexpected. Retrace his steps. Back through the passage, re-emerging into the main panic room. That room, I knew from the plans Zoe had sent through, was large, built for extensive use. Away from its control desk, it had seating, tables, cupboards, bedding, a kitchenette, and a restroom. No one was searching it now. The Whistler could hide there while the search for him raged outside. Once he assessed the coast being clear, likely after nightfall, he'd exit the underground area via the boat ramp portal, and steal away along the shore, in the darkness.

I'm not going to let that happen.

I couldn't access the second room from the front as it had a unique security code, known only to the brothers, so I headed out via the ramp, doubled around the outside, and into the forest. The wind was wilder than before, and I winced. *That's the last thing we need.* Due to its proximity to the Strait of Juan de Fuca, I knew it was not uncommon for the island to be hit by powerful windstorms. I pressed on, pushing against it, my hair streaming out behind me. As I reached the place where the fake drain exit was located, I cupped my comms, contacted Will, and hurriedly explained my theory.

"Are you certain?" he asked.

"No."

"Okay," he said. "The men with me will continue the search along the coast but I'm heading back."

"I'm at the forest exit now."

"Wait there for me," Will commanded.

I slid down through the hole; it was only a short drop. The passage was large enough to stand and wide enough for two people to move through it side-by-side. Tiny bulbs embedded in the walls emitted a dim light.

I knew I should wait for backup as instructed and as per all protocols and training. Will could only be fifteen, maybe twenty minutes away on foot.

That's twenty minutes in which the Whistler could decide to make his run.

Slowly, quietly, with my eyes focused intently on the winding passageway and with my pistol drawn, I moved forward.

* * *

Zach's way of dealing with his anxiety, while waiting for further word from Will, was to pace. Back and forth.

Marcia, by contrast, had a stillness about her, watching Zoe, who in turn was shooting her gaze from one of the multiple screens to another, her hands flying across her keyboard.

"Themis has been crunching through that data I asked for," Zoe said, "on all business purchases or start-ups in the year after Sebastian received his trust money." She sounded out a low, brief whistle. "Over 10,000 businesses sold, over 600,000 new business start-ups."

Zach and Marcia looked at her expectantly, and then, swiveling in her chair to face them, she said, "The system cross-referenced every detail from those businesses with every scrap of data we have on this case."

"I didn't think there was going to be anything–"

"Neither did I," Zoe cut Zach short as he and Marcia stepped closer to the monitor. "But out of all of that, there is a link. One name. Just one."

Zach's eyes widened as he focused on the words on the screen.

* * *

As I approached the point where the passage enabled me to access the panic room, I became aware of the strong odor. Gas. Why was there gas back here, drifting from the main safe room?

If I was right and the Whistler was in there, what was he…?

I froze in my tracks, my mind reeling back through everything I knew about Sebastian Rivera. Always a step ahead.

I thought of the boy. Dantes. The orphanage.

Sebastian entered that orphanage and led Dantes away, right under everyone's noses, invisible amidst the chaos caused by the inferno he'd ignited for just that purpose. Victor Gonzalez had used the same method years before when he'd taken the young Sebastian out of the juvenile detention center.

That's how he intends to escape from Whidbey Island. Creating a diversion on a scale that will shield him from the search.

Now I knew I couldn't hold back and wait for Will or the Navy chopper or the motorboats that were converging on the coast.

The round steel door that separated the passage from the panic room was open, the gaseous odor stronger as I inched through the opening.

There he is.

On the other side of this panic room was an alcove with the kitchenette. The Whistler dropped a match into a pot of cooking oil which brought forth a burst of flames.

Pumping in gas to mix with the oxygen in a confined space and subjecting it to rising flames, created the perfect storm for a catastrophic explosion.

"Smother the flame, Sebastian," I ordered, "and turn around slowly, hands in the air."

The Whistler spun around, a pistol in his hand, as the flames from the pot whooshed higher.

Even though he wore the wide-brimmed hat, from this distance and with the overhead light bathing him in light, enough of his face was visible.

I gasped in disbelief.

Apart from old childhood photos, I had never seen Sebastian Rivera but this was a face I *had* seen, a face I knew.

Chapter Fifty-Six

Brendan Davis glared back, his blonde-tinted stubble a distraction from his dark eyes and South American complexion.

In that instant, my mind whirled with dozens of fragments shifting into place. Accessing his trust fund in the US at age twenty-one, Sebastian had adopted an alter ego. He'd purchased a small skydiving firm, added helicopter flights and expanded it, the franchises mostly based at airports. He'd kept this world, as Brendan Davis, completely removed from his other lives, as Sebastian Rivera and the Whistler. Never suspecting for one moment that his first victim was his biological father and the man who had set up the trust fund.

"The Montesinos gifted me the perfect escape," he said, exhibiting no surprise on seeing me. "Pipes with pressurized gas. A room full of weapons and of course flammable cooking materials. And I'll be out there, fading into the distance while all hell breaks loose."

"Was it pure chance that Roger Islington became one of your skydive customers?"

"Not at all," he sneered. "I saw to it that he was sent half-a-dozen free skydives as part of a promotional mail-out."

"As the proprietor of the skydive, you knew you wouldn't be a suspect."

"I planted a few false trails."

"Victor Gonzalez, masquerading as Ken Rossi, was something far more than you're aware of. He had an affair with your mother–"

"I know that."

"What you don't know – what your aunt knew but never revealed to you – was that Victor Gonzalez was also your father."

His dark eyes bore into mine, the intensity so powerful I felt as though it could suck me in, envelop me in his warped reality, an inner realm of fury and anger and infinite torment. He didn't dispute my words or exhibit shock, and I wondered if he'd known or suspected, or whether he simply didn't care.

"Even if that's true," he said, "do you think it matters to me? Gonzalez was a monster, not a father. He caused my family's destruction. Now the Montesino empire that supported him, and so many others like him, is finished."

"This isn't the way to get justice, Sebastian."

"It is *my* way."

Through his clenched teeth, his voice seething with anger, I could detect the snake-like hiss of the Whistler just beneath the surface and I felt the hairs on the nape of my neck lift.

The flames were spreading.

"Drop the gun, Sebastian, hands in the air and I take you out of here before this whole place goes up."

"You won't be taking me anywhere," he said and he fired the pistol at point-blank range.

The first bullet grazed my shoulder. I sprung sideways, gun still aimed squarely at him, shouting, "You don't want to do this!"

The second bullet, seconds after the first, struck me in the chest and I was hurled backward. I hit the wall and slid down to the floor.

My thoughts tumbled around my head as I slid. *What have I done?*

"You were never a target," he said, "but you keep getting in the way." He rushed past me and through the passage doorway as the fire surged in the kitchenette. And he was gone, slamming the round steel door closed behind him.

Chapter Fifty-Seven

The bullet had been absorbed by the Kevlar vest beneath my jacket, something the Whistler didn't know, but the impact was still enough to leave me winded and bruised. I gasped for breath, the gas weakening me further, but I knew I had to push through that, and I drew on every last vestige of inner strength, lifting myself to my feet.

On wobbly legs I turned to the escape doorway — would there be enough time left now? I had to reach the exit before the flames and the gas ignited and sent a fireball flashing through the tunnel. I attempted to open the round steel door to the passageway, but it wouldn't budge. It had wedged shut when Sebastian slammed it behind him.

The entire kitchenette was alight, spraying sparks and smoke across the room. I glanced momentarily at the door on the other side, the portal to the outer trap room. The gas had dispersed earlier in there, with the way now open to the boat ramp exit. I didn't know the code to open this inner door between the two panic rooms but I thought I should be able to open it from the computer console. I hobbled across to it, pulse racing, the flames rising around the edges of the bench and licking at the sides of the computers. Any second, they'd be destroyed. I tapped the keys, and the screen showed a command column. I scrolled through it, desperately, saw 'door', navigated to 'open', and clicked the icon. Would it work? The PC metal was hot to the touch, the heat of the flame like a furnace blowing its heat onto my face and stinging my eyes.

I heard the click of a lock and the doorjamb shifted and partly slid aside, but not the whole way, its mechanism already compromised by the heat. I rushed to get through, the narrow opening just enough to fit in – part of the way, not all the way, too tight, I was wedged – I eased back out, hurriedly removed my flak jacket and Kevlar vest and cast aside the shotgun and then pushed through again. This time I just managed to squeeze through to the other side.

There were deafening cracks and pops as the furniture in the room behind sizzled and the metal and plastic of the equipment melted. And then an enormous blistering surge of heat and flame.

I ran out of the trap room, hurtling across the bunker, and as I did, I heard the deafening roar and felt the powerful force of the explosion.

I was knocked off my feet. Debris began flying and falling all around me. I struggled to my feet again, a chunk of granite smashing against the side of my face, and I ran, covered in dirt and ash, blood gushing from my cheek. I burst through the bunker exit and dropped onto the cool sand of the beach.

Lying there, catching my breath, I looked back up the steep hill to the Montesino homes. Dio's house, the one immediately over the brothers' underground system, was rocked by a series of explosions as the fire raged through the whole structure. The windows blew out and as the fire flamed through every opening, the walls began to crumble. Several more explosions followed, casting a cloud of shattered metal, wood and glass through the air like a tornado wreaking havoc.

I took hold of my phone and called Emergency, watching as the flames leaped and hissed and the surrounding treetops began to blaze. This was what the Whistler wanted. Total pandemonium, a massive firefighting effort as the surrounding region was threatened. But even he couldn't have anticipated the sudden windstorm coming off the Strait.

The Navy chopper flew overhead, and I first heard then saw the Navy motorboats zooming across the water.

I was on my feet again. I had to navigate my way back around to the point where the Whistler would have exited the passage into the forest. I started to run but I was faint, my legs weak, my vision blurring. *Damn, got to push through…*

And then the blackness rushed in, and I crashed down onto the sand.

* * *

Will sighted the drain hole exit in the forest floor ahead as he dashed through the scrub.

Where is Ilona?

Then there was movement and the Whistler clambered out of the hole.

Less than ten minutes before, as he'd made his way back to the house, Will had taken a call from Zoe. She told him what she'd learned from Themis's search of businesses purchased during the year after Sebastian accessed his trust fund. One name had a connection with the murder of Roger Islington at the skydive operation.

Pistol raised, Will shouted, "FBI. Stand down, Sebastian, or should I say *Brendan!*"

The young man in the long-tattered coat sprang away into the undergrowth with barely a backward glance like a startled deer fleeing from a predator.

Will gave chase. The woods were thick and the long grasses, shrubs, and ferns, whipped into a frenzy by the wind, had quickly obscured the Whistler from Will's line of sight. He pushed forward, determined the killer would not elude him in this heavily wooded landscape, when all of a sudden there was a loud crack and a bullet whizzed past dangerously close to his head.

Will sprang to his left, scrambling behind the cover of a wide, gnarled trunk and another bullet struck the tree, splintering and showering strips of bark.

He's armed himself with weapons from that control room. And he knows how to use them.

He inched stealthily from one tree to the next, alert to the fact he couldn't see his prey and that another bullet could find its mark. And then he heard a rustle of leaves and caught a flash of movement, not at ground level but higher.

He charged forward scanning the treetops, and saw the Whistler climbing one of the trunks, speedily disappearing into the low-hanging spread of the forest canopy.

"Give it up, Sebastian," Will called out. "We have the area surrounded. It's over." He didn't expect a response and he didn't get one. He craned his neck, looking up. He couldn't sight him from down here.

Must keep track of him.

I need to be up there.

He shed the shotgun to lighten his weight. He found a trunk with lower-hanging branches than those surrounding it and began to climb, one hand over the other, legs wrapping around parts of the trunk where possible, scrambling for any footholds and handholds.

He was twenty feet off the ground – *too slow, I've lost him* – when a bullet smashed into the bark of the branch that was holding him and he almost lost his footing, reaching out, grabbing hold of an intertwining branch. Mobilizing himself, he lowered his body, angling to get some cover from further shots.

There was a deafening roar and a powerful gust of heat and air tunneled through the trees. Branches swayed, leaves caught alight, and flocks of birds squawked, rising out of their hiding places and taking to the sky.

Will squinted through breaks in the foliage which gave him a narrow line of vision to sections of Dio Montesino's nearby mansion. It was on fire, enormous plumes of smoke billowing out. Then there was another explosion, more deafening than the first, and as though hurled by a flamethrower, several balls of fire surged through the trees, fanned by the windstorm, igniting large swathes of the forest.

Will was stunned by the rapid escalation that followed, giant flames leaping up around him, a sudden inferno hungrily devouring the vast expanse of green. He knew better than to try and stay on the Whistler's tail, he knew how quickly you could become ensnared in a raging forest fire. He lowered himself to the branch below, beginning his descent but as he did, a further explosion ripped through the woods, and the branch he was hanging from snapped.

He fell, toppling down through carpets of leaves, and slammed into the ground.

He was bruised and heavily scratched, his ribs ached and there was blood all over his hands though he wasn't sure where it was coming from. He groaned and gasped for breath and pushed himself unsteadily to his feet, straining against the ever-increasing gale. The air was thick with swirling smoke, and the flames leaped and hissed all around him.

Will half-ran, half-limped, narrowly navigating the areas not yet alight, heading in the direction he hoped was the one that would lead him most quickly to open ground.

A burning branch thudded down across the trail ahead of him and he jumped back, the heat licking his face like a living thing. He altered his direction, coughing now from the polluted air, wondering whether he could find his way out before the speed and ferocity of this inferno driven by winds consumed everything, including him.

Finally, he stumbled out onto a road with level fields beyond it, a section of the land on a ridge above the area where the Montesino properties were located. He ran across the road to the field and raised his phone to his ear, calling for help.

Chapter Fifty-Eight

The Whistler jumped from one branch to the next, confident at first he would out-leap, out-swing, and then on the ground, out-run the hellfire racing across the canopy toward him. But as the flames leaped all around and then ahead of him, propelled by the explosive fireballs of the gas explosions and the sudden ferocity of the wind, he regretted the time wasted, perched in the treetops, firing the pistol at the federal agent.

The sweep of the fire was pushing him away from the coast, deeper into the forest, not the way he needed to go. Then one wrong footing. The snap of a branch already sizzling with flames, another sonic boom erupting from the house, and he fell, spiraling down through the foliage, bouncing and rolling off the branches and the trunks until he smashed like a flailing doll onto the earth.

* * *

He lay on the ground, the wind knocked out of him, coughing violently from the intake of smoke, blood in his mouth, pain rippling throughout his body, his vision blurring. All he could hear was the seething hiss of the flames as they snaked across the ground around him like the coiling body of a reptile. At that moment he was no longer either of his alter egos, no longer Brendan Davis, no longer El Silbón, the Whistler. He was Sebastian. Just Sebastian.

He pushed his bruised and aching body to his feet despite the agony. The wind was fierce, the air acrid. He ran, ignoring the pain, maneuvering between the flames. Was he heading toward the coast or away from it? Further from the worst of the firestorm or closer to it? He'd lost his bearings.

He forced himself forward, his movements slowing, his body heavy, gasping for air but inhaling smoke.

As his eyes blurred further and his other senses dulled, he had the impression of everything around him slowing to an unnatural flow, and he dropped, first to his knees then onto his side.

He thought of Dantes, his brother, his family…

I rescued you from that orphanage, you will be okay… Dantes, you will be okay…

Through the swirling smoke and the fog of his faltering sight, he imagined a tall man in a long coat, his face shadowed by the brim of a tattered hat, standing in the flames. A vision. Watching, whistling.

The figure raised its arm. *Come with me…*

Despite the heat, the smoke, the lack of air and the darkness enshrouding him, the young man felt a strange calm descend. He'd avenged his parents, he'd brought Victor Gonzalez to justice, he'd destroyed the network that had disguised and shielded so many evil people, and he listened now to those eerily repetitive seven notes, hearing the song he'd taught to his young brother.

The years have passed
Your time has come…

Chapter Fifty-Nine

I opened my eyes and groaned. I felt as though I was coming out of a deep and drugged stupor, my mouth dry, my limbs rubbery. I was on a blanket that had been spread over the sand, looking up into the eyes of Will and Detective Radner.

I groaned again and Will handed me a flask of cold water. I sat up and gulped down several mouthfuls.

"I had to go in," I said to Will, wiping my mouth, "Sebastian was using the gas to create" – I waved toward the fires burning up on the hill – "all this–"

"He didn't make it."

"What do you mean? He must've…" My voice trailed off, my eyes searching his.

"He made it out and into the treetops."

"What happened?"

"We believe he fell and was trapped."

"The firefighters found his body not far from the house," Radner said.

I nodded. An image sprang to mind. The Whistler was caught and trapped by the same inferno that he'd started to enable his escape. It mirrored the deaths of the Montesino brothers, trapped and murdered in the same gas-filled outer safe room they'd designed for their enemies.

It occurred to me that with Sebastian Rivera dead, we were robbed of the chance to interview him, to delve into his psyche, to determine what truly made him tick. He'd been a highly intelligent but troubled teenager with a violent streak. Would he have still become a merciless killer if it wasn't for the financial scam that destroyed his parents, and the discovery of the criminal network that enabled that scammer, Gonzalez, and others, to escape? Once he'd completed his self-styled mission, would he have gone on to find other reasons to commit further murders?

"The fire and rescue workers are out there," Radner offered. "There's a way to go but the wind's dying down and they believe they can contain the fire in the next few hours."

"What about the boy?" I asked.

It was Radner again. "The chopper pilot reported the motorboat idling just off the opposite shore, near a marina. No sign of the boy."

"Must have jumped in and swum the rest of the way," Will said.

"We've narrowed our search down to a somewhat rickety old, unused fishing boat out along the far edge of the jetty there," Radner said. "We think it's the easiest place for Sebastian to have joined up with the boy."

"Tell your officers not to board it," I said, "just to watch. Until I get there."

"Ilona," Will said, his hand on my shoulder. "The detective's men can handle it."

"This boy suffered the loss of his parents and the abusive environment of a corrupt orphanage," I said. "I'm not sure if he knew Sebastian was his older brother, but he most certainly saw him as his friend, his savior. And the boy's out there, alone, frightened, waiting for the one person he relates to. Will, I want to be the one who talks to him first."

* * *

The fishing trawler was a seventy-year-old, forty-foot wooden boat.

The cabin door's old-fashioned lock had been picked and the door swung open with a creak. I motioned for the police officers to be quiet and remain on the deck. I went into the cabin, past the galley, and down the companionway and pushed open the door to the first of the three berths. The boy was sitting on the bunk and his eyes widened with shock when he saw me in the doorway.

"It's okay, Dantes," I said softly. "My name is Ilona and I'm here to help you."

I knew that, even though he was a minor, the boy would be charged as an accessory to Sebastian Rivera's crimes and there would be consequences. Nevertheless, I would speak on his behalf and ensure the courts were fully aware of his extenuating circumstances. I wanted to make sure Dantes received the necessary counseling and the chance to start a new life.

Unlike Sebastian, who'd recognized me on the Portland roof, Dantes did not know I was the mystery woman who'd been warned not to follow them. "You won't find El Silbón," he blurted out defiantly. But he was not certain of his own words, and his eyes were fearful.

"Dantes," my voice was gentle, "I've got some bad news, some very bad news for you, I'm afraid."

He didn't respond. He just glared at me. I sensed that, as young as he was, he'd been through a great deal already in his short life, and he knew what I was going to say.

"I'm so sorry to have to tell you that Sebastian was caught… in a fire in the woods over on the island."

Tears welled in the boy's eyes. "He's dead, isn't he?" It was as though it was something he had long been expecting.

I nodded and then reached out, my hand touching his shoulder. "I'm here to make sure you're going to be okay, Dantes, that you'll be looked after by good people."

I sensed that Sebastian hadn't told Dantes they were brothers, and I wondered if that was something Sebastian had been planning to reveal later, once his mission was complete, and the boy was a little older. It was not something I intended to reveal to the boy. I wondered if, in fact, it would be better if he never knew.

There was silence for a short while, neither of us spoke and then Dantes began to cry. He allowed me to take him in my arms and hold him close.

"It isn't fair," he sobbed.

"No, it isn't," I agreed, choking back tears of my own. I felt the dreadful sadness this innocent child was suffering.

"Sebastian wanted justice," the boy said after a while. "Justice for his father and for mine, justice against the criminals."

"Justice is a noble thing to seek, Dantes" – my tone comforting – "but Sebastian wasn't seeking justice, even if he told you he was. Even if, in his own way, he believed it. He was seeking revenge, which is not something any of us should be consumed by because it *doesn't* lead to justice." I clasped his hand tightly. "Would you do me a favor, Dantes?"

His eyes searched my face as though he was looking for the answers to a whole host of questions. "Okay…" he said tentatively.

"Let me tell you about justice," I said. "About what it really is, and how we should go about achieving it, about how my colleagues and I at the FBI take it very seriously and want it as much as you do. Would you let me talk to you about that?"

The boy regarded me quietly. And then he nodded his agreement.

Chapter Sixty

Aftermath

Will ushered me into his office and not for the first time it struck me that the décor in here – or rather lack of it – was exactly like the man. Practical. Orderly. Down-to-earth. Even the framed photo on his desk, of his graduation from the FBI training academy at Quantico, and the painting that hung on his wall, a montage depicting the country's proud history – the US flag, the Declaration of Independence, the White House – all were extensions of his career and his passion for law and order, all part of his overarching sense of self.

"Nothing wrong with the feel of your office," I said, "but it couldn't hurt to have something a little on the personal side in here, something that isn't Bureau-related. Have I mentioned it could use a woman's touch?"

"Three times, not that I'm counting," he replied with just the trace of a grin on his lips. And then it was down to business. He gestured for me to sit. "One of the men who abducted yourself, Brooke, and Sharpe the other night… one of the men we're interrogating–"

"The one who's talking."

"They're both talking now that they know the brothers are gone," Will explained. "This man, Valdez was with them for over twenty years. The Montesinos didn't have an inner circle, but Valdez was about as close to them as you were going to get. Personal bodyguard, security controller, and he undertook a range of criminal activities for them, including, of course, the warehouse abduction of yourself, Brooke, and Sharpe the other night. Under questioning, he let something slip about you."

"Like what?"

"That it wasn't the first time."

I rocked forward in my chair. "What did he mean?" I recalled the words the tall man had spoken to me that night. *"And so we meet again."*

"Ilona, he's revealed that he was one of the men who kidnapped you when you were fourteen."

"What? Why? Under instruction from the Montesinos?"

He nodded slowly, choosing his words carefully. "He believes the Montesinos were carrying out the kidnap on behalf of someone else, a favor for someone with whom they had a connection."

"Who?"

"Firstly, take a look at these." He pushed a folder overflowing with papers across his desk toward me. "Working directly with the computers we confiscated from their offices, Zoe's been able to do some deep digging into the Montesino archives. Lists of accident victims' addresses, sensitive personal data given to them, as we suspected, by various accident investigation authorities over the years."

"Many of these are the people we saw the Montesinos with, in those photos."

"Yes."

I swallowed hard. "Including Robert Wheeler?" I could barely imagine the trauma for Ben Wheeler discovering something like this about his father.

"I'm afraid we've confirmed that," Will said. "And with Themis digging up every item of available data on Robert Wheeler from the past two decades we believe we know just how he's come to be blackmailed by the brothers. There's a string of massive gambling debts that were conveniently paid after the Montesinos began receiving information about the Ven Air passengers and then, later, other airline accident victims.”

I sighed. *This can’t be happening.* “What has that got to do with my kidnap?”

“As you know, the FBI was involved in assisting with the missing plane investigation,” Will elaborated.

“And Ross Grande was the agent attached to that.”

“Yes. Grande was working closely with Wheeler and scrutinizing every aspect of the investigation,” Will said. “We believe he discovered Wheeler’s leaking of that material to the brothers and found out about the blackmail. Some documents show he visited and interviewed the Montesinos, but rather than report the incident or follow through with an investigation, there’s nothing. The file was closed.”

“Grande did a deal with them,” I guessed.

“He’s kept their criminal activities hidden from investigators in return for using their services for his own agendas.”

My shoulders slumped. “One of which, years later, was my kidnap, to place my father in an impossible situation and for Grande’s career to benefit.”

“It wasn’t the only time he compromised others for his own gain,” Will said. “Valdez’s testimony and a string of other documents from the Montesino archives have revealed… many other crimes he commissioned from the brothers. *But, Ilona,*” he stressed, “there’s no suggestion Robert Wheeler knew about your kidnap or even what the Montesinos were using the accident victim data for.”

I started flicking through pages and pages of names – crime figures who had been the Montesinos’ clients.

“Robert Wheeler’s arrest is imminent and I’m in talks with DC about how we proceed with A.D. Grande,” Will added, “but I wanted you to be aware before anything else progresses…”

I nodded my appreciation, flicking him a glance but momentarily lost for words. I had always wanted to solve the case of my kidnap, but not like this, never like this…

My eyes wandered and I tucked a loose strand of hair behind my ear. The last thing I could have imagined was that the Whistler's victims would be linked to Robert Wheeler.

The Montesino computers contained both the real and the corresponding deceased SS names of their clients. "Those lists have been sent to field offices in a dozen states," Will further explained, "and local agents will conduct raids and make arrests. By tomorrow morning the news will break nationwide."

I was stunned, not just by the extent of the operation throughout the US and South American countries, but also by its growth in the past few years to include fleeing crime figures from the UK, Europe, and some Asian countries. The Montesinos had used their growing international network of contacts to spread their tentacles further and further.

"Do we know how many impostors we're talking about?" I asked.

"The team is still crunching the numbers but it's already over a thousand and it's growing by the minute."

I reflected on this. "It's been going on for over twenty years and Ross Grande has known about it all along." I shook my head in disbelief.

* * *

Back in my own office, I was attempting to make a start on the paperwork when Brooke appeared in my doorway. "Ilona… hi. They said to come straight through."

"How are you feeling, Brooke?"

The reporter moved into the office. "Me? I'm fine, Ilona. I came in to see how you were. The guys told me what happened."

"Because you're plaguing them relentlessly with phone calls, drop-ins, and questions."

"Well, yeah—"

I cut across her, motioning to pull up one of the visitor chairs. "As you're here, take a seat. We need to talk." It was unmistakable from my tone that this was no casual chat.

Brooke sat. "Okay…"

"You were keeping close tabs on the previous Piper investigation," I said, my gaze on Brooke intense. "You were a big help but just because I'm forever grateful for how that turned out, it doesn't give you carte blanche to stalk me and the team, digging for confidential case data and hoping to be on the spot when we break a case."

"Ilona—"

"Am I making myself clear, Brooke?"

"Yes. But, Ilona, the reason I wanted to keep an eye on your movements…" Even though her eyes were locked with mine, her voice trailed as she considered her words.

"Yes…?" I prompted impatiently.

"I was fishing. I felt… there was something bigger going on."

"Something bigger?"

"You and Agent McCord and the others… you're not just one of the regular field office teams here, are you? I suspected something after the Piper case and then, with this investigation… You're some kind of special unit."

"I can't discuss internal Bureau business with you, Brooke. You know that."

"You can't tell me if you're a special team or what the focus is?"

"Here's what I'll tell you," I said. "You are not to follow or spy on myself or Agent McCord or any agent or consultant. I sympathize that you've suffered traumas of your own and that, in part, is driving you. I'll make one concession to you, and one only."

"Okay…"

"If and when there's releasable information on any case I'm working on, I'll endeavor to see that you're the first reporter to be advised. But there's no guarantee and it's only provided you back off and conduct yourself professionally. Do we have a deal?"

Brooke didn't smile, she mirrored the solemn, serious expression on my face. She nodded her agreement. "We have a deal."

Chapter Sixty-One

There are calls a federal agent has to make, calls they dread. Calls that deliver devastating information to families and survivors.

I didn't have to make *this* call. Not in any official capacity at least, but it was a call I *had* to make nonetheless.

As soon as Brooke left my office, I tapped Ben Wheeler's number and a moment later he answered.

"Ilona, hi."

"Ben, there's something I need to tell you."

"Okay."

"It's something that is… happening right now. I expect it will be on breaking news reports in the next hour or two. I just… wanted you to hear it from me, first."

"Ilona, you sound awful. What is it?"

"It's going to come as a hell of a shock, so if it's okay with you, I'd like to meet with you privately. Not at your office. If we could meet at your apartment in a little while, I can give you the background, explain how this has all come about."

"Ilona, what on earth are you talking about?"

"It's about your father, Ben. Federal agents are at his house. He's being arrested."

* * *

Ben Wheeler stood in his living room, a glass of straight scotch in one hand, his remote in the other, watching the TV news broadcast. Twenty years after its disappearance, Ven Air Flight 387 was in the news again. Only this time for a very different reason.

He grimaced at the sickening sight of his father in handcuffs, being taken by police from his beachside home.

He aimed the remote and switched off the set. He couldn't watch.

My father?

He walked out onto the balcony of his apartment. He glanced down at the name he'd brought up on his phone display. It was over an hour since her phone call. He'd left his office after the call, headed back to his apartment, and he knew she was heading over and that she'd be here soon. He wanted to call her. His finger hovered over the 'call' icon.

How can I have a friendship, or even something more, with Ilona Farris?

None of this was her fault. She'd simply been doing her job, a job he approved of, but ultimately her investigation had led to the downfall of his father. The man he'd looked up to for all these years. The man whose career steps he'd followed. The man now exposed as harboring a dreadful secret.

It wasn't Ilona's fault.

Ben liked Ilona and had wondered if something more serious might develop with her. He tried to imagine holding her, kissing her. He tried to visualize walks along the coast at sunset. But every time he did, he was instead assaulted with the scenes of his father in handcuffs, the police arriving at the Stinson Beach home, the yet-to-come newspaper headlines about the investigator who'd betrayed the victims and the families of one of the world's greatest aviation disasters.

Damn all of that, he thought.

He raised the phone, placing the tip of his finger on the 'call' icon. The unwanted images flashed through his mind – a permanent, flowing mural imprinted on his psyche.

He walked back into the living room, his finger hovering, and then in an uncharacteristic move he flung the phone against the wall and its glass display panel shattered.

With a heavy heart, he realized that he could never start a relationship with Ilona. This catastrophic family event, her role in it, and the images burned into his memory had created an emotional divide that would always be there, for him, at least.

The pain of seeing all of that every time he looked at her would be too great. The regret he felt was like a knife twisting in his gut. Would he still feel this way tomorrow, or the day after that? He didn't know.

She had said she was on the way over to talk to him about how all of this had unfolded. Bewildered, he'd said, "Okay."

But I need to be alone.

I need to speak to my father. I need to think this through.

I need…

He wasn't sure what he needed, but he didn't want to be here when Ilona arrived, and he couldn't bring himself to make the call and hear her voice on the other end of the line.

He grabbed his car keys and headed out. He drove aimlessly with no destination in mind, his hands clenching the steering wheel in frustration, confusion, and despair.

Perhaps he was being irrational but there was a part of him that already knew it would be best to make a clean break now before he formed any deeper feelings. It would be best if he never saw nor spoke to Ilona Farris again.

Chapter Sixty-Two

I was in a familiar spot, standing by the large, wide window at the corner of the corridor, gazing out on the city skyline, when Marcia found me.

"Reflecting?" she asked.

I continued to stare at the view. "There's a lot to take in."

"Have you been in touch with Ben?"

"I haven't heard from him," I said matter-of-factly. After a pause, I revealed my frustration. "I've phoned and left messages but no response. His office said he's taken extended leave."

"You and he built up quite a good rapport."

"Yeah."

Marcia's hand came to rest on my shoulder. "Maybe he just needs time. It would have been a hell of a shock, discovering his father's secret."

"And I played a part in that."

"Doing the job you had to do," Marcia reminded me.

"Lucky me."

We watched the night sky in silence for a few minutes and then Marcia gave my shoulder a gentle squeeze. "Time," she repeated, her voice soft.

"I think, Marcia," I said, "that all the time in the world isn't going to be enough."

My phone buzzed. "It's Will," I said to Marcia as I answered the call.

"I'm upstairs with the bosses," he said. "Word has just come through from the Directors in DC."

* * *

This was not something Will wanted on his resume.

He wanted to be known for heading up the fledgling UCU. He wanted recognition for reducing the cold cases of tomorrow by solving them today when all the analysis predicted that was unlikely.

He wanted his legacy to be for solving some of the country's most baffling mysteries.

But not this. Not for uncovering a conspiracy that stretched into the heart of the Bureau and ensnared one of its most senior men. Not for leading the field of agents that arrested one of their Assistant Directors.

The word that had come through the night before was that he was to be in Washington DC early morning, where he'd have a full team from the DC office at his disposal.

* * *

I'd insisted on going to DC to observe. I'd flown overnight with Will and now I stood across the street, watching as the agents led A.D. Grande out of his home in the exclusive suburb north of the city, his wife of thirty-five years looking on horrified, in her bathrobe, from their front door. True to my word, I had informed Brooke Goodman, who was outside the house with a photographer from the *Chronicle* and a TV newsman from a DC channel. What was that about? I grimaced. How had she arranged all this so quickly? But then, that was typical Brooke.

I wanted to look away, disgusted by this man's extraordinary deception, but I couldn't. Deep inside I knew that for a long time now I'd been drawn to the darkness, and this was just as dark as the deep hole I'd been imprisoned in as a fourteen-year-old.

As he was being maneuvered into the back seat of an FBI vehicle, Grande momentarily raised his head, spying me across the street, and our eyes locked for a brief moment. I saw no emotion there, just a mask of arrogance and indifference, one of the many masks, I thought, that

Grande had worn throughout his life and career, throughout his 'friendship' with my father and his mentoring of me as a young agent.

I wanted to ask him to his face how he could have betrayed us, all of us, but deep within I already knew the answer. He was an ambitious man, hungry for power, good at his job but impatient and unwilling to leave his progress to the natural processes.

I reflected on what I'd learned from Zach about the El Silbón legend. The nineteenth-century people of the Venezuelan plains had feared the ghostly whistler. At that moment, I wondered what was the real definition of someone like the Assistant Director. Were men like him any different from that nightmarish, whistling wanderer in the dark who was also a vicious killer? Grande presented one face to the world, hiding his real self – his other, much darker persona – behind closed doors. Someone whose self-serving, corrupt practices had aided and abetted a vast criminal conspiracy. Someone I believed I knew and now discovered I knew nothing about at all.

I drew a deep breath. I watched as the car carrying Grande sped away and I closed my eyes, questioning myself, questioning the world.

What do I call someone like you? A man? Or a monster?

No, I shook my head, *what you are doesn't even deserve a name.*

Straightening my shoulders, I turned and walked away.

THE END

If you enjoyed this book, please let others know by leaving a quick review on Amazon. Also, if you spot anything untoward in the paperback, get in touch. We strive for the best quality and appreciate reader feedback.

editor@thebookfolks.com

www.thebookfolks.com

Also in this series

THE PIPER'S CHILDREN (Book 1)

A boy is found wandering in the woods, dressed in medieval clothes and speaking a strange language. When another child turns up, it doesn't shed any more light on the mystery for FBI agent Ilona Farris. Only by digging into her own past will she begin to work out what is going on, and who these children are, seemingly lost in time.

THE STORM KILLINGS (Book 3)

As tornado season gets under way, the FBI's advanced computer system highlights an anomaly in the casualties. It looks like someone is using the chaos caused by the weather as cover to kill unsuspecting women in their homes. Special Agent Ilona Farris heads into the eye of the storm to catch them in the act.

FREE with Kindle Unlimited and available in paperback!

More fiction by Iain Henn

DEAD SET ON MURDER

Eighteen years after disappearing without a trace, Jennifer's husband's body turns up, yards from her home. Apparently without aging one bit. She knows something is seriously amiss. Fortunately homicide detective Neil Lachlan shares her concerns. But when the case overlaps with a manhunt for a serial killer, it will put Jennifer's life on the line.

FREE with Kindle Unlimited and available in paperback!

THE GREATEST BETRAYAL

Liz Carter is the proud owner of a successful advertising business when she begins a whirlwind romance with handsome airline pilot Callan McKenzie. Yet after his estranged ex contacts him, he disappears without a trace. Liz resolves to move on with her life, but a chain of events has been set in motion that threatens all she holds dear.

FREE with Kindle Unlimited and available in paperback!

Other titles of interest

A KILLER AMONGST US
by Mark West

When her husband invites Jo on a couples' hiking weekend, despite disliking camping she accepts, hoping they'll rekindle their former closeness. But her hopes are shattered when the group starts to argue amongst themselves, and then the unthinkable happens… a happy holiday quickly turns into a desperate fight for survival.

FREE with Kindle Unlimited and available in paperback!

BOUND TO RUN
by **Robert McCracken**

A romantic getaway in a remote Lake District cottage turns into a desperate fight for survival for Alex Chase. If she can get away from her pursuer, and that's a big if, she'll be able to concentrate on the burning question in her mind: how to get revenge.

FREE with Kindle Unlimited and available in paperback!

Sign up to our mailing list to find out about new releases and special offers!

www.thebookfolks.com